A Grave Prediction

THE PSYCHIC EYE MYSTERY SERIES

THE GHOST HUNTER MYSTERY SERIES

A Grave Prediction

· ·

A Psychic Eye Mystery

· ·

Victoria Laurie

AN OBSIDIAN MYSTERY

OBSIDIAN

OBSIDIAN
Published by New American Library,
an imprint of Penguin Random House LLC
375 Hudson Street, New York, New York 10014

This book is an original publication of New American Library.

First Printing, July 2016

For more information about Penguin Random House, visit penguin.com.

LIBRARY OF CONGRESS CATALOGING-IN-PUBLICATION DATA:

Names: Laurie, Victoria, author.
Title: A grave prediction: a psychic eye mystery/Victoria Laurie.
Description: New York, New York: New American Library, [2016] | "An Obsidian mystery."
Identifiers: LCCN 2016005201 (print) | LCCN 2016010349 (ebook) | ISBN 9780451473882 (hardback) |
ISBN 9780698186613 (ebook)
Subjects: LCSH: Cooper, Abby (Fictitious character)—Fiction. | Paranormal fiction. | Women psychics—
Fiction. | Women detectives—Fiction. |
BISAC: FICTION / Mystery & Detective / Women Sleuths. | GSAFD: Mystery fiction
Classification: LCC PS3612.A94423 G73 2016 (print) | LCC PS3612.A94423 (ebook) | DDC 813/.6—dc23
LC record available at http://lccn.loc.gov/2016005201

Printed in the United States of America
10 9 8   7 6 5 4 3 2 1

Penguin
Random
House

For K-Lo,
who has always been my Huckleberry

Acknowledgments

Writing is a bitch of a way to make a living. It's a bitch on the writer, but it's probably even more of a bitch on those people who love and support the author.

That's what's so fabulous about writing the acknowledgments. It's our opportunity to say, *Sorry! No, really . . . sorry, sorry, sorry, sorry!!!!!* See, during the book creation process, we writerly types are simply awful to live with. To work with. To be around. To be near. To be in sight of. To be at a distance from. To be friends with on Facebook. We're so often curmudgeonly, unkempt, disheveled, and malnourished that it takes a certain hearty soul to continue to love us throughout the cranking out of several hundred pages.

So, at the start of every book, I'm so happy to have the opportunity to tell all the people in my life who routinely put up with me at my curmudgeonly worst how much I love them, adore them, need them, and hope they continue to bring home a pizza every now and again.

To that end, I will begin with Jessica Wade, who has been so incredibly patient and understanding. This book came with particular difficulty, and I so appreciate all the compensations for extra time you extended me, Jessica. I also sincerely appreciate all the wonderful insight you gave to the editorial process. Your comments are always spot on, and you really, really help bring out the best story possible. I've worked with you on only two books so far, but I've so enjoyed the partnership, and I'm looking forward to many more experiences to come.

Also, thank you to my amazing publicist, Danielle Dill, who is simply wonderful in every single way. Both at her job and as a person. She's amazeballs.

And to the rest of the team at Penguin, thank you so much for your dedication, hard work, and keen insights. I love my publishing house, and I hope you all know that.

Next, I'd like to thank my wonderful agent, Jim McCarthy, who is simply invaluable as a creative partner. He always knows *exactly* the right thing to say to me at the precise right moment. One of the true gifts of my life was securing Jim as my agent and eventually getting to call him my dear, dear friend. I can't think of a thing I'm more grateful for.

Finally, I'd like to thank the people in my personal life who constantly support me even when I'm running myself ragged trying to make a deadline. Brian Gorzynski (I love you, honey. I'm the luckiest woman in the world with you at my side.); my amazing sister, Sandy Upham; Steve McGrory; Matt and Mike Morrill; Katie Coppedge; Leanne Tierney and Karen Ditmars; Nicole Gray; Sandy Harding; Terry Gilman; Catherine Ong Kane; Drue Rowean; Sally Woods; John Kwaitkowski; Matt McDougal; Dean James; Anne Kimbol; McKenna Jordan; Hilary Laurie; Shannon Anderson; Thomas Robinson; Juliet Blackwell; Gigi Pandian; Martha Bushko and Suzanne Parsons and all my homies at Stars and Stripes CrossFit, who just throw a wall ball at me when I'm getting too cranky. ☺

A Grave Prediction

Chapter One

. . .

The thing I hate about the future is that it's so freaking unpredictable.

I know, I know—that's not something you usually hear from a psychic. I get it. But it's a fact. Yep. It's a stinky, irritating, frustrating, annoying fact that the future is far less predictable than even I like to admit.

Still, as much as I may whine about how hard it is to nail down what's coming up in the next few months for a client, it's always *super*cool when something that I say will happen . . . actually does.

I suspect that the reason the future is so nebulous—even for those of us well practiced at predicting it—is that destiny itself isn't a thing that's set in stone, and on some levels, that's pretty counterintuitive.

I know that most people who believe in psychic ability might think the future itself is a direct path forward—like a paved road. The truth is that the future looks and feels a bit more like a flowing river with lots of twists and turns, surprise tributaries, calming pools, a few beaver dams, and even some waterfalls. All that energy hinders our innate intuitive ability to predict it with a hundred percent accuracy, and sometimes even telling people what their future holds allows them to change it on the spot, much like paddling a little more on the left will steer your canoe to the right.

The fact that the future is so malleable is, quite frankly, why I perform readings in the first place. I like to think that I'm allowing people to make informed decisions about what's coming up and am giving them the opportunity to alter course if they'd like.

Sometimes a course can't really be altered very much, if at all, and I have no idea why there are such distinct exceptions to the rule. Some destinies are simply set, and there's no opportunity to alter the outcome. That's the part that's most frustrating—when I get the rare client who seems to be set for an end that has no alternative.

It's even more frustrating when it happens on a case I'm working. Yeah, that's the part I haven't mentioned yet—along with doing private sessions for clients, I also do a little consulting work for the Austin FBI cold-case division.

My work with them is strictly on the down-low—I mean, can you *imagine* if it got out that the FBI had a *psychic* on the books? There'd be mayhem. Madness. Governments would topple, heads would roll, chaos would reign, villages would be pillaged, and innocents everywhere would suffer. . . .

That enough sarcasm for you? Good. It's pretty eye-roll worthy for me too.

Anyway, as I was saying, most cases I work on, we get results. I wouldn't say in any way that I'm solely responsible for solving the various cold cases that come our way (we've got some *amazing* agents on our team), but I would (proudly) declare that I'm a valuable asset, and I do contribute to the investigations. We have a great track record, so the results speak for themselves.

In fact, it's those results that led me to my earlier comment on being frustrated when nothing I seem to say or do alters an outcome. You see, it was because of those stats that I was asked to an early January morning meeting with my boss, Brice Harrison.

Brice is not only my boss; as the Austin bureau's SAIC (special agent in charge), he's also my husband's boss. And as long as I'm confessing how tricky my relationship with him can be, I should probably mention that Brice is *also* my BFF's husband. (How's that for convoluted?)

Now, when Brice and I first met, we maaaay have clashed a weensy bit. Sort of the way Godzilla clashed with Tokyo . . . Ahhhh, good times.

Whatever. We got over it and discovered a bit of respect for each other, and then we discovered that we genuinely liked each other. Since those early days, Brice has had my back on more than one occasion, even when his job was on the line, and I think of him like a brother, so there's not a lot I wouldn't do for him.

"No way, Brice. No *way* am I'm doing that!" I yelled after he pitched me his proposal that early morning in his office. (What? I said "not *a lot* I wouldn't do . . . ," not "*nothing* I wouldn't do. . . .")

"Cooper," he said, lacing his fingers together on the desk to regard me with steely, stubborn determination. "You can't say no to this."

My eyes narrowed. "I think I just did."

"Yeah, but you need to take that back and say yes."

"No," I repeated, just to show him I could.

Brice sighed loudly and shook his head. "Do you give Dutch this much of a hard time?"

"Only when he says something stupid." Wagging my finger, I dropped my voice to add, "Abby, you can't say no to this really dumb thing I want you to do."

Brice chuckled before he cleared his throat and focused intently on me again. "It's not dumb. It's an honor. I mean, what could be better for your reputation than an invitation from another bureau for you to come out and lend a hand on some of their toughest cases, while teaching their agents how to become better investigators by helping them develop their own intuition? Seriously, what could be better?"

I rolled my eyes. "Oh, gee golly, Brice. I don't know—maybe something like getting punched in the face."

Brice sighed. "Come on, Abby. It's an honor. It really is."

I sat forward in challenge. "An honor to go where I'm not wanted to teach a bunch of reluctant, skeptical Neanderthals to use their own intuition—something they don't even *believe* they have—to solve cases? I think not, sir. I think not."

"I never should've mentioned the part where the agents threatened to quit if you showed up, huh?"

"Not your best sales pitch," I told him, crossing my arms over my chest.

Brice rubbed his temples. "For the record, Candice told me to leave that part out too."

"You should listen to your wife, Brice. She's smarter than you."

"That's true. But I wanted you to know what kind of an environment you were walking into. I wanted you to know that you'd have to win those L.A. bureau agents over just like you won these guys over." For emphasis, Brice waved in the direction of the open cubicle area behind me, where the seven other agents who made up our group sat.

"See, the problem with that logic is that when I came *here* to Austin, I had you and Dutch on my side. From what you've just told me about this proposed assignment, I won't have *anybody* in La-La Land who's going to be on my side when I get there."

"You'll have Whitacre," Brice reminded me. "The way I

heard it, he practically had to beg Gaston to let him borrow you for a couple of weeks." Greg Whitacre was the Western regional director for the FBI. Bill Gaston was the Southern regional director, and the fact that these two had come up with this scheme to loan me out made me think it'd been conceived over a round of golf during the last Big-Brass-Shield convention. It irked me that I was being passed around like a goody bag.

"Is Whitacre going to be there the whole time?" I demanded.

"Probably not," Brice replied. He knew there was no lying to me. "But he'll be there at the beginning and his presence alone should keep the other agents in check."

"Until the second he leaves and I'm given the cold shoulder, no one comes to my classes, and I'm assigned to the broom closet to shuffle through case files, where any leads I hand off to the agents won't be followed up on."

"Yep," Brice said, tossing up his hands. "That's probably exactly how it'll go. You'll have two good days followed by twelve days in hell, but still, Abby, you have to go."

"Why? Why do I *have* to, Brice? I'm a consultant. If I don't want to work for you, I don't have to."

"That's true," he said. "But part of our budget is approved by people with a much higher pay grade than even Gaston's, and if two of the four regional directors like having a psychic on the books, then the part of our budget that gets earmarked for your hourly rate doesn't get slashed and I can keep you employed by the FBI."

"I can live without the FBI," I said flatly. I liked the paycheck from this consulting gig, but I didn't especially need it.

"I'm sure you can live without us, Abby, but the real question is, can we live without you?"

That gave me pause.

Brice sat forward and laced his fingers together again. "The thing I know for sure is that you've saved lives since you've come on board with us. Actual lives, Abby. There are men, women, even children, alive today because you got involved in a case that brought a murderer to justice. You've also given closure to dozens of families that've been denied it for years because the cases of their loved ones went cold. If I lose you to budget cuts and politics, knowing you could've saved even more lives and provided even more closure . . . that would haunt me the rest of my career."

Shit. He'd brought out the big guilt guns. It was my turn to sigh. I dropped my gaze to my lap, scowling fiercely. "You play dirty," I muttered.

"Gaston needs you to do this," Brice said. "Politically, it needs to happen."

I lifted my gaze. I realized he'd just given me a hint to what was really at play here. The real clue was the word "politically." "Someone wants me off the books," I said, feeling out the ether. "Someone with clout who has something to gain by having me removed from this bureau. A senator? Congressman?" It suddenly dawned on me that the game was much bigger than I'd realized.

Brice's lips pressed into a thin line. It was all the verification I needed. "You can't say no."

"Then let Dutch come with me," I said.

Brice shook his head. "I can't allow that."

"Why?" I wasn't backing down. I needed Dutch.

"Because the last thing I'd do to you is send your overprotective husband into that den of wolves to kick up a lot of testosterone, which would only cause problems between our branch and theirs. You go in solo, kiddo. Sorry, but that's the deal."

I glared at Brice. He'd backed me into a corner, and I wasn't much liking it. "Fine. Then I'm taking Candice."

"No," Brice said before I'd even finished speaking his wife's name.

"Oh, come on!" I yelled. "Why can't I take Candice?"

"For almost the exact same reason I won't let you take Dutch, except that the body count would probably be higher."

I couldn't resist a smirk even though we both knew it was probably true. Candice was super protective and I was glad for it. "What if I can't solve any of the cases they're gonna make me work on?"

"You have to solve at least one," Brice replied. "There's no walking away from this, Cooper. You have to pull out a valuable clue that these guys either have not seen or have overlooked. It's what you do best, and you've gotta bring your *A* game to California and stay until you help solve at least one of their high-profile cases."

My jaw fell open. "You're kidding," I said to him. He'd *never* handed me a case and told me I had no other option but to solve it.

"Unfortunately, I'm not. If you don't prove yourself as a valuable asset, then we'll lose you. We need Whitacre to go to bat for you. To do that, he's got to have something that he can point to. Something that makes him look good."

I drummed my fingers on the arm of my chair, considering Brice's statement. And then I did what came naturally to me—I looked into the ether again and checked out a little more of what was really going on. "Someone's pissed," I said. "Someone powerful is personally pissed off at me."

Brice shrugged noncommittally.

"Why?" I asked. "What've I done?"

"You exposed an injustice," Brice said simply. I had a feeling Gaston had told him to keep the political details to himself.

I peered again into the ether and expelled a small gasp when I saw the truth. "Skylar," I whispered. Months before, I'd worked on the case of a death-row inmate wrongly convicted of murdering her son. I'd never dreamed I'd make a powerful political enemy for doing the right thing.

"Lots of heads rolled," Brice said—his way of telling me I'd hit the nail on the head. "Lots of money went to the settlement. It cost someone their political clout, and they have powerful friends who're now making waves."

I lifted my chin defiantly. "Screw them," I said. "If the FBI wants to fire me, that's fine. I can work for you guys off the books and no one has to know. You can send Dutch home with a case file here and there and I can have a look. I'll even do it for free."

"That's very generous of you, but you should know that it's not just your name and reputation on the line here, Cooper. All of us who've gone to bat for you, who've insisted on working with you, we're in the line of fire too."

My shoulders slumped and I turned to look behind me. There were seven agents at their desks, not including my husband, Brice, or Gaston, whose reputations could be called into question. All because they believed in me. Taking a deep breath, I turned back to Brice and said, "Okay, then."

"Yeah?"

"It's not like I have a lot of choice here, Brice. You need me to play nicey-nice with the L.A. bureau? Fine. I'll do it. But I get an expense account."

"You do," he agreed. "Seventy-five dollars a day not including hotel or your hourly rate."

He said that like he thought it was a generous offer. "Gee, Brice . . . the timing on this is a little awkward, but I think I need to inform you that my hourly rate just went up."

My boss raised an eyebrow. "It did, huh?"

"Yep. Inflation. You know, a gallon of milk is getting crazy expensive these days."

"How much?" he asked me, clearly unhappy that, even while forced to accept an assignment against my will and better judgment, I was trying to negotiate a better deal.

"Well, as I'll be spending two lonely weeks in L.A., away from my paying clients—"

"You can do readings by phone," he said, because he knew full well I could.

I adopted a mock smile. "Oh, you mean those clients I already have scheduled during the day? Yeah, how about you clear that with the L.A. bureau? Tell them I'll just need a conference room all to myself for a few hours four days a week while I make my way through my private client list."

Brice dropped his chin and rubbed his temples. "Can't you just reschedule them, Cooper? You do it for us all the time."

"Oh, I'm going to reschedule them, but I'll have to put them off for two weeks or schedule them for a session at night after I finish up putting on the dog and pony show for the L.A. frat boys, which I definitely don't want to do, and all of *that* will be a huge pain in my ass and not something I'm willing to do without some form of compensation."

He stopped rubbing his temples and eyed me curiously. "You have two full weeks of clients already on the books?"

I smiled genuinely this time. "I have six full *months* of clients already on the books, my friend."

"Damn," he said with appreciation. "Word's really getting out about you, huh?"

I brushed my knuckles against my shirt. "Told you I had mad skills."

He laughed. "Okay, okay, what's this gonna cost us?"

"Eight grand," I said, going for broke.

Brice rolled his eyes. He knew I was pushing it. "Four."

"Six," I countered, setting my jaw. No way was I taking less. "And you can double that lame-ass food allowance while you're at it. *And* no crappy motel in some seedy neighborhood either. You put me up someplace nice or no dice, Brice." I bounced my eyebrows to emphasize my point . . . and of course my exceptional rhyming skills.

In turn, Brice lowered his brow and frowned hard at me.

I squared my shoulders and raised my chin to show him I wasn't scared of him. (Much.)

With a grin he suddenly put out his hand. "Deal."

I let go a little breath of relief and before offering my hand, I said, "I totes would've taken five."

His smile widened. "I would've gone up to seven."

I was about to pull my hand away when he grabbed it and shook it quickly. "A deal's a deal, Cooper," he said.

I got up and waved at him dismissively. "Yeah, yeah. If you need me, I'll be at home packing. Oh, and Dutch is going to take a long lunch today, so don't give him any crap when he's not back by one."

"Does he have an appointment or something?" Brice asked.

"Yep," I told him. "He's not going to see his wife naked for the next two weeks. I suspect he'll want to make a memory that'll last him till I get back."

Brice actually blushed and I chuckled all the way to the exit.

My hubby drove me to the airport at three, which was good because I was still trying to reschedule the last few clients I had on the books for the next two weeks. Dutch's lunch hour was stretching to half the day, but at least we both had contented smiles on our faces. "You don't have to go, Edgar," he said, using his preferred nickname for me (coined after he read a book on famous psychic Edgar Cayce).

"Yes, I do," I replied.

"No," he insisted. "If you get kicked out of the consulting pool, so what?"

"It's not me getting kicked out that I'm worried about."

Dutch made a face. "So they kick me out too. Who cares? Milo and I are making enough on the side. With a little planning, we wouldn't even feel the lost income."

Dutch was far more irritated that I'd been pushed into this deal with the L.A. bureau than I was. "Okay, allow me to amend my earlier statement. It's not me or you getting kicked out that I'm worried about. Brice wouldn't be Brice without that job. If he got kicked out, he'd stay home and mope, which would drive Candice crazy, which would drive me crazy, which would have serious consequences for a certain stubborn cowboy I happen to love a whole hellofa lot."

Dutch pursed his lips. "I see all roads lead back to me."

"Don't they always?"

"They don't have to. Only the one that brings you back home."

I leaned over to rest my head on his shoulder. "Sometimes you say the most perfect thing."

"I'll work on coming up with a few more for when I pick you up in two weeks," he said, kissing my forehead.

I lifted my head and eyed him suspiciously. "You're banking on the fact that I'll be willing to get naked with you if you're super-sweet to me, even though you know I'll be crazy tired when I land, aren't you?"

"Nooooo," Dutch said.

My inner lie detector hit the red zone. "Oh, really?"

"What if I also promise to cook you dinner as I ply you with sweet nothings?"

That piqued my interest. "What'd you have in mind?"

"Spaghetti alla carbonara," he said immediately.

Damn him. He knew I loved all things bacon and pasta. "There you go, exploiting my weaknesses," I told him.

Dutch adopted his best Humphrey Bogart and said, "I plan to miss yous, sweethot."

"We'll see," was all I committed to. The truth was we both knew I'd be naked before the pasta was al dente, but this whole flirtatious banter stuff was part of our ongoing courtship, and I enjoyed making Dutch wonder if he could really coax the clothes off me on my first night home.

Dutch dropped me at the Delta skycap and I checked the two bags I was bringing, got my boarding pass, and meandered inside. While I was waiting in the security line, my phone beeped and I thought about ignoring it but gave in and answered the call on the last ring before it went to voice mail. "Hey, Brice. I'm about to go through security, so if you're calling to check up on whether I actually went to the airport, you can rest assured that I'm a woman of my word."

"I never doubted it," Brice said.

My lids lowered to half-mast. "Really, Brice? Really?"

"Okay, maybe I put the odds at fifty-fifty, but that's not why I'm calling."

"Not the sole reason at least," I muttered.

"Have you seen or heard from my wife?"

"Candice?" I said. "I sent her a text to let her know that you guys were banning me from my beloved Austin and sending me away for two weeks of purgatory in La-La Land to defend my honor against some FBI boys ready to receive me with pitchforks and torches, but I haven't heard back from her."

"Glad you kept the drama out of it and just stuck to the facts," Brice said.

"I'm a colorful and expressive person. You want the facts, just the facts, fire me and hire Joe Friday."

"Hire someone less of a pain in my ass than you, Cooper? Why would I ever want to do that?"

"I don't know. . . . You like boredom? Predictability? The wrath of your wife if you ever actually do fire me?"

"*No one* wants that last part, Cooper," he said. "No one."

"True that. Anyway, I haven't heard from her," I said, inching forward and trying not to look suspicious enough to be pulled out of line and strip-searched.

"Yeah, well, she's not answering my calls," Brice said. "Or my texts."

"She's probably working a case." Candice was a licensed PI, and she and I shared an office and often worked cases together, but I hadn't joined her on anything since before the holidays.

"You know more about her cases than I do," Brice said. "Did she mention what she's working on?"

I barely held in a sigh. I wanted to reply that it wasn't my turn to watch Candice, but Brice had been a little on edge about his wife's whereabouts ever since she'd disappeared on us to run off to Vegas and do some undercover stuff for a mobster. It's not as bad as it sounds, but it's close. "No, I don't know what she's working on, but I'm sure she'll call you back soon. She just needs to wrap up whatever she's working on and she'll be home for dinner."

At that moment I felt a sinking feeling in my gut—an intuitive sign that what I'd just said wasn't going to happen, which wasn't especially odd as Candice sometimes worked very late, especially if she was on surveillance. "Or maybe a nightcap," I amended. Again I got that sinking feeling. Hmmm, that was curious. "Midnight snack?" I tried. Sink. Sink. Sink. "Well, crap. That's weird. Breakfast tomorr—?"

"Cooper, what're you even talking about?"

"Nothing," I said quickly. Candice was probably fine. She was always fine. Nothing was wrong. Just because she wouldn't be home for dinner or by midnight was not a reason to freak out. "Listen, security is calling me forward. I gotta go."

I hung up on Brice and moved through the security line— managing to avoid the strip search while I was at it. (Score!) After getting some chips, a Snickers, mints, bottled water, and Excedrin for the two weeks of headaches I was bound to incur, I made my way to my assigned gate and sat down with a sigh.

After unwrapping the Snickers and taking a satisfying bite, I dialed Candice's number and waited for the inevitable voice mail. She picked up on the first ring. "Sundance," she said easily. "How you doin', kiddo?"

I sat up a little, surprised that I'd reached her. "Brice is looking for you," I said by way of hello.

The honeyed sound of her laughter echoed into my ear. "I'll bet," she said cryptically. "I'm assuming, given the background noise, that you're at the airport."

"Yep," I said, chewing another bite of the Snickers. "This whole deal sucks."

"It does," she agreed. "You doing okay?"

"Yeah," I said, slouching again. "Stupid politics these bureau boys play. Why don't they all just pull out their winkies and some measuring tape and leave us the hell out of it?"

She chuckled again. "Want some company?" she asked.

I eyed the tarmac moodily. "Brice said I had to go alone."

"Oh, did he, now?"

"Yeah. I begged him to let Dutch come with me, but he said it'd only cause problems. You know, too much testosterone from the hubby might send the fists flying."

"I'll be your Huckleberry," Candice said, smooth enough to make Val Kilmer swoon.

My radar pinged. It suddenly occurred to me that I could hear some pretty distinct noises coming from Candice's side of the conversation. Then the hair on the back of my neck prickled like when you get that feeling that someone's looking at you. I sat up straight again and swiveled in my seat. Coming down the corridor was my gorgeous partner in crime, turning heads as she glided along trailing a carry-on behind her. I broke into a wide grin before getting up to race toward her and throw my arms around her.

"You are the best friend *ever*!"

She laughed in surprise and hugged me back, then said, "Easy, Sundance. People are starting to stare."

I let go only long enough to grab her by the elbow and drag her over to my seat. "What're you doing here?" I asked, following quickly with, "Not that I'm not happy about it, I mean . . . obvs, but still, what made you think you needed to come with me?"

Candice pulled up her phone, tapped the screen, and began to quote a text I'd sent her. "'Candice, your total ogre of a husband is forcing me against my will to go to L.A. to teach a bunch of bureau pretty boys Intuition One-oh-one. He's already admitted no one out there wants me to come and I'm only going as an experiment. They'll probably tar and feather me before the first day is over. Or burn me at the stake. Or shove me in a trunk, drive me out to the desert, and let the vultures pick my bones clean. He says that you and Dutch can't come, and that I have to solve some impossible cases or we'll all lose our jobs! But, no pressure . . .'"

I gulped. Brice was right. I was a little heavy on the dramatics. "And you thought that meant that you should buy a ticket and come with me?"

Candice stared levelly at me before shifting her gaze back to her phone and quoting the next text I'd sent her. "'Without you there to have my back, how the hell am I supposed to do this? After I fail, it'll be my fault when our branch closes, and our husbands lose the only jobs they've ever loved! This is nothing but a fast train to Divorce Depot, I tell you!'"

I winced. "You should know by now that I'm given to exaggeration."

She placed a hand over her heart in mock surprise. "Say it ain't so, Sundance."

I offered her the bag of chips as a consolation prize. "Okay, okay. I'm sorry. But this assignment sucks. I don't want to go it alone."

"Like I said," she purred. "I'll be your Huckleberry."

"Brice is gonna go ballistic," I said when she settled back to open the chips.

"He should know better than to force you into something like this alone and to forbid me from having your back."

I pointed at her. "You're so right. He should've expected exactly this scenario."

She nodded. "Damn straight."

At that moment Candice's phone rang. I recognized the ringtone as the one she'd assigned to her husband. Her only reaction was to arch an eyebrow while she peered into the bag of chips, ready to select one.

"How long are you gonna make him sweat?" I asked when the call finally went to voice mail.

"Not sure," she said. "How long's the flight?"

Chapter Two

. . .

I could hear Brice yelling through the phone pressed to Candice's ear. It made me want to giggle meanly. But then I decided that maybe it wasn't so cool that I was the cause of an issue between the married couple. I mean, I'd been at the center of enough angst between Candice and Brice over the years. Maybe I was pushing the limit.

"I'll take that under advisement," Candice said smoothly, without a hint of the anger that I knew was simmering beneath the surface. Candice doesn't cotton to being yelled at. Brice is about the only person who can get away with it and live to talk about it.

There was a little more yelling from Candice's phone before I reached over and gently pried it away from her. "Brice? It's Abby," I said, holding the phone so that Candice could hear too. "Before you start yelling at me, you should consider how often I fly off the cuff when put into an uncomfortable situation like the one you're sending me into. And you should also consider that the only thing that usually keeps me in a calm, reasonable, and professionally courteous frame of mind is Candice. I'm not the only one who needs her here with me, Brice. *You* need her here with me too."

There was a lengthy pause, then, "Fine, Cooper. *As usual*, you and my wife get your way. But if any word from Whitacre gets back to me about the two of you causing trouble, I'm going to yank both of you back here and discard your FBI credentials so fast it'll make your pretty little heads spin."

"Promises, promises," Candice said, grabbing the phone again to hang up on Brice.

We walked in silence through the terminal to the tram at LAX. Well, I walked. Candice mostly stomped.

A while later, after we'd gotten our bags and boarded the shuttle that would take us to get our rental car, I said, "I don't get why Brice has got his panties in such a wad over you being here with me. I mean, we work together on bureau cases all the time."

Candice glared out the window. I had a feeling Brice had said something that'd really pushed a button with her, but I couldn't figure out what it might've been. She revealed it when she said, "It's Whitacre. He made it clear that I wasn't welcome in his territory."

I blinked. "Wait, what? Why would he do that? Do you two know each other or something?"

Candice shifted her steely gaze to me. "He oversees the Vegas bureau too."

"Ahhh," I said as understanding dawned. "Yeah. They don't love us so much out there, do they?"

Candice rolled her eyes. "Oh, they love you, Abby. It's me they have a major grudge against."

"Because of that Mafia guy who wanted to take you out to the desert, bury you up to your neck, and let the coyotes use your face as a chew toy if you didn't prove to him that you were really his loyal and trusted friend?"

The woman next to me turned her head sharply to look at us. "Yeah," Candice said. "Because of that."

There was some shuffling in the shuttle as the woman got up and moved several seats away. Some people are so sensitive. "So what does Whitacre not wanting you in his territory mean, exactly? You're not allowed to come with me to the L.A. office?"

Candice had been standing for the ride, holding the pole in front of me. She let go of it and scooted into the seat next to mine. "Not sure, Sundance. What does that radar say about the situation?"

I switched on the old radar and focused on the dilemma for a minute. "We're damned if we do and we're damned if we don't," I told her.

"Then let's be damned if we do," she said.

I considered her stoic expression. "Your being here is politically dicey territory for Brice, right? Because it's gonna remind Whitacre about Vegas and your . . . connections."

She pointed a finger gun at me. "Nothing gets by you."

"Then what're you *doing* here, Cassidy?" I said softly, using my favorite nickname for her.

"You needed me more than Brice needs me to stay home," she said simply.

"That's true," I said, because it was, but the guilt of it still tugged uncomfortably at me.

The shuttle bus pulled to a stop and we waited our turn to get off and head over to the express kiosk to check in and get our keys for the rental car.

"There," Candice said minutes later when we were searching for the car.

"Huh," I said, a bit surprised. Brice had reserved an SUV. Definitely a pricier car for a two-week rental.

Candice gave my arm a nudge. "Underneath all that cold, professional armor, Brice does his best to look out for you."

"You both do," I said, heading over to the driver's side.

Candice beat me to it. "How about I drive?" she said sweetly.

"Uh . . . ," I said. "This is awkward. See, I was sorta hoping to arrive at the hotel in one piece."

"You were, huh?" she said, never moving away from the door and holding her hand out expectantly for the set of keys I was currently clutching.

"Yeah. *Crazy* as this may sound, Candice, I had my fingers crossed that today wasn't going to be my last. And if I let you drive, that sorta cuts my odds in half."

"I drive you all over town at home," Candice said.

"True, but this is L.A. And L.A. traffic is unforgiving. And your driving calls for a *lot* of forgiving." Candice glared at me. "Just sayin'," I added hastily.

"Fine," she said. "You drive. But don't ask me to help you navigate."

"No problem," I said. We hopped in and I smiled sweetly when I noticed the onboard navigation system. "No problem at all."

That got me a scowl from my bestie, but I wasn't at all sorry. Candice drove like a person with an attitude like, "You only live once!" and "Only the good die young!" and "Booyah, mother firecrackers!" In other words, recklessly. It was a miracle we'd been in only a *couple* of accidents together.

Still, driving in L.A. will make you wish you'd let someone else—even someone reckless—take the wheel. And I now know that from experience. By the time we arrived at the hotel, I needed a drink. Something stiff, strong, and accompanied by an identical twinsie. "Oh, God, let there be a minibar!" I whispered as I parked the car in the hotel lot.

"This is nice," Candice said, looking up at our digs.

"Maybe there's a hotel bar!" I said.

"When do you have to meet with Whitacre?" she asked.

I got out of the car and made my way to the back to get my

bag. "I don't know. Brice said Whitacre would call me. Probably tomorrow morning." At that exact moment my phone rang. "Son of a peach pit," I growled.

Candice appeared amused. "You better answer," she said when I simply stood there, scowling at my phone.

"Crap on a cracker," I muttered, then swiped my finger across the screen. "This is Abby."

"Mrs. Rivers," a male voice said. "This is Director Whitacre. I trust you've landed safely and arrived at your hotel."

My eyes narrowed. We'd done exactly that, and I wondered that he seemed so certain of it. "Yes, sir, thank you."

"After you check in, I'd like you to come to the office and meet a few members of my team. You'll be working with a select group of agents at first and I'd prefer to make the introductions as soon as possible."

Double crap on a cracker. "Of course, sir. Give me about an hour and I'll see you at your offices."

"Good. Oh, and please leave Ms. Fusco behind to enjoy her visit to L.A. She might consider taking in some sightseeing while she's here. We'll only be needing your expertise for now."

Before I could even answer, the director hung up. "Good Lord," I said, staring at my phone. "*What* an asshole!"

"What's the deal?" Candice asked.

I scowled. "Whitacre told me to come alone. He thinks you should go be a tourist."

To my surprise, Candice chuckled. "Yeah, I figured he might play hardball."

"I'm not leaving you behind," I said. "Either he lets you come with me or I don't work for him."

Candice swung her arm across my shoulders and pulled me gently toward the entrance to the hotel. "Abs, you gotta learn to pick your battles, honey. I'm here for moral support and backup.

That doesn't require me to follow you around like a puppy. I can hang out until you need me."

I glanced sideways at her. "You say that like you're pretty sure I'll need you."

She shrugged. "Don't you always?"

"No," I said firmly. "Sometimes I need Dutch. Or Oscar. Or even Brice."

"Noted," she said with a hint of mirth in her voice. "Come on, let's get our room keys and check out that minibar."

"I have to meet Whitacre in an hour," I reminded her.

She winked. "Did he tell you to come sober?"

"I kinda think that was implied. He's probably assuming I'll show up fresh as a daisy and sharp as a tack."

"Men and their assumptions," she said, making a *tsk*ing sound.

Exactly one hour later I came out of the parking structure next to 11000 Wilshire Boulevard on steady feet but thirsty for a martini. There'd been no minibar in the room, but there had been a restaurant bar on the main floor and Candice had sauntered in like she owned the place. She'd ordered me to eat something before I left to meet Whitacre, and I'd scarfed down a cup of clam chowder and an iced tea while she'd sipped on a glass of single malt that was definitely going on the room tab. I had a feeling the bar bill would climb steadily over the course of our stay.

Trying to find my second wind, I approached the massive Federal Building and realized that it'd been used in many a backdrop for dozens of movies and TV shows I'd seen. For the record, it's even more impressive up close.

I tried not to feel intimidated as I headed across the pavilion and into the massive lobby. By contrast, our bureau office in

Austin is tiny. I mean, we're across the hall from a dermatologist and an insurance company. The Wilshire Federal Building is a *huge* structure almost entirely devoted to government business. It'd make any newcomer quake in her modest three-inch heels.

Once I was through the doors, I looked around for a directory or someone I could ask to point me in the direction of the FBI offices, but before I could even get my bearings, I felt a light tap on my elbow and someone said, "Mrs. Rivers?"

I turned and saw a woman with brown hair and thin features, dressed in a smart navy blue business suit. "It's Cooper," I said. Her brow furrowed. "I mean, I am Mrs. Rivers, but my professional name is Cooper. Abby Cooper."

She offered me a slight nod and I realized I hadn't even said hello to her. "Sorry. I've been struggling with the decision to take my husband's last name or keep my own, and I think I'm finally settling on leaving it alone." Her brow furrowed even more and I added, "I'm babbling, aren't I?"

"You're fine," she assured me, and pointed me forward through the lobby. We began to walk and she said, "I'm Special Agent Hart. I've heard a great deal about your fortune-telling abilities, Ms. Cooper, and I have to confess I'm pretty skeptical about what you claim to be able to do, or how you might be able to help us."

"Did they tell you about the levitating?" I asked.

I saw her gaze flicker sideways. I kept my expression neutral. "Levitating?" she repeated.

"Yeah. On the night of the full moon, I levitate and my head spins around a hundred eighty degrees and I spit fire. It's wicked cool."

Her finger came up to press against her mouth and stop the laugh that I knew she was close to giving in to. "Lucky for us, then, that there's no full moon for the next three weeks."

"Bummer," I said. "I always feel it's important to give a lecture and a show at these things. Maybe next time."

"I'm assuming you encounter a lot of skeptics," she said, slightly chagrined, as we stepped onto an elevator.

I widened my eyes. "Gee, what gave it away?"

"Okay, okay, maybe I deserved that. How about if I promise to keep my skepticism to myself while you give your little demo?"

I shook my head. We were the only two people on the elevator and Agent Hart had just confirmed what a total pain in my ass this was going to be. "How do you like the new car?" I asked her.

Again, she looked sharply at me. "What?"

"Your new car. It's silver, right? You also have a black car, but it's much bigger, like SUV size. I'm surprised you'll be keeping it, because I only see you driving the new silver car. And I can't say that I blame you. It's fast, cute, and sporty. There's also something luxurious about it too. Maybe you opted for the leather seats, or got the navigation package—something made it a little bit extra special."

It was her turn to widen her eyes.

Now that I had her attention, I kept going. "The new car heralded in a celebration. Not a birthday per se, but a rebirth of some kind. Professionally, you've done very well over the last twelve months, but personally you've had a hard year. A relationship ended, but you were happy—or maybe I should say relieved—that it did. Still, it dragged out for some reason. I see legal docs, so I'm assuming it was a divorce. The car was to celebrate being not just free of a relationship that'd soured, but being free of the legal entanglements that followed."

Hart's jaw dropped, and at that moment there was a ping to let us know we'd arrived on our floor. The elevator doors opened and I flashed her a slightly evil grin before practically prancing out of the elevator. *Booyah, bitch,* I thought.

And then I remembered Brice's warning to play nicey-nice with the kiddies in L.A. If his job hadn't been on the line, I would've grabbed my bag and gotten back on the plane for Austin, but I believed him when he said there was trouble brewing for our division and I needed to bring home a win. So I reined it in. Just an eensy, weensy bit.

"Nice," I said, indicating the impressive open floor we'd landed on when Agent Hart had recovered herself enough to follow me out of the elevator.

She was still staring at me in amazement, but at least she wasn't all slack-jawed. "I . . . uh . . . we . . . ," she said, eventually managing to motion with her hand in the direction we needed to go.

We walked side by side in silence, and it was hard but I managed to keep the smug smile off my lips all the way down the corridor. It probably helped that as we walked past there were nudges and whispers from the men and women standing about. People had turned out for my appearance, it seemed. Awesome.

At the end of the corridor, Agent Hart motioned to a closed door and moved ahead of me to open it. "In here, Ms. Cooper."

"Thanks," I said, passing by her into a conference room with a large mahogany table and about a dozen of those weird-looking ergonomic chairs.

I moved to the far end of the table and pulled out a chair before setting down my purse and taking a seat. When I looked up, I saw that Agent Hart was standing there with a puzzled expression on her face. "Are other people joining us?" I asked.

Hart pulled a little on her left ring finger—which was bare of any ring. "Yes," she said, but it was clear she wanted to say something more. "It's just . . . I paid cash for the car. And I bought it at one of our FBI auctions. It's not on my credit report or any public record. I haven't even registered it yet."

I stared at her dully. "Your point being that even if I had researched the financial and public records of every single agent in this office—which, if I actually *had*, would've landed my ass in serious hot water—I couldn't have known about the car, right? I mean, even *besides* the fact that I just found out about this assignment this morning, and between hearing about the assignment and getting on a plane, I obviously had no time or even access to a database that would've shown me exactly who was employed here—not to mention the time to memorize enough details to toss out a few very specific and accurate facts about you, individually, Agent Hart, upon meeting you for the first time, without knowing that it was *you* who would be greeting me. Is that about the gist of what you're thinking right now?"

Her face flushed and she bit her lip. "I seem to have severely underestimated you, Ms. Cooper."

"Don't sweat it. You're definitely not alone, and after you, I'll be dismissed just as easily by every person in this office. So how about you bring in the firing squad and we get this dog and pony show on?" I clapped my hands and rubbed them together for emphasis, and Agent Hart dipped her chin and scooted back out of the room, probably to gather the other pitchfork-wielding villagers.

While I waited, my phone beeped. It was Candice.

How's it going?

I sighed. Exactly like we expected.

So, they're being complete douchewaddles. . . .

"Douchewaddle"? That's new.

I'm three drinks in. You get what you get.

Got it. Yes, they're being total DWs.

Need a Huckleberry?

Not yet, but how about you lay off the booze and sober up in case I need one later?

Roger that. Hang in there, Sundance.

I put my cell away but not the smile that hearing from her had brought on. Candice had this way of making me feel smarter, stronger, and more confident than I usually could feel on my own. Maybe it was because she was so smart, strong, and confident that some of those qualities rubbed off on me. And I had no doubt that she was in fact totally sober. The "douche-waddle" and three-drinks-in thing was just an effort to get me to laugh and chill out in an otherwise stressful situation. God love her, it'd worked.

By the time the door opened and a line of men in crisp, starched dress shirts, ties, and slacks all marched in, I was fairly relaxed. Still, I kept my expression neutral lest the smirk I wanted to adopt get us off to a bad start.

The first man through the door came around to the other side of the table directly across from me and stuck out his hand. "Ms. Cooper, I'm Special Agent in Charge Manny Rivera."

I stood and shook his hand, adding a nod for good measure. "A pleasure, sir," I said. (I figured it didn't hurt to be polite.)

Pointing down the row of men as they came in to pull out

chairs from around the table, he said, "These are special agents Kim, Perez, Williams, Robinson, and Simmons."

I nodded to each of them and I noticed that all the agents had carried in one thin folder apiece, which they set on the table in front of them before taking their seats. Just as I'd settled back into my chair, Agent Hart came back into the room and looked around the table. I'd noticed that the men had all taken up chairs opposite me, gathering around their leader, SAIC Rivera. The message was easy to see. It was them against me.

There was one last seat at the end of the table next to Agent Simmons for Agent Hart to take, but she surprised me—and it seemed her peers—when she came to my side of the table and pulled out the chair just one down from mine. Hmm . . . maybe I'd underestimated her too.

I dipped my chin in thanks at her, but she didn't acknowledge it. Instead she rested her hands on the conference table and looked expectantly to Rivera.

"Well," he began in the slightly awkward silence that followed. "Now that we're all here, I think we should start by seeing what you're capable of, Ms. Cooper."

That's doubtful, I thought, but held my tongue.

Rivera pushed forward a very thin file toward me. "This is a case that Agent Simmons has been working. We'd like to see what you can tell us about it."

I stared at the closed folder, trying very hard not to give in to my first impulse to yell "Bullshit!" After counting to ten, I opened the folder and considered the first page. It was a photo of a young man, maybe late teens to early twenties, with ginger hair, a dusting of freckles, and slightly crooked teeth but a smile as wide as Texas. He looked the picture of innocence, appearing happy and like he had his whole future ahead of him with endless possibilities. Nothing about his image spoke to the truth about who he was, however. That I picked up right away as a series of images flashed through my mind.

There was a typed-up bio on the inside of the folder. It stated that the young man's name was Sean Anderson. He was nineteen. His dad was a locksmith. His mother was a tax accountant. They lived in Van Nuys.

"God, I hate being tested," I said softly, closing the file to fold my hands over the top of it and stare dully at Rivera.

His brow furrowed slightly. "How do you think you're being tested?" he asked carefully.

I pushed the file back toward him. "That's a closed case, sir. And it's a waste of my time to give you my impressions on a case you've already solved. Granted, if any case might've tested my abilities, it'd be one where Opie from Mayberry gets turned by Islamic extremists into a homegrown terrorist, but, sadly for you folks, today's the day I pass with flying colors." The room had been quiet before I'd spoken, but now there was an extra sense of stillness to it. Most of the people around the table were trying to hide their stunned reactions. Some of them squinted at me and pressed their lips together, while others looked at Rivera as if he would provide an explanation, but he was staring at me as if trying to figure me out. Like I was some kind of puzzle that just needed the corner piece to orient the rest of the picture.

I've seen that look a lot in my life. It gets really, really wearisome after a while, because the answer is so simple. . . . I really AM fucking psychic, people. But, whatevs. I'd owe the swear jar a mental quarter later. For now, I had more proving ground to cover. I switched my focus from Rivera to the guy at the end of the table. Snapping my fingers and pointing to him, I said, "Slide your case file over here, Agent . . . ?"

"Kim," he said with a hint of irritation.

I nodded and motioned impatiently with my hand to have him give me the file. He looked to Rivera—who nodded—before sliding it (with a bit of force) across the table toward me. I slapped it with my hand before it could get by me, then opened it and stared at the photo for like two seconds before closing it firmly. "Dead," I said of the man pictured inside. Then I pointed at Kim and added, "And you know it. Granted, I don't think you've found your body yet, but you will. It's belowground, but not buried. Look at a family member, like a brother or a cousin who was like a brother. There was a familial connection between the murderer and the victim, but neither of the two men were saints. Just the opposite. This guy was connected to organized crime out of Russia . . . no . . . maybe Croatia, and the only person he trusted was his brother. Stupid. The brother was Cain to his Abel and wanted to take over the business." Kim opened his mouth as if to say something, but the needle on my snappish and rude meter was already in the red zone, so I gave his folder a good shove back to him and turned my focus to the remaining agents. "Who wants to go next?" I asked them.

The agent on the left side of Rivera stood and handed his folder to me. There was unspoken challenge in his eyes. I took the folder and opened it. A woman with long ash-blond hair and pretty green eyes stared out at me from the inside cover. The bio said that her name was Chelsea Brown; she was single and living in Inglewood. Her energy was somewhat "loud," and by that, what I mean is that she had energy that was very easy for me to pick up on and sort through. As I studied the photo and the energy attached to the woman, I got a series of images that caused me to frown. Looking up at the agent, I said, "Agent . . . Uh, sorry, what was your name again?"

"Perez," he said.

"Yes, Agent Perez, why is this woman being investigated? She's done nothing wrong."

His eyes widened and he didn't even try to cover it up. I realized immediately that he knew she was a law-abiding citizen.

That sparked some anger from me because I could feel that he'd been interacting with her quite a bit. "Listen," I said, leaning toward him. "You need to back the hell off this woman, Agent Perez. She hasn't broken a single law and *you* know it. Now, I can't understand why you're investigating her, but I sense your energy *all* over hers and I don't like men who stalk women on the pretense that they're investigating them for some trumped-up charge."

"I'm not stalking her, Ms. Cooper," he said.

"Bullshit," I snapped. "You're very aware of her daily comings and goings, and I have the feeling you're not going to back off either. For God's sake, man, the woman's pregnant! She's in a vulnerable situation right now and the last thing she needs is you breathing down her neck!"

Perez looked taken aback—obviously he hadn't known she was pregnant. Still, he offered up no further information, and that made me even madder. Pointing a finger at him, I said, "I think you should know that after this little party winds up, I intend to place a call to Director Gaston about you and this woman."

Perez's eyes widened a little more. He looked to Rivera, who also seemed pretty surprised by my outburst. I pointed my finger next at him and said, "She didn't do anything wrong, Agent Rivera. She's broken *no* laws."

"Thank you, Ms. Cooper," was all he said.

I glared hard at him. I could tell he didn't intend to do anything about it, so I closed the file and made a show of tucking it into my purse. If I had to, I'd drive out to the address listed in the bio and warn the woman myself. I very nearly walked out right then—I mean, I had no intention of being a part of any abuse of power by these L.A. chuckleheads—but Rivera put up his hand in a stopping motion as if he sensed I was ready to bolt and said, "Ms. Cooper, I'll explain why we needed your feedback on Chelsea Brown later. For now, if you'd please hand over that file and indulge the rest of our agents?"

I tapped a finger on the table while I thought about it. It seemed that Rivera was sincere about talking to me afterward, but if he was going to try to protect Agent Perez, then I didn't really need to stay.

On the other hand, my intuition was telling me to stick it out. Why, I didn't know, but every time I don't listen to my gut, I regret it, so I compromised. I pulled out the file from my purse, opened it to the address listed, and memorized it; then I slid the file back to Perez. "Fine," I said, crossing my arms to show Rivera that I'd stay, but I wasn't happy about it. After taking a deep breath to settle myself, I nodded across the table to where the only black agent in the room sat. He had a beautiful face, with sharp, intelligent eyes. He could've easily been a model or a movie star, but he'd chosen this for a career, which earned him a teensy ounce of respect from me. Pointing to him, I cocked an eyebrow in silent question.

"Robinson," he said.

Shifting my hand slightly to point at the folder underneath his right hand, I asked, "May I?"

He pushed the folder forward and I flipped it open to look at the photo and corresponding bio. I took in the image of a Hispanic man in his mid-fifties with a goatee and squinty eyes. "Drugs," I said when I felt that familiar oily, bitter taste at the back of my mouth. Sometimes, my intuition interprets things through my other senses, and the fingerprint of drugs in the ether always leaves an oily, icky taste on the back of my tongue. In my mind's eye I saw a crown being placed on the man's head. "He's a kingpin," I said. Then I saw a pair of wings and my symbol for Mexico. I closed the file and pushed it back across the table. "You've been working this case for a while, right?" I asked.

"Yes," he said. I could tell my four-word assessment of his case file hadn't overly impressed him.

"That," I said, pointing to the folder, "is not a closed case. But it sure as hell should be. You'll never catch him." Agent Robinson shifted in his chair and his energy suggested he was totally resisting my message. It didn't stop me from giving him more of my opinion, of course. "He's already flown the coop and gone back to Mexico, and no way are you gonna be able to tempt him to come back across the border again."

Robinson cocked an eyebrow and pursed his lips ever so slightly in silent challenge to my statement.

I shrugged. "I know he's got family here, right? A wife and two girls who're in their teens, right?"

Robinson's other eyebrow joined its raised twin, but he didn't give me a yea or a nay on that.

"You think that this guy is gonna come back over here one more time for them, and I'm here to tell you he's already abandoned his family. He finds clever ways to send them money, but emotionally, he's completely divorced himself from his wife and daughters, and soon even the money's gonna stop. He'll never set foot on U.S. soil again, and you're not going to get the Mexican authorities to hand him over either. I think you'll chase him for a while, though, because you're just the kind of man who won't quit until you bring in the bad guy, but it'll cost you something in the long run. I'm thinking the price you'll pay is something in the form of a promotion when it comes time for your turn. Your superiors don't think you know when to give up a dead case and focus on one you can actually resolve."

I felt a wave of anger emanate off Robinson, but he gave no outward sign of it. Instead his expression became a blank mask and then he did something that even I didn't expect. He moved his chair back, got up, tucked the chair back into place, and walked calmly out of the room.

No one spoke as he exited. They didn't need to. We all understood his absolute dismissal of me, and while I pretended not to care, deep down I'll admit that the insult stung. It was too reminiscent of being summarily dismissed by my parents when I was a child, and it made me question again why I'd even bothered to come out here to do this. I looked at Rivera, who was still staring at the door as if he was thinking of the lecture he'd be giving to Robinson later.

The whole atmosphere in the room was beginning to change too. With Robinson's departure, there was a palpable hostility circulating, and I suddenly felt very vulnerable and alone.

I figured I'd really blown it until Agent Hart came to my rescue. She slipped her folder toward me and I noticed that it was actually much thicker than any of the other files. "Ms. Cooper, I'd like to get your impressions on this case, please."

I took the file and opened it and saw that it was set up in the standard format of all the files that came across my desk when I worked cases back in Austin. Encouraged by the familiarity, I read the first few paragraphs of the file brief on the left-hand side of the page.

The case in question had to do with stolen artwork. There was a gallery owner, Mario Grecco, living in the Hollywood

Hills, who was being investigated for possibly fencing stolen art-work out of Europe. According to the bit of text I read, the FBI hadn't found a single solid lead to pin him to the crime. None of his clients would cop to the fact that they'd been approached to purchase the artwork, and it was still a mystery as to who Grecco's contacts in Europe were. It was estimated that he could be responsible for fencing between ten and one hundred million in stolen artwork.

I looked up from reading the brief and asked, "What's Grec-co's connection to wine?"

Hart seemed confused by my question, but then she said, "Actually, he collects it. It's one of his hobbies."

"He may be a collector, but he's also a forger," I said. "I keep seeing wine paired with my symbol for forgery."

While Hart pondered that, Rivera said, "Why is that rele-vant, Ms. Cooper?"

"Because you're not going to nail Grecco by following the stolen-art trail. The clients who buy these works from him know full well they're buying something stolen. But the clients who purchase a super-pricey bottle of wine from him will roll right over if you can prove to them that the wine isn't the rare vintage he's claiming it to be. My gut says that he's forged labels for wine that he probably picked up in the grocery store, then sold those bottles to at least a few of his stolen-art-buying clients. If you offer them immunity on possession of the stolen artwork, they'll be willing to testify against him.

"And I know you're after the bigger fish—the ring of art thieves that's supplying him with the pieces to fence—but you're looking in the wrong place. These guys steal from all the coun-tries where they don't actually reside, which is how they keep such a low profile."

Hart leaned in toward me; she seemed very interested in what I had to say. "We've been looking for them in Milan and Verona because so much of the stolen artwork comes from there."

"Nope," I said, closing my eyes to focus on the map that was forming in my mind's eye. "I'll go out on a limb here and say that none of the artwork comes from Switzerland, am I right?"

There was a pause; then Hart said, "No. Nothing from Switzerland."

I opened my eyes and smiled at her. "Everybody trusts the Swiss. Have your contacts work the European trail from the beginning. I'll bet the first pieces were stolen from countries that surround Switzerland—Austria, Germany, France, and Italy. The trail is also older than anybody realizes. Go back another decade and you'll start noticing a pattern. I keep seeing a set of skis, so if I were a betting woman, which I am, I'd lay money down that your thieves work at some sort of ski resort, which allows them access to wealthy European clients to target. They'd never hit close to home because that'd be too risky for them, but I'll bet that every ski season they target a few of these tourists, gather intel on them, and hit their homes a few months later when they can be sure that their vacation to Switzerland won't seem relevant. If you work this case from both ends, Agent Hart, I'm pretty sure you'll shut this whole ring down."

It was her turn to smile at me and just like that, we bonded. "Thank you, Ms. Cooper. That was fairly incredible."

I chuckled, waving a hand. "Oh, please. This is what I do. I pinpoint directions that'll lead to results, and when I'm *trusted*, good things can happen."

Hart's gaze shifted slightly to her boss across the table, and a flush touched her cheeks. I had a feeling she'd disobeyed orders by bringing in an actual, bona fide case for me to look at and not some lame photo and bio in a folder. I declined to look at Rivera but turned to one of the last agents I hadn't yet spoken to. Motioning to the thin file in front of him, I said, "Want me to take a look?"

Before he could answer, the door opened and in stepped a giant of a man. I pegged him to be perhaps a little over six and a half feet tall. He literally ducked to come in the door. His features were square and there was a hardness to him that made me want to back away a little from his presence.

He had large hands to go with his big frame, but he didn't move like the extra body mass was hard to lug around. In fact, I was surprised to see a bit of grace in his movements as he shut the door and walked to the head of the table. "Agents," he said to the group still gathered at the table. "I'd like a word with Ms. Cooper, please."

I recognized the voice as that of Director Whitacre. I hadn't been prepared for someone so tall and imposing, and it took a minute for me to mentally reconcile his image with that of Director Gaston, who was fairly short as men go, right around five-eight or thereabouts.

Still, there was a little something extra to both men that couldn't be measured with a yardstick, and that was an essence of authority that permeated the space around them. Gaston had a little extra essence on Whitacre, I noticed, but maybe that was because Gaston was perhaps the more dangerous of the two. I had no doubt that Gaston had used deadly force when he worked for the CIA. I also had no doubt, in fact, that when ordered to, he'd killed quickly, quietly, and most efficiently and he hadn't lost a moment's sleep over it.

I liked Gaston. A lot. But I was also a teensy bit terrified of him.

Whitacre scared me only because he could cause damage to

my husband's career and that of my friend if he wanted to. There was reason to be cautious and careful around him, but not in a way that would make me sleep with one eye open.

The agents got up and began to abandon the room. Perez was the second-to-last person through the door, and just as he was about to pass Whitacre, the taller man put a hand on his elbow to stop him for a moment, then bent to whisper something in his ear. Perez nodded, then continued out with Rivera on his heels, finally leaving me alone with Whitacre.

The second the door closed, I began to feel out the director's energy, which might've been an invasion of privacy, but he was the one testing me, so I figured I had the right. "Director," I said. "It's nice to finally meet you."

Whitacre stood above me—an intimidation tactic for sure. I did my best not to look the least bit afraid, and a slight smile played at the corner of his mouth. "Ms. Cooper," he said. "Thank you for coming out to L.A. on such short notice."

"Least I could do to save my job and those of my husband and boss, Director."

The slight smile got a teensy bit wider. "There's been a lot of chatter about you," he said, moving to the chair opposite mine and taking a seat. "Bill Gaston has taken a pretty good ribbing from the rest of us."

"Not surprising," I said, because it wasn't.

"He practically dared me to put you to the test," he continued.

When he didn't say anything after that, I said, "And?"

"And that display in here was, at the very least, impressive."

I sat back in my chair and crossed my arms, then looked around the room. No obvious sign of a camera, so I tilted my chin and eyed the corners. The cameras were small, hardly noticeable, and tucked into all four corners. I had no doubt that there were hidden microphones about the room too. "Thanks," I said before resting my elbows on the table and lacing my fingers together. "Now what?"

Before Whitacre could answer me, we heard a buzz and he looked down at his belt. Lifting his cell phone, Whitacre answered the phone and said, "Yes?" There was a long pause, during which the director smiled again, adding a small shake to his head, and he finally said, "Very good, Hector. That's excellent news." He then hung up the phone and said, "You were right about Chelsea Brown. She's pregnant."

That ignited a little fire in my belly again. "You need to talk to Perez," I told him. "Chelsea Brown has done nothing wrong. I don't even think she's connected to anyone who's committed a crime. She seems totally clean and all her associates seem . . ." My voice trailed off as I expanded my intuitive view of Chelsea. I saw a badge and a wedding ring. "Crap," I said with a shake of my own head when the obvious hit me. "I missed that one. She's married to Perez."

Whitacre tapped the table. "Yes," he said, clearly amused. "And Agent Perez had no idea of the surprise waiting for him when he got home tonight. He told me that Chelsea had planned to tell him over dinner."

"Well, I'm only sorry that I ruined her surprise. I'm not sorry about calling Perez out on his fabricated file. I mean seriously, sir, I'm used to being tested, but if someone like Director Gaston wants to vouch for me, don't you think that's worth at least a *little* courtesy at our first meet and greet?"

Whitacre appeared to consider that. For a long time. Finally, he held up his hands in apology and said, "You're right. I know and respect the hell out of Bill. Which is why his championing of you has seemed so out of character. He's far too smart to be taken in by a charlatan. At least, that's what we all thought until conversations of you came up. But he's sworn all along that the reason his team in Austin closes so many cold cases is because of your influence. And the numbers have been consistent for the past two years now, ever since that office opened. The stats are impressive to say the least, and Bill's peers and superiors have all been asking how he's doing it. He's never tried to hide the fact that he employs a psychic. Learning that you're also married to one of his top field agents made us even more curious, and I was the one to volunteer for a demonstration."

That wasn't quite the apology I was looking for, but maybe I'd have to pick my battles while I was on loan. "Okay," I said. "So, assuming I've passed the test, how about you let me look at a real case or two? You know, so that I can tell Harrison that I played nicey-nice with the other agents."

Whitacre stood up. "Agent Hart already brought you one of those, Ms. Cooper. I don't know what you said to her on the way up here, but whatever it was convinced her not to use the dummy folder I'd had her prepare for your audition. As for the other cases I'd like you to look at, I think we can start on those tomorrow. I'll need to speak to the other agents privately now. You know, to settle a few ruffled feathers."

I understood he was specifically referring to Agent Robinson, but maybe I'd ruffled a few other feathers too. I'm really good at that, actually. I've got "make 'em mad" skills, I tell ya.

Getting to my feet, I said, "Sounds good. What time would you like me to come back in the morning, Director?"

"Nine a.m.," he said, moving ahead of me to open the door for us. As I passed through the doorway, he added, "I hope you won't mind working late this week, Ms. Cooper. I have a feeling we'll be running quite a few cases by you."

Freaking perfect. There went much of my free time. "Not at all, Director. See you in the morning."

With that, I left him and, once at the elevator, I dialed Candice. "Sundance," she said smoothly. "How goes it?"

"Great!" I lied. "We got along so well they've asked me out for drinks and nachos."

Candice laughed. She knew when I was kidding. "It went that well, huh?"

"You seem surprised."

"Who could possibly resist your charms?"

"Riiiiight? Anyway, I don't think I'm gonna go. You know how these L.A. people can be." The woman in business attire next to me in the elevator offered me a sideways glare. I smiled sweetly and added, "Yep. I'm just making new friends everywhere I go!"

"How about if *I* take you out for drinks and nachos and you can tell me all about it?" Candice asked.

I gave in to a sigh of relief. "There's a reason you're my best friend. See you in half an hour?"

"Deal."

Chapter Three

. . .

Candice had done her homework, and by homework, I mean she'd scoured Yelp for the best nachos in all of L.A. and found *the* place to eat them. The restaurant was called Tinga—a relatively small eatery with tons of character, bright colors, funky lighting, and some *seriously* fine nachos.

Over a plate of said seriously fine, I told Candice all about the meet and greet at the L.A. office, emphasizing the many ways I felt I'd been mistreated and disrespected. At the end, she wadded up her napkin and tossed it on the table. "I'm not sure I understand why you're so worked up. You knew they were probably gonna try to trip you up, right?"

"Of course I knew. But that doesn't mean that they had to treat me like I was a joke from the get-go, does it, Candice? In the end it's a choice to either treat me like a human being with some pretty great credentials and offer me a little respect for our first introduction or to be total douchewaddles, as you so elegantly put it. And I wasn't naive about how this was going to go. Of course I was expecting them to bring a healthy dose of skepticism, but not all the judgmental condescending bullshit, which they didn't even try to hide, I might add. I mean, how about you be polite, courteous, professional, and let me look at an actual active case file before you start deciding what I'm all about? Coming into that meeting all assholes a-blazing put me immediately on the defensive."

"Oh, I think you were already on the defensive."

I frowned at her but had to consider that. "You may have a point. But they still didn't have to be so shitty about it."

"Of course they did," she countered. "Abs, this is L.A. There's a psychic on every street corner and most of them suck. You know that."

"Yeah, but *I* don't, Candice!" I snapped. "And it's not just my word they had to take into account. It's the *entire* Austin bureau *and* Director Gaston!"

Candice let me verbally thrash around in frustration for a bit longer before she looked at me sadly and said, "Abby, no one wants everyone to accept you more than the people who know you and love you, but the world isn't ready for someone like you. You're asking not just this person or that person to change their approach to you, but the entire planet to come at you differently. What you don't get is that you *are* different from most everyone you meet, and that's why they're wary when you first tell them you're psychic. They don't know anything about what that actually means or if you're perhaps certifiably crazy. And while I can't imagine what it'd be like to exist in a place where I'm constantly judged, underestimated, and maligned, I think that this frustration you have over wanting the whole world to approach you differently could eat you up pretty good if you let it."

My defenses were still up. "So I should just *let* them treat me that way? I should just accept it and not allow it to affect me?!"

"Yes," she said.

My jaw dropped and I stared at her in stunned silence.

Candice reached forward and put a hand on my arm, squeezing gently. "Sundance," she began, "whatever opinions, thoughts, or preconceived notions other people have of you, they're *other* people's stuff. You don't own *any* of that. You only own your stuff. It's not up to you to fix, resolve, or change other people's minds or even prove to them that you're the real deal. It's only up to you to be *you*. And you are the best you that I know, and I'm damn proud to be your friend."

I looked down at Candice's hand on my arm. "It's just so hard to walk into all that doubt, Candice. It was so hostile in there."

She squeezed her grip a little to reassure me. "I totally get it. But you know you don't have to mirror that attitude, right? I mean, wouldn't it be better to be your own dazzling portrait rather than someone else's reflection, Abby?"

She paused for effect and I had to admit that her analogy struck a deep chord with me. I wanted to respond to that, but Candice wasn't quite finished doling out the wisdom, and she continued by saying, "If you can simply allow everyone else to think or feel about you how they will, it will free you up completely to just be you and not the mirror image of the person you're busy sniping back at. And, just so you know, girl, you're not so bad to hang out with when you're not in the mood to rip someone's head off their shoulders."

I offered her a crooked smile. "I can be delightful. . . ."

"Yes. Yes, you can. You can also be a total pain in the ass. The choice to be one or the other is completely up to you. What you need to understand is that it costs you less overall to remain unfazed by whatever attitude someone else wants to throw at you while you're simply being you."

I heard everything that Candice was saying and I grudgingly had to admit that she made a whole lotta sense. I was super thin-skinned. I got that from being told I was less than acceptable and totally unwanted by parents who *never* should've

had children. The adult me (over)reacted to nearly every per-
ceived slight because I was always walking around on the
defensive. I found plenty of people willing to slight me, too,
and I wondered if maybe I'd brought a lot of that on myself.

Mentally I went back over the meeting at the L.A. bureau,
and I realized that if I hadn't actually called the agents out on
their bullshit, perhaps I could've ingratiated myself with them
by simply giving them my feedback without all the verbal
finger-pointing and crying foul.

"You're right," I said at last. "I mean, I hate to admit it, but
you really are right."

Candice beamed. "I never get tired of hearing that."

"So, what do you think I should do to repair things?" I
asked her, realizing I had two weeks ahead of me that were
already off to a bad start.

"That's the best part. You don't have to do much of anything other than be yourself."

"Really?" I said. "You don't think I should try to mend fences
or apologize or anything?"

"Nope. What's done is done. Plus, these guys don't need to
hear an apology, which I don't really think you owe them anyway. In fairness to you—they did start it. But that only means
that it'll be easier for you to walk in there, head held high, and
get to work doing what you do. Everyone who works with you
eventually comes around, Sundance. Just focus on being the
amazing psychic you are, and the rest will follow."

"You make it sound easy," I said.

"It's as easy as focusing on what's important. The cases are
the thing you came here to work on, so get to work on them."

"I'm also supposed to teach these agents about harnessing
their own intuitive gifts to make them better investigators," I
reminded her.

"You can work on that next week," Candice said easily. "This week, it's all about the caseload."

Most of that night, I thought about everything that Candice had said to me. No surprise, I didn't sleep well. Her words about being my own portrait instead of somebody else's reflection kept reverberating through my mind. I've been picked on and bullied a *lot* in my life, and when faced with a new, possibly hostile situation, I tend to shoot first and ask questions and bury the dead bodies later.

What Candice had so kindly pointed out was that not every new encounter with disbelieving jerkholes had to be the O.K. Corral. I could meet fire with apathy. After a while and some practice, I might even be able to meet it with compassion, understanding, and empathy.

So, the next morning when I again arrived at the bureau and was met by Agent Hart, I was all smiles and relaxed attitude. "Good morning, Agent Hart," I said. "How're you?"

"I'm very well, Ms. Cooper, thank you for asking," she said warmly while motioning toward the elevators. "And thank you also for your insights yesterday. I did some preliminary checking and discovered that Grecco offers some of his wealthier clients a bottle of rare wine as a thank-you for their purchase. A few of those clients he's offered to sell even rarer vintages to."

There was a slight gleam in Hart's eye when she revealed that to me, and I suddenly put together why. "Let me guess," I said. "Grecco doesn't have a license to sell liquor."

She winked at me. "Bingo."

"So you can obtain a warrant on that alone and dig into his records and the wine he sells."

"Yes," she said, that gleam in her eye brightening even more.

"I'm going to arrest him later this morning after the judge signs the warrant. The local authorities will be working jointly with us on this, and we'll search his home and gallery thoroughly for evidence of more crimes."

"He's tricky about the wine," I said as my radar pinged. "He keeps it belowground."

"I've learned that the house he owns has a wine cellar."

"Those are rare in California, right?"

"Generally," Hart said, pushing the button for the elevator. "The hardest part may be finding the wine cellar. We have only a suggestion from the archives that the old home, once owned by Errol Flynn, has a hidden wine cellar."

"Ah," I said, stepping onto the elevator when the doors opened. "Well, good luck with that."

Hart stood next to me and eyed me sideways. "I was thinking . . . ," she said.

I chuckled. "You want me to come with you to help you find it."

"The director said it would be fine to take you if you'd agree to go."

"I'm game," I said, happy to have at least one ally in the office.

"Perfect," Hart said. "Oh, and Rivera wanted a moment of your time. You're set to meet with him first."

"Not Whitacre?" I asked.

"No, he's headed to Arizona this morning. One of his SAICs had a heart attack last night and Whitacre went to see about her and assess the situation."

My radar pinged again and I frowned. "Oh," I said.

"What?"

"I don't think she'll pull through. Her situation looks very grave."

Hart stared at me in shock. "Sara's going to die?"

"You know her personally?"

"I do, but not well," she said, still looking stunned. "We met a decade ago at a conference where she gave a speech about the difficulties of being a female agent at the bureau. The ratio back then was eight to one. Today it's better, about six to one, but still not great. Anyway, I approached Sara—Agent Barlow—after her speech, and we struck up a conversation and even had dinner together at the end of the conference. We kept in touch here and there. I sent her congratulations on her post as the SAIC in Phoenix; she sent me one when I received a commendation. I'd call us friendly acquaintances at best, but I've always admired her. I can't believe she won't recover. She's still relatively young."

I tapped my chest. "Her heart hasn't been well for a while," I said. "The stress of the job and genetics feel like they finally caught up to her."

Agent Hart dropped her gaze to the floor, and I felt bad that I'd sprung the dismal prediction on her.

A moment later the doors opened and, before we got out, I placed a hand on her arm and said, "I'm really sorry. If it helps, I don't think she's even aware anymore. She feels very distant from her body right now."

Agent Hart nodded and we stepped out. We walked in silence along the same route we'd taken the day before, but as we were approaching the conference room, Agent Kim came up to us, wiggling his phone. "The director sent an update on Barlow's condition," he said. "Sorry, Kelsey, it doesn't look good."

"Thanks, Lee," she said. "I already heard it was bad." For emphasis, Hart looked at me.

Kim seemed to register that I'd been the one to tell Hart

about Barlow, because his mouth formed an O and then he backed carefully away, as if he didn't want to catch my cooties.

I felt a flame of anger ignite in my chest, but Candice's sage words from the night before came back to me. In my mind's eye I saw a painting of myself, wearing a pleasant expression, set next to a mirror, which reflected a fearsome creature similar to an Orc from *The Lord of the Rings*. Just like that, I felt the fire die away and I said, "Should we head to the conference room?"

Agent Hart nodded absently. I could tell her mind was still on the special agent in charge in Phoenix. She didn't say anything further about it, however; instead she led me to the conference room, where I saw that Rivera was already seated and waiting for me. He looked up from his laptop as we entered. "Your warrant just came in, Hart. Gather your team and let me know when you're ready to go."

"Yes, sir. Thank you." She was kind enough to nod to me before she turned and left the room.

Rivera made a motion to the chair I'd occupied the day before and I headed for it. As I took my seat, I concentrated on keeping myself calm and unruffled by remembering the image of the portrait and the mirror in my mind's eye. When I looked up at Rivera, I thought the technique was working because he was eyeing me curiously and said, "You good, Cooper?"

"I am, sir, thank you."

"Glad to hear it," he said, closing the lid of his laptop to lean forward and rest his elbows on it. "Agent Hart has requested you to go with her to Grecco's home and help sniff out this wine cellar he's got hidden somewhere in the house."

"She briefed me in the elevator, sir."

"Good. When you get back, I believe Agent Perez and Agent Robinson have a case that they'd like your . . ." Rivera's voice trailed off as he seemed to struggle with what to call my intuitive input.

"Insight?" I offered.

"Yes," Rivera said. "A case requiring your insight."

"Are you sure Agent Robinson wants my input?"

"I'm sure we'd all like your input on this particular case, Ms. Cooper," Rivera said, his tone growing a little flinty. He was probably waiting for me to challenge him further, especially after Robinson's abrupt departure from the room the day before.

"Of course, sir. I'm here to help."

"Good," Rivera repeated. There was a small awkward pause; then he said, "Ms. Cooper, I think you should know that, even given that exhibition of yours yesterday, my team remains skeptical."

I ran down a list of possible retorts and went for simple. "I see."

"Director Whitacre has asked me to keep him in the loop about your progress here. However, he's leaving the decision to keep you on for the full two weeks up to me. I want you to know that we'll be proceeding with you as a consultant for now, but I'm reserving the right to dismiss you and send you back to Austin on a moment's notice."

I sat with that for a long moment and everything that Candice had said to me the night before rang in my ears. Mentally, I stepped back from the tone of Rivera's words, and the second I did that, I was able to see his barely contained hostility—and that of his team—in a completely different context. One that didn't attach itself to me personally, but more as a group of serious professionals expressing their collective fear about something they didn't fully understand and couldn't yet relate to. The minute I saw myself through their eyes, it was like a lightbulb

ignited over my head, and I began to think about Rivera inform-
ing me he'd be ready to dismiss me at a moment's notice as
something that was actually kind of funny; I mean, did he think
I'd be *upset* about being allowed to go back home? Just like that,
I felt all that tension and anxiety I'd been walking around with
since Brice ordered me to L.A. fall away. "Of course, sir," I said
smoothly. "I'd expect nothing less."

He nodded curtly and stood up. I got up too. "Agent Hart
should be waiting for you at her cubicle. She won't leave for the
Grecco residence until you join her."

"Excellent," I told him, turning for the door with a great deal
more enthusiasm than when I'd entered. Not only was I confident in my abilities to help these people, but now I didn't care
what they thought. I'd do my job and not give a crap about the
obvious skepticism wafting off every agent save Hart. And if I
got sent home—so be it. All I could do was all I could do.

Hart spotted me in the aisle leading to her cubicle and got
up to meet me. I noticed she'd swapped her suit jacket for a
Kevlar vest. "Expecting trouble?" I asked.

"Not really," she said, belting her gun holster. "But we go
in prepared."

"Do I get a vest?"

Hart smiled. "Not today. We have no plans of putting you
in harm's way."

"Comforting," I told her, returning the smile. "Are we
ready to roll?"

"We are," she said. "I'll fill you in on how this'll play out in
the van."

I followed Hart down to the parking structure located underneath the building, which was where two large dark blue vans

were lined up, engines running. Hart motioned me to the first van and I pulled open the door to see agents Kim and Robinson already buckled into their seats. Robinson glared at me with open hostility, while Kim's expression remained carefully neutral, and I could tell he was working to avoid my gaze.

"Hey, guys!" I said brightly. "Ready to have some fun?" (Okay, okay . . . so sometimes I like to poke the dragon.)

Behind me I heard Hart chuckle. "Don't tease them, Cooper. They bite."

I continued to grin winningly at the two men, hopping into the van to take a seat in the back without further comment. Hart took up the seat next to me. A moment later, agents Simmons and Perez joined us, and as Simmons closed the van door, Perez patted the shoulder of the driver to motion him to go.

Once we were under way, Hart said, "We'll have you stay in the van until we secure the residence. At this point we don't know if Grecco is at home or at work, but if he is home, we'll remove him from the premises until we can finish our search. I'll do a sweep of the whole house first and see if the wine cellar is somewhere obvious. If I can't locate it, I'll call you on your cell and ask you to come inside."

"Got it," I told her.

"It may be a while before I call you, though," she said.

I wiggled my cell phone and said, "Candy Crush. Level four forty-two." I could easily lose track of time playing Candy Crush; it was the crack of all online games.

"Excellent," Hart said.

We rode the rest of the way in silence and I busied myself by staring out the window. Eventually we arrived in what appeared to be a very wealthy community, where the privacy fences were crazy tall, and only the rooftops of most houses were visible.

"Grecco lives pretty high on the hog, huh?" I asked Hart.

"He does," she said. "But not for long. I can't wait to show this guy his new twelve-by-twelve-foot digs."

"Been chasing him for a while?"

"Far too long," she said.

At that moment the van slowed and began to make a sharp right turn. I looked out the window again and saw that we'd entered the top of a driveway with a gate and call box. The driver of the van lowered his window, pressed the call button, and exchanged words that I couldn't quite catch with someone in the house. The gate opened a moment later, so whatever he'd said to get us in, it worked.

The driveway was long and the house was big. It was pale white stucco with a Spanish clay-tile roof and a fountain centered steps away from the entrance. The driver of our van parked right at the front door and every agent in the van got out quickly and headed up the steps. Hart lingered only as long as it took her to say, "Sit tight. I'll call you with a status as soon as I can."

I saluted to her and got busy crushing some candy.

Time passed—I had no idea how long, but when my phone did buzz, I jumped and answered with a hasty, "Hello?"

"Cooper, it's Hart. Come on in. We can't find the wine cellar."

"On my way." Before pocketing my cell, I noted the time: They'd been inside for almost two hours. "Wow," I muttered. "That was a time suck."

My knock on the front door was answered by Agent Kim. He wore that same blank expression, but he did say, "Agent Hart is waiting for you in the kitchen. Follow me."

I tagged dutifully along behind him as he led me through the large house, which I ogled as much as I could get away with. The place was gorgeous, with bright white walls to display a ton of art, and furnishings that didn't distract from the stuff on the wall. We passed several rooms that I would've loved to explore, but Kim kept a pretty good pace. I did take note of one room along the way that held a particularly large aquarium set into the wall, which hosted a bounty of richly colored fish. "So cool," I whispered to myself.

The kitchen was at the back of the house, and it was as marvelous as all the other rooms we'd passed. Open and airy with marble countertops, slate gray cabinets, double ovens, a cooktop range with a gajillion burners, and one of those refrigerators that costs more than most cars. Dutch—who's definitely the cook in the family—would've loved it.

"Awesome," I said, looking around.

Hart, who was over by the sink with agents Robinson and Simmons, looked up as we entered. "Thanks for coming inside," she said. "We've gone through every room, closet, bathroom, and storage space and there's no sign of a wine cellar."

I noted Hart's expression and the slight flush to her cheeks. She was frustrated and maybe a little embarrassed. I could feel the tension wafting off her, and I understood. The rest of her peers were expecting this search to pay off, and she needed a win. I figured I did too.

So I held up my finger and stared down at the ground while I opened up my intuition. The first thing that popped into my head was a fish. At first I wondered if I might just be curious about the aquarium and that's why the image came to mind, but when I focused again, asking myself where the wine cellar was, the image of the fish became a little more intense. "Did you check behind the aquarium?" I asked.

Kim, Simmons, Perez, and Robinson stared at me like I was an idiot, but Hart at least indulged the question. "No," she said. "It's built into the wall."

"You sure?" I asked her.

Hart looked confused, while Simmons rolled his eyes and

nudged Robinson, who shook his head and sighed. I ignored them and said to Hart, "How about we check, just to make super-duper sure?"

Hart bit the inside of her cheek. I knew she must've been feeling like I was putting her on the spot—I mean, if my hunch didn't pay off, she would likely be seen as a fool by her team—but I had faith that there was something about that aquarium that would lead us to the cellar.

So, before she could even answer me, I turned on my heel and walked back the way I'd come. Behind me I could hear the patter of lots of footsteps and I couldn't help but smirk. The guys thought they were going to see my hunch come up empty, and they wanted to be there to witness it. But I thought that Hart probably was really hoping I was right, and damn it, I didn't want to disappoint her.

After entering the spacious room where the aquarium was housed, I paused in front of the tank and looked around. Behind me, all the agents had come to a stop at the entrance, and they were each staring at me as if wondering what the hell I'd do next. I ignored them for a moment and studied the wall the tank was set into. The blue of the water was set off beautifully by a dark wood-paneled wall. Then, I backed up and turned in a circle, studying the architecture around me. "This room is at the very center of the house, right?"

Hart and the other agents looked around, but only she nodded. "Yes," she said.

I moved over to the tank and saw that there was a plastic piece at the top that swiveled, allowing the fish to be fed. I pushed at it and tried to peer through the opening, but it didn't seem to house any secrets. Then I moved to the side of the tank and tapped on the wall next to it. I had a feeling there was a hollow space behind the paneling, which sort of made sense when I thought about it, because the aquarium would need to be cleaned every once in a while, and no way could that be accomplished just by pushing the piece of plastic up above the tank. Looking back at the tank, I could tell there was no obvious way to access it fully from where I stood, so there must have been some other way to get to the tank. Someplace hidden behind the wall. Backing up again, I pointed my radar right at the tank, willing my intuition to guide me to an access point, and like a trusted friend, it came through. Feeling a tug on my right side, I moved over several steps to the right of the tank and then moved close to the wood paneling again to study it. "Eureka," I whispered, then put my hand on the panel in front of me and gave it a small push.

There was a click and then a narrow door that had been all but completely obscured opened up. I put my head through the opening to see what was inside, then turned around with a flourish and swung the door all the way open, revealing a room behind the tank with a stairway leading down to what I knew was the wine cellar.

Every agent standing in the entrance stared at me with mouth agape.

I made a point of wiping my hands together before walking toward them. As I approached the line of agents, I said triumphantly, "All yours, boys and girls, my work here is done. Anybody needs me, I'll be in the van getting my Candy Crush on."

Booyah! I thought. I beat my chest twice before giving a peace sign, then passed through the line of stunned agents and yelled, "Cooper out!"

Chapter Four

. . .

Two hours and many Candy Crush levels later, Hart opened the van door and peeked in at me. "You hungry?"

"Freaking famished," I said with a sigh.

"Good. I'm taking you out for something to eat. My treat."

"I'm totes in for that." Then I pointed over my shoulder toward the house. "The boys still inside wondering how I did that?"

Hart chuckled as she settled into the seat next to me. "Yeah. They're on their way and they haven't stopped talking about you since you dropped the mic and walked off the stage."

I bounced my eyebrows. "I have that effect on the mens."

"You don't say?"

I sighed dramatically. "It's a curse."

"Robinson hasn't said a word all afternoon," she confessed.

"He strikes me as the strong, stubborn-like-bull type."

"I think you really rattled him. And I know you freaked Perez out. Did Rivera tell you that his wife, Chelsea, was the one he gave you for his test case and he didn't even know she was pregnant until you told him and he made a phone call home?"

"He told me something about that," I said.

Hart shook her head in disbelief. "You're amazing, Ms. Cooper."

"Could you call me Abby?" I asked. I was sick of all this "Ms." business.

"I'll call you Cooper in front of the others, because that's how we talk, but when it's just us, I can certainly call you Abby if you'll call me Kelsey."

I put out my hand for her to shake. "Deal." After we shook on it, I said, "So, Kelsey, how was the wine cellar?"

She rubbed her hands together. "A gold mine! Not only did we find evidence that Grecco is creating forged labels for the wine stored down there, passing off what looks like cheap homemade vino as rare bottles of some of the world's most expensive wines, but we also found a journal that might actually be a record of Grecco's sales in stolen art. It's mostly written in shorthand, but some of the names he listed in the journal match with who we suspect had purchased stolen art from him. I'll have my analyst look at it and try to pin down the shorthand, but we should be able to put Grecco away for a long time."

"Congratulations!" I told her, feeling genuinely happy for the big win she'd be bringing home to Rivera.

"I couldn't have done it without you," she said. "That whole thing you did in there with the hidden panel, like you knew exactly where the wine cellar was all along—that was amazing."

I felt my cheeks heat with a blush. "It wasn't that hard," I said. "I mean, you guys probably would've figured it out soon enough."

"No, Abby," she insisted. "And that's the point. The search warrant was only good for five hours and none of us even took much stock of the room you led us to. We kept looking around the perimeter, not the middle of the house, for the entry to the wine cellar."

"It makes sense to put it in the middle of the house," I said. "It'd be the most stable place given California's earthquakes, right?"

She shrugged. "Maybe. I'm not a structural engineer, but that makes sense. Anyway, I don't think we would've found it in the time allotted. You saved my ass in there and I owe you."

"Happy to help," I said, and I was kind of surprised to discover that I actually *was* happy to have helped.

The door to the van opened and several agents began bringing in boxes filled with wine bottles and paper sacks marked with evidence tags. Hart helped organize them all in the back of the van, and it wasn't long after that that we were able to leave Grecco's residence.

Hart was on the phone with someone the moment we were under way, and from what I could tell about the conversation, it sounded like she was on the line with local law enforcement. "You've got him?" she said at one point. "Great. Put him in a cell and I'll be there first thing in the morning to interrogate him."

After she hung up, I said, "Grecco?"

She nodded. "Yep. I had LAPD pick him up. They'll hold him until I can get to him tomorrow. He'll lawyer up, but it doesn't really matter. We've got enough evidence for a solid win on this one and that means he might be open to a deal."

"Ah," I said knowingly. "You want the name of his accomplices."

"I do. I also want the names of his clients." When I looked at her curiously, she explained, "No way should these rich assholes who bought stolen art from Grecco get a pass."

I nodded in appreciation. Kicking the one-percenters' hornet's nest guaranteed one quite a few WASP stings, and I hoped Hart was up for that. I was about to say as much when Agent Kim turned in his seat to face Hart and he held up his own cell. "Kelsey," he said to her, "I just got word from Rivera. Agent Barlow didn't make it."

Next to me, Agent Hart paled and her eyes immediately watered. I saw her struggle to keep it together and she managed— barely. "Thanks for letting me know, Lee," she told him.

The van was quiet for the rest of the way back to the bureau. Once we were there, everyone chipped in to load the collected evidence onto three double-decker carts, which were then sent down with an equal number of crime lab techs responsible for tagging and booking the items. Hart had a few words with one of them to let him know what she specifically needed for her interrogation of Grecco the next day, and then she waved to me to follow her to the elevator.

"You okay?" I asked when we were alone in the elevator.

"I will be," she said, attempting a smile that didn't quite get there. "It's tough to hear something like that, even though you told me how it'd turn out."

"I can be wrong sometimes," I admitted.

Her gaze slid sideways to me. "Oh, yeah? How often?"

"Not very," I said. "But sometimes. It happens."

She sighed sadly. "I would've believed you had a special talent even if you'd been wrong about Sara," she said.

"I'm sorry for your loss," I told her, mostly because I was and I didn't know what else to say. "We can skip going out for a meal if you're not really up for it."

"Abby, I think the *only* thing I'm up for right now is a drink with a friend."

It made me feel pretty good that Kelsey thought of me as a friend. "Thanks," I told her. And meant it.

Over plates of delicious pasta and bread so good I wanted to marry it, Kelsey and I got to know each other a bit better. She impressed me on a number of levels, mostly by the way she was so dedicated to her job—a job that requires a certain hardness in a person, and yet, Kelsey had a really lovely soft side. She was sweet and genuine and earnest and I liked her immensely. In some ways she was a little like Candice, but in other ways not so much.

Candice can sometimes play fast and loose with the law, and she has close friends who play even faster and looser with it. I highly doubted that Kelsey had ever come close to bending the law, much less sending a yearly holiday card to a mob boss (true story).

Still, I had the sense that I should introduce these two women to each other. Call it a gut feeling. "My best friend would love this place," I said casually, intending to steer the conversation in that direction.

"Your best friend?" Kelsey said. "You mean Candice Fusco? Persona non grata around the office?"

I frowned. "You've heard of her, huh?"

"Oh, yeah," she said with a knowing smile. "I'm a little surprised you didn't ask me if it was okay that she meet up with us for lunch."

"So, you also know that she's here in L.A. with me, huh?"

"There's not a lot we don't know about you, Abby. We were given a full briefing by the director before you even boarded the plane from Austin."

"Seriously?"

"Seriously. Whitacre wasn't too optimistic about your chances of lending us a hand, and he wanted us to know exactly what we'd have to deal with. It's why your reception was a little on the chilly side."

I laughed. "I like that you think it was only a 'little' chilly."

"Yeah, sorry about that. If it helps, I'm now a believer."

"It helps," I admitted. "What do you think the odds are that any of your peers will be willing to give me a chance?"

"Before you found Grecco's wine cellar, I'd have said they were slim to none. Now I'd put them at about even."

"Well, that's better than I would've thought, at least."

"The one to work on would be Agent Robinson. He's the most respected agent in our department."

I grimaced. Robinson seriously disliked me, and I didn't need to be psychic to pick up on it. "Why's he the leader of the pack?" I asked her.

"He closes the highest percentage of cases, and he's known for not letting go of a case until he brings in the bad guy. That's why what you said to him yesterday about Alejandro Cortina was such a blow to his ego. It's a trait that, until recently, had been seen as something to be respected, but as the Cortina case continues to go nowhere, I think he's afraid it's starting to become a liability. Basically, you fed into his worst fears."

"Awesome," I said flatly.

"Did Rivera tell you that you'd be working on his case next?"

"He did," I confessed.

Kelsey nodded. "Just do your thing, Abby, and you'll win him over."

"It's not the Cortina case, is it?" I asked, a little worried that, in spite of my warning, he'd ask me to find a way to lure Cortina here.

"No," she said. "It's another case entirely."

"What's it about?"

She cocked a playful eyebrow. "You mean, you don't already know?"

I resisted the urge to roll my eyes . . . but just barely. People are always attempting to use a bit of "psychic humor" with me, and I'm pretty sure they don't realize just how often everyone else does it, or, after years and years of enduring it, how *totally annoying* I find it. "No," I said levelly, and left it at that.

Kelsey's eyebrow lowered and she cleared her throat. "You get that a lot, I'll bet."

"More than you know."

"Sorry," she said. "Robinson and Perez have partnered up to work a series of bank robberies happening in and around La Cañada Flintridge and Pasadena."

"Where's that?" My knowledge of the local geography was pretty limited.

"North," Kelsey said, thumbing over her shoulder to indicate the direction.

"Huh," I said. "What do you know about the case?"

"We have weekly meetings to brief Rivera and the team on each of our case files, so I know a fair amount, but I think I should let Robinson and Perez explain," she said, placing her napkin on the table. "And on that note, I think it's time we got back. Rivera's going to lend us some latitude with the late lunch after bringing in a win like we did today, but he's not going to let us push it."

We arrived back at the bureau around four o'clock, but it felt much later to me. It was more than just the time change; I was tired and drained. So I was hardly enthusiastic when Rivera called Kelsey and me into the conference room again for a debriefing about the search at Grecco's house.

Kelsey did most of the talking, thank God. And she gave a lot of the credit to me, which I seriously appreciated. Rivera did little more than grunt as he listened and looked over the list of evidence sent up from the crime techs.

At last he leaned back in his chair and said, "Great work, Agent Hart. You can get back to your prepping for your interrogation of Grecco in the morning."

Kelsey hesitated to get up. It was clear that Rivera was dismissing only one of us, and I thought she might've wanted to stay with me in a show of support. I was quick to smile at her like I wasn't worried in the slightest about spending more time with the special agent in charge. "Good luck tomorrow," I told her.

"Thanks, Cooper," she said. As she walked past my chair, she squeezed my shoulder to let both me and Rivera know that she valued my contribution. It meant a lot to me that she continued to demonstrate such strong faith in me when we'd really only known each other two days.

After she'd gone, Rivera studied me silently for several long moments. I made sure to return the stare. "So, you're a snowboarder?" I said to him.

He blinked. Then blinked again. "What?"

I pointed to him and sorted through a few of the images flickering in my head. "Snowboarder. You're going snowboarding soon. Not locally, though. You're headed east a bit."

Rivera blinked several more times. "What the hell are you talking about?"

I reached into my purse and pulled out some lip balm. Casually I swirled the balm over my lips as I replied, "Purple mountains majesty. Colorado. Rocky Mountain high." I paused the swirl long enough to smile, both at how much fun it was to tease Rivera and at the look on his face.

Tucking the lip balm away, I sighed wistfully. "I'm not much of a skier or a boarder. And it's been a while since I've even seen snow. You'll have a great time, though. Late February is the perfect time for that kind of a trip."

Rivera made a sound, a sort of expelling of breath combined with a snort, and then he simply shook his head. "Okay, Cooper, you can knock that shit off. I get it. There really is something to this whole psychic stuff."

"For reals?" I said, leaning forward to put my elbows on the table. "Just like that, you believe me?"

"It's not just like that," he said. "After you left with the team this morning, I took the time to make some calls and check up on you. It appears that you do have some sort of ability, but whether that ability can be harnessed by anyone but you, or can be used to help us solve more cases, is what I don't yet know."

I shrugged. "Only one way to find out. Put me on the next case and if I prove myself, let me coach your team about developing their own intuitive abilities. It won't turn any of them into professional psychics, but it will make them even better investigators."

Rivera squinted skeptically at me before taking out his cell and tapping out a text. He then set the cell on the table and went back to eyeing me keenly. The door opened a few moments later and in walked agents Robinson and Perez. Both of them looked like they'd just been given detention. Once they'd taken a seat at the table, Rivera addressed the two men while motioning in my direction. "You're to give her a brief history of the Pasadena/Flintridge robberies, then follow up on any leads she provides. Answer any questions she may have honestly, and don't give her a hard time about it. I'll be expecting some progress by the end of the day tomorrow."

With that, Rivera got up and left us alone together. Joy.

I leaned back in my chair and laced my fingers together, while looking expectantly at the men. Robinson was his usual stone-faced self, while Perez was sweating nervously. I wondered if he thought I was a witch who might put a spell on him. After a long moment where no one spoke, I tapped my wrist and said, "Time's a-wasting, gentlemen."

Perez looked at Robinson, but that man didn't seem to mind disobeying a direct order. He continued to sit there and gaze at me with dull, flat eyes. Finally, Perez said, "We've been investigating a series of bank robberies."

"Okay," I said, glad that at least someone was moving the train forward.

"Five banks in five weeks around Pasadena and La Cañada Flintridge."

"Five in five weeks?" I repeated. "That's a pretty aggressive schedule."

"It is."

My radar was buzzing. The energy around their case was electric, and that was good. It usually meant I wouldn't have to work too hard to draw out a clue. Neither Robinson nor Perez had brought in a file for me to look at, so I took it upon myself to peer into the ether and see what I could tease out. "This isn't just one robber," I began. "There're multiple people involved. They're organized, like a gang of thieves." Across the table Perez was nodding slightly. "I feel like they're very systematic about things. They have a routine that is always the same. The same number of robbers each time taking up the same positions within the bank, and I keep seeing a clock in my mind, which means they probably rob the place in exactly the same number of minutes each time. Like, down to the second. And it's the same bank being hit each time, just at different branches."

Perez's mouth fell open. The cynical side of me thought that these skeptical bureau boys really were a bit too easy to impress.

"The sixth robbery hasn't happened yet," I continued. "They're off the pattern."

"Yes," Robinson said.

I was a bit startled that he'd spoken, but I tried not to show it. "And you guys don't know why they're off said pattern. In other words, you don't know if that means they've moved on to another city, or if they're taking a break or even if they've given up robbing banks altogether." Focusing on Perez, I said, "How long has it been since the last robbery?"

"Two weeks."

I tapped my finger on the conference table. "Hmm. That's interesting." Purposely, I didn't elaborate. If these two wanted more of my input, they'd need to ask. Politely.

"That it?" Robinson said after a lengthy pause.

I sighed and stood up. "No. There's a whole lot more. But I'd like a look at the crime scenes before I comment further."

"Now?" Perez said, glancing at his watch. I knew it was just before five.

"No," I repeated. "Not now. Tomorrow. Nine a.m. In the meantime I'm going to head back to my hotel and rest. It's been a long day and I'm tired. I think you guys need a break too. At least a break from being total hard-asses. Tomorrow how about we all meet back here and at least pretend to play nice, m'kay?"

With that, I left them to glare at my backside.

Candice met me in the hotel bar at six. "Sundance," she said smoothly, sidling up to take the barstool next to mine.

"Huckleberry," I replied.

"How's things?"

"Peachy."

She motioned to the bartender and pointed to my margarita.

He nodded and while he got busy making her a goblet of goodness, she considered me critically. "Brice and I have a bet, you know."

I inhaled deeply and let it out slow. "You don't say?"

"Yeah. He bet me you wouldn't make it past the first week."

I turned my head to arch an eyebrow at her. "*Did* he, now?"

"Yep. Dutch has you down for ten days, though."

I chuckled. "Glad my own husband has such faith."

"I have you down for the full two weeks," she said.

"How much?"

"Last time I checked, the pool had five hundred bucks in it."

"There's a pool?"

"There is," she said. "Oscar thinks you'll crack the day before you're scheduled to leave, while Cox didn't think you'd even go. He laid money down that you'd head west all right, but he thought you'd bypass L.A. and make for Hawaii."

I laughed and shook my head ruefully. "So, now that you've told me about the pool, you're thinking that I'll stick it out to the end *just* to let you, oh, true friend of mine, cash in and split the winnings with me, right?"

Candice picked up the margarita the bartender had set in front of her and took a demure sip before answering. "Actually, I was just counting on the first part of that scenario."

I made a dismissive sound. "No way, Huckleberry. If I make it to the end of this nightmare, I get half of that pot."

"I suppose that's fair," she said. "Although I might be more motivated to help you stay focused and on track if the split was closer to say . . . seventy-thirty."

"Only if that seventy percent comes this way, darlin'," I said, pointing to my chest.

"Fifty-fifty it is," she said.

"I thought so." We sipped on our margaritas in silence for

a bit before Candice said, "I take it today was as tough as yesterday?"

"Not really," I admitted. "Actually, today was pretty good. I scored a big win helping Agent Hart with her case against the stolen art fencer. I was the one who found his hidden wine cellar, where the team discovered a ton of evidence to convict the art dealer's sorry ass and send him away for a long, long time."

"Abby, that's great!" Candice said, patting me on the back. "And it must've gone a long way toward convincing these L.A. Feds that you're the real deal."

I rolled my eyes. "You know, you'd think that would be the case. However . . ."

"Really?"

"Yeah, they're a stubborn group."

"So what's next on their agenda for you?"

"A series of bank robberies. There's a ton of supercharged energy around the crimes, so I'm thinking I'll be able to do some solid good on the case. Tomorrow, we're going to visit the banks where the robberies took place."

"Sounds promising," she said. I nodded and she added, "So why're you here with that sad face and this big-ass margarita?"

I swirled the drink and frowned. "Because nothing I do seems to be good enough for these guys. I mean, Agent Hart is awesome. We had a late lunch together and I swear you'd like her too, Candice. But the other ones . . . Man! They're just cold, you know?"

"Why do you need them to be all warm and fuzzy toward you?"

I made a face at her. "Come on, Candice, you know me better than that. I want them to think I'm awesome because I'm emotionally needy. Like . . . duh!"

"Ah," she said. "Yes, I forgot. Your parents didn't love you and the rest of the world has to pay."

"Can I help it if I had a crappy childhood that left me broken and damaged beyond repair?"

She grinned. "No, I suppose not. And for the record, you are neither broken nor damaged beyond repair. Dented, maybe, but not broken."

"That, right there, is the reason I love you. You just get me." For emphasis, I saluted her with my drink. And then I got serious. "You're right, though, I suppose. I've been trying all day to keep in mind what you said last night about it being their stuff, not mine, if these guys are so skeptical. Still, it's really tough to work in a hostile environment."

"Is it really hostile?" she asked curiously.

"I'd have to say that it is, and it makes me uncomfortable. It's tense and it's angry and no one but Agent Hart trusts me. I was fine this morning, Candice, I really was, and I thought after I brought in the home run on the Grecco case that the boys would ease up, but they're not. It's as hostile as ever and when it's coming from all directions, I have a hard time ignoring it."

"You can bring me in, you know," Candice said seriously. "I mean, fuck this Whitacre dude who wants me to stay out of his bureau. If you need me, then I'll go with you tomorrow."

I had a brief flash of Candice being physically removed from the building by Robinson and Rivera—the two biggest men at the bureau. That wasn't sure to end well . . . for them.

"No," I said with a sigh. "It'd only cause trouble for both of us."

"So what can I do?" she asked.

"Hang out with me for a while tonight, give me a pep talk in the morning, and tell me it's all gonna work out in the end."

She wrapped an arm around my shoulders and pulled me in

close to her. "It's all gonna work out okay, Sundance. You just go in tomorrow, bring home a big win on that bank robbery case, and those bureau boys will have no choice but to come around. Just remember, you won Brice over, and nothing says more about your capabilities than that."

She was right about that. Brice had been the *worst* when I'd first started working his cases. He'd put me through all sorts of seemingly impossible scenarios—which I'd passed—before finally coming around. And the boys at my own bureau back in Austin had also been really tough nuts to crack. Candice reminding me of that actually bolstered my confidence. "When you're right, you're right," I told her. "I'll just go in tomorrow and blow their minds while bringing in another big win."

"Easy peezy," she said.

And we both drank to that.

Chapter Five

• • •

The drive to the first bank in La Cañada Flintridge the next morning felt interminable. Of course, that might have been because Robinson and Perez forgot to bring along their sunny dispositions, opting instead for Mr. and Mr. Grumpy Pants.

Such an unpleasant couple, I thought as I stared meanly at the backs of their heads. I'd even offered to treat them to a coffee if they'd been willing to stop at any one of the five gazillion Starbucks that we passed along the way, and they'd both looked at each other like, "Does she really think we're doing that?" and kept driving.

And because I'm not someone who can just let an obvious insult go (you're reeling in shock right now, I know . . .), I'd taken to humming a merry tune. I'd started with "Ninety-nine Bottles of Beer on the Wall," segued rather elegantly into "Row, Row, Row Your Boat," and lightly flitted over to "The Itsy Bitsy Spider" before Robinson had turned his head to glare hard at me and said, "If you don't stop, I'll throw you out of this car."

"Like I'm scared of you!" I'd snapped in return. Still, I'd

stopped humming. When one is faced with being tossed from a moving vehicle, it's probably best to *fermez la bouche*.

At last we arrived at the bank in question and Perez parked near the rear. The boys got out first, buttoning their suit jackets to hide their badges and guns. The move wasn't lost on me; they didn't want anyone to know they were FBI with me in tow. They were probably afraid I'd get inside the bank and start speaking in tongues.

I was tempted to pull something like that out of spite, but then, I didn't really know what speaking in tongues was all about and quite frankly it sounded like a lot of work, and I hadn't even had a decent cup of coffee yet.

With a reluctant sigh I followed them into the bank and after coming through the doors, I moved off to the left near a potted ficus tree, as much to find a quiet place to feel out the ether as to get away from the señores Grumpy Pants.

The bank had only two patrons in it, but there was a tense energy to the place. I figured the staff was still very much on edge after their ordeal. It occurred to me that I didn't know much about the robbery other than what I'd already felt out about it the day before. Neither Robinson nor Perez had shown me anything from the case file: no photos, video, descriptions, witness statements. Nada. Which was fine—I mean, I could still pick stuff out of the ether on my own—but it would've been nice to have had something tangible and relevant to the case shown to me prior to our hopping in the car and driving all the way here.

"Whatever," I muttered as I shrugged off my irritation and got busy doing my job. Taking three deep breaths, I got calm and centered and focused all of my intuitive prowess on the interior of the bank.

My attention was pulled in a completely different direction. "Weird," I said quietly. Turning toward the window that I was standing in front of, I looked out at the parking lot. It, like the bank, was mostly empty.

"Did you need some assistance?"

Looking away from the window, I saw a woman about my age with long blond hair and clean, somewhat angled features, smartly clad in a black business suit, addressing me. "No," I said, attempting to smile. "I'm good." My radar hummed and my attention was pulled back toward the window and outside.

"Are you sure?" she said.

There was a nervous hitch in her voice and I realized that I might look like someone who could be casing the joint. To put her at ease, I pulled out the lanyard from inside my coat with my FBI consultant ID attached. "I'm here about the robbery," I said.

She flinched ever so slightly before steeling herself; then she leaned forward and looked closely at my ID. "You're a consultant to the FBI?"

"I am," I said, then pointed to Dumbledumb and Dumbledumber. "They're actual agents."

She turned to look and took in the sight of Robinson and Perez standing off to the other side staring dully at me. "I think those two were in last week," she said. "They spoke to the bank manager. Would you like me to get her?"

"Not right now," I said, and swiveled once again toward the window, unable to keep my attention away from the parking lot for some reason. "What the heck is out there?"

"Out there?" she repeated, that nervous hitch back in her voice. "Nothing. I mean, it's the parking lot."

Still distracted, I said, "Yeah, but there's something. . . ." I moved away from the ficus and over to the entrance. Something from outside was pulling at me and my intuition wasn't letting it go.

"Where's she going?" I heard Perez say when I pushed on the door to head outside.

"I guess we're leaving," Robinson replied.

But I wasn't leaving so much as following my gut. Once outside, however, I was at a bit of a loss. There were four cars in the medium-sized parking lot. None of the cars felt suspicious to me. So what was it that had called to me so urgently from inside?

I scanned the parking lot, trying to feel from which direction that intuitive pull had come from, and finally settled on straight ahead—but there wasn't a car parked in any slot straight in front of me. Just several spaces and a hill that appeared to lead up into the mountains.

Walking forward a few paces, I puzzled over what my intuition was trying to tell me. I felt like I needed to look at the ground, so I did, sweeping my eyes back and forth over the pavement, searching for anything resembling a clue, but there was nothing, not even a bit of litter.

"Dammit," I said, irritated.

"What are we doing, Cooper?" Perez asked me. "Are we leaving and going to the next location?"

I waved at him impatiently. He needed to shut up so that I could focus. "Not yet," I told him while I scanned the ground again. Walking forward several more paces, I tried to find the clue, but something felt very off about where I was looking. "This is so weird," I said to myself. Then I looked up at the horizon and put my hands on my hips. In the distance at the top of the hill that abutted the parking lot was a bulldozer, trudging along near the base of what appeared to be a plateau of land about a hundred meters up and away from where I stood. All of a sudden I sucked in a breath because a series of images was popping into my mind like flashbulbs, and none of those images meant anything good.

"Agent Perez?" I said, staring up at the bulldozer.

"Yeah?"

"Was someone killed during any of the robberies?"

"No," he said.

"Are you sure?" I asked.

"Yeah, I'm sure," he replied with a note of irritation.

"Weird," I muttered, walking forward again, my gaze still on that bulldozer. I have a distinct sign for murder—it's the image of a smoking gun—and it kept appearing in my mind's eye like an annoying strobe light. The closer I walked to the hill, the more the image flashed. I wondered if maybe the driver of the bulldozer had committed a crime, but I wasn't sure that felt right either.

Behind me I heard Perez say to Robinson, "Where's she going?"

"No idea," came the reply.

I didn't bother to turn around and explain it to them. At that moment I was totally focused on following my intuition.

It kept leading me forward and when I reached the edge of the parking lot, I didn't stop. Lifting my leg over the metal guardrail that separated the hill from the lot, I moved into the deep grass and began to ascend the slope.

It was a steep climb, but the ground was firm from the recent drought, which was good since I was in heels, but at the top the view was a bit unexpected. There was a large swath of flat rect-angular land that'd been cleared of trees and scrub. There was also a sign posted about ten feet away announcing the new de-velopment of a series of homes starting in the mid–seven hundred thousands. A mock-up of the type of house about to be built was also on the sign, but what was really weird was that the sign appeared to me to be both new and then something aged and faded.

I blinked hard and when I focused again, I saw that the sign had to be brand-spanking-new, but then it seemed to fade again right before my eyes, becoming dirty and weatherworn. I shook my head and there it was again, crisp, clean, and promising luxurious homes for an affordable price.

"What the hell?" I asked myself. I felt a little dizzy and disconnected as I gazed at the sign, so I pulled my gaze away from it and back to the cleared land, and that's when I saw the graves.

There were four of them. They were freshly dug, side by side, without markers or ornaments of any kind. At the sight of them, my breath caught and my heart seemed to skip a beat. I knew that the graves held the bodies of four young girls. It was as if someone had told me that as a fact, and it caused me a bit of nausea. "Oh, God," I whispered.

And then I realized that the bulldozer was headed right for the graves. In a panic I rushed forward onto the freshly tilled earth. Slipping in my heels, I began waving at the driver, trying to get his attention. He wasn't stopping or even slowing down; he simply kept a steady pace directly for the four graves. "Hey!" I yelled. *"Hey!"*

A moment later the bulldozer ran over the first grave. *"Stop!"* I screamed, and tried to run faster. My feet were covered in dirt and my ankles kept twisting as I ran in the damn heels, but I wasn't fast enough to reach the bulldozer and he ran over the second grave a moment later. *"Stop! Stop! STOP!"* I screamed.

"Cooper!" I heard behind me. Perez or Robinson had obviously come up the slope—I didn't know which of them was calling to me, nor did I care. At the moment I was completely focused on getting to the driver of the bulldozer before he crushed the bodies of all four victims. Just as he was about to plow over the fourth victim, however, he must've heard or seen me, because the bulldozer came to an abrupt stop, rocking on its giant tread as the driver pushed hard on the brake.

I was panting and out of breath when I caught up to the big machine, and I was still waving my arms, trying to get him to back away from the fourth grave, as well as get off the first three.

"Cooper!" I heard again, but I continued to ignore Perez and Robinson.

At last the door to the bulldozer opened and the driver leaned out a little. I pointed to him and said, "Get back! Get back off the graves!"

He blinked. "What?" he said, turning off the loud rig so he could hear me.

I pointed to the front of the bulldozer. "You just ran over three graves! The women have been murdered and you're destroying evidence!"

The driver's eyes widened in shock and he got out of the cab, stepping onto the tread of the wheel to look out over the shovel of his truck.

I ran forward to the front to point to the remaining grave, but when I rounded the rig, I came up short. In front of the shovel, the dirt was perfectly flat. "Dammit! You ran over the fourth one too!"

"Cooper!" came that voice again. Now that the bulldozer was silent, I could tell that it'd been Perez who'd been shouting to me.

"Shit!" I swore, and moved quickly to the other side of the shovel to look underneath the big truck, but it was too dark to see anything.

By now the driver had jumped down from the tread and had

come around to my side. "Lady, what graves are you talking about?"

"There were four mounds of dirt here!" I said, in a bit of a panic about them. "How could you not see them?"

The driver took off his ball cap and squeezed it nervously. "I didn't see any graves!"

"What's going on?" Perez demanded, coming around the bulldozer.

I was actually a little relieved to see him. "There're four women buried here," I said.

He looked down at the ground, then back at me. Robinson came around the bulldozer at that moment too. "What do you mean there're four women buried here?" Perez said. That made Robinson skip a step.

"When I was in the bank, my intuition kept pulling me up here, and when I crested the hill, I saw the bulldozer about to run over the graves of four young girls."

Robinson, Perez, and the driver looked down to where I was pointing, which was right in front of me. I could've sworn the fourth grave was there, but again I figured it was underneath the dozer's shovel. "You need to move this thing," I said, hitting the shovel with the flat of my hand.

The driver nodded and started to walk toward the cab, but Robinson called to him with, "Hold on a second. Somebody explain to me what the hell this is all about."

I moved away from the shovel, past Robinson and Perez, without pausing to explain. When I was clear of the bulldozer, I motioned to the driver to get up into the cab and back the thing up. I figured the explanation would come when I could see the graves more clearly, if they weren't already smunched level.

Luckily, the driver seemed to think I might have more authority than Robinson (although why he thought that was anybody's guess), and he moved up to the truck, hopped in, and started the engine. Perez and Robinson came to stand next to me, and as the bulldozer was very loud, it prevented them from yelling at me.

We all waited until after the bulldozer had backed up several meters and then the driver cut the engine again and came back down to us. I moved over and stared at the ground. There was a tugging sensation in my gut and I pointed to a section of dirt. "There," I said.

"There what?" Robinson asked, his tone low and even with barely veiled fury.

I directed my answer to Perez. "There are four women buried here," I said. "Murder victims."

Perez looked at me like he thought I was crazy. "Says who?"

"Says my intuition," I told him.

Perez turned to the driver. "You see any dead bodies around?"

The driver got even more nervous and fidgety. "No, sir! No, I didn't see anything. I've been leveling off the grade here all morning, and I didn't see nothing."

Perez looked from the driver to me, then back again. "You got a hand shovel we could borrow?" he asked.

"Back at my pickup," the driver said. "It'll take me a couple of minutes to get it."

"Please do," I told him. If the only way to convince these clowns was to dig a little into the dirt, then I was willing.

The driver nodded to me and took off at a slow jog. I was grateful for his help at least.

Perez's phone buzzed and he answered it immediately. "Yes, sir," he said into the phone. "We're at the La Cañada Flintridge target with her right now, but she's led us to some plot next to the bank where she says four women were murdered and buried." There was a pause, then, "Yes, that's correct sir. That's what she said."

I rolled my eyes. I knew he had to be talking to Rivera, and the way he'd explained the situation made me sound cray-cray. A moment later, Perez handed me his phone and said, "Rivera wants to talk to you."

I took the phone and before he could even address me, I said, "Agent Rivera, I'm not wrong. My gut is telling me there are four young women buried here. I believe they were all murder victims."

"What evidence do you have to support that?" he asked me.

"Nothing yet, sir. But the driver of the bulldozer who's been leveling the grade has gone off to retrieve a shovel from his pickup truck."

Rivera sighed. "Is this like your hunch about Grecco yesterday?"

I knew he was asking me if what I was sensing now was like how I'd sensed Grecco's hidden wine cellar was behind his fish tank. "It's a much stronger sense, sir. I *know* these women are buried here and that they were murdered."

After a long silent moment in which Rivera was obviously considering what I'd just told him, he said, "Fine. Please hand the phone back to Agent Perez."

I did as instructed and Perez listened to Rivera for a minute and didn't seem to like what his boss told him. He walked off to try to argue, but either he was hung up on or Rivera shut him down quickly. He came back to Robinson and me, wearing an angry expression.

I turned away from the agents, picked up a stick, and began to mark off where I thought all four graves were. By the time I was done, the driver had returned with the shovel. There was an awkward moment where we all looked at one another to see who was going to do the actual digging, and when both agents eyed me, I lifted one heeled shoe and wiggled it at them.

Perez scowled and grabbed the shovel, handing me his suit coat and rolling up his sleeves before he began to dig. I watched him with bated breath, waiting for that awful moment when his shovel would find flesh and bone, but also dreading it as well.

He dug steadily for a good fifteen minutes, and removed a fair amount of dirt in that time. Pausing to wipe his brow and look at me, he said, "How far down is she buried?"

I frowned. Something was again lighting up my intuition, but not in a way that made any sense to me. I felt strongly that we were digging in the right spot, but there was something odd about the ether—something off. "I can't tell," I admitted. "She might be down a few feet farther."

Perez muttered an expletive under his breath and got back to it. His phone rang again and he stopped to unclip it from his belt, look at the screen, then toss it to Robinson.

Robinson had been standing off to the side a bit, glowering at me with crossed arms. He seemed really irritated by the whole scene. He caught the phone, though, glanced briefly at the display, then answered it with, "Rivera? It's Robinson. Perez is still digging. . . . No, sir. Nothing. There's nothing but dirt."

I glared at Robinson. *Oh, ye of little faith,* I thought, turning away from him to focus once again on Perez.

We all stood around for another ten minutes, and Perez had moved even more dirt by then, but I could tell he was really beginning to tire. Pausing to wipe his brow again, he looked up at me from the hole he'd been steadily digging and said, "There's nothing here, Cooper."

I moved over to stand beside the hole he'd made and put my hands on my hips. Something again felt off and I was now feeling the pressure of the fact that we hadn't found a body, even though Perez was about six feet down. The truth was that I hadn't expected Perez to need to dig so deep. It'd initially felt like the girls were only two or three feet under the surface, but now there seemed to be nothing in the grave that I'd marked off. And yet the feeling of someone being buried there was so strong.

"I'm not wrong," I said.

Perez glanced at Robinson. "Your call," he said.

Robinson pointed to the bulldozer. "We've got a better tool at our disposal."

"No!" I told them. "You'll wreck the crime scene!"

But Robinson appeared to be unfazed. "What crime scene?" he asked me.

Perez climbed out of the hole and stood dirty and sweaty next to Robinson. "He's right," he said to me. "Without a body, there is no crime scene, and if there is someone buried here, and she's buried deep, our best bet is to let the dozer remove some of the dirt so we can take a look."

The driver shifted on his feet again. "I can dig you a twelve-foot hole in six minutes," he said.

"Do it," Robinson and Perez told him.

I pressed my lips together, so angry at their willingness to destroy a crime scene just because they didn't believe me. I hoped they'd be sorry when the first girl was uncovered.

The driver moved back to his rig and started up the engine. The agents and I stepped well out of the way so that he could do his work, and he hadn't been kidding when he'd told us he could dig a deep hole in relatively little time.

Within a matter of minutes we were staring at a square hole, a good fifteen feet down in exactly the spot I'd indicated. The hole dug by the bulldozer was wider than the grave, so it should've exposed the other girls buried next to our target, but there was nothing in the earth. Nothing but dirt.

My brow furrowed when the driver backed his rig up again and for the first time since I'd seen the graves, I started to get really nervous. We should've discovered at least one of the bodies by now, and no way would the murderer risk being seen burying a dead body by standing around for an hour or two digging a hole that was below six feet.

"I don't get it," I said to myself, and moved over to the edge of the hole.

"There's nothing down there," Robinson said, his voice now filled with disgust. "You led us on a wild-goose chase and wasted the whole morning."

"No," I said, shaking my head adamantly. "I'm not wrong." Stubbornly I moved to the edge of the hole, ready to jump in and start digging myself, but when I reached for the shovel, Robinson caught my arm and held me back.

I looked up at his angry face, then pointedly down at his arm. "Oh, hold me closer, tiny dancer," I snarled.

He tightened his grip and snarled back, only his was perhaps a weensy bit scarier than mine.

"Darnell," Perez said softly. "If she wants to dig some, let her."

Robinson's hand unlatched itself from my arm and he turned away in disgust. I glared at him for a moment before picking up the shovel and very carefully made my way down to the bottom of the pit. The hole dug by the bulldozer sloped a little as it got deeper, which allowed me to half shuffle, half slide down to the bottom. It smelled mossy and dank and I wondered how my intuition could insist there was a dead body buried someplace that showed no evidence of that. I mean, I *can* be wrong, and I have been, but not about something that felt so certain.

So definite. So substantive. I couldn't reconcile it and I didn't know even how to explain it.

Still holding the shovel, I made a few attempts to move aside some dirt, which was very difficult, given that it was so packed in at this depth, but at least I wasn't hitting bedrock. I figured centuries of mud and dirt rolling down the mountain during the rainy season had deposited quite a bit more earth here than just a little further up. It was obvious that a murderer hadn't dug a grave here, but I felt compelled to keep scratching at the ground and stall for time while I tried to think about what else to do. If I went back to Rivera after having claimed to have visions of four dead girls who didn't seem to exist, I'd be sent home with my tail tucked between my legs and egg on my face.

"Come on, Cooper," Perez said. "Get out of there so we can let this guy get back to his job and we can get back to ours."

Frustrated, I jammed the shovel one last time into the bottom of the pit, and it caught on something. Like a root. Or . . .

I bent over and scraped with the shovel a little more.

"Cooper!" Robinson barked. "Get out of there or I'll come down and drag you out."

I turned to glare up at him. "You want me to come out?" I snapped. "Then come on down, Agent Robinson. And while you're here, maybe you can explain *this*." Very carefully I propped the blade of the shovel underneath a hard lump of earth and pried out of the dirt a skeletal hand.

It would've been seriously gross if I'd thought about anything other than my relief at having been right.

For their parts, Perez and Robinson stared down at me and the hand sticking out of the dirt with such shock that I wanted to take a picture and show Candice later. I resisted of course. But only just barely.

Then Robinson lifted up his cell and made a call. "Yes, sir.

It's me. She was right. We found remains. Better send the techs to us and I'll alert the local PD."

With a satisfied sigh I moved away from the hand so as not to further disturb the scene and carefully edged my way back up out of the hole. When I was on level ground again, the driver stared at me in awe. "Well, I'll be damned," he said. "I'll be damned."

Chapter Six

. . .

Hours later, and draped in a blue and yellow FBI Windbreaker, I stood in the center of a storm wishing like hell I'd never come to L.A.

The crime-scene techs had unearthed a body all right, but the medical examiner—a man with thirty-two years of experience no less—had pronounced the deceased as anything but a murder victim.

It seemed that I'd led the investigators directly to the ancient remains of a Native American tribesman, who'd perhaps lived in the area some five hundred to a thousand years earlier.

The surrounding terrain was now swarmed by local news reporters, archaeologists from UCLA, and, of course, the owners of the development project, who were fit to be tied.

Pointing angry fingers at me (thanks to Agent Perez, who'd let it "slip" that I was the one who'd insisted there were remains to be found, and enlisted the help of the bulldozer driver), they'd yelled for a good half hour. With the discovery of the remains, the entire area quickly became a war zone of jurisdiction between the developers, the UCLA archaeologists, and representatives from the Haramokngna American Indian Cultural Center, who were claiming the remains belonged to a member of the Tongva tribe, and as such, no one but them could touch it or excavate the area until they had.

With a sigh I eyed the large sign announcing the new homes starting in the seven hundred thousands. There was no way anything would be built on the property for at least a few years. No wonder I'd seen the sign faded and aged. And no wonder the developers were furious at me. The substantial outlay they'd put out to secure the real estate would very likely be tied up in the courts for years, and of course there'd be legal fees involved.

It all made me feel not so great about things, especially as I'd obviously disturbed a Native American's burial site. He or she should've been left in peace.

"Hey, there," I heard someone to my right say.

"Hey," I replied with a sigh.

"How's things?"

"Peachy, Candice. Isn't it obvious?"

She chuckled softly and draped an arm across my shoulders. "You're all over the news."

"Swell."

"So what's the real story?" she asked. "I mean, I know you wouldn't have used that radar to dig up ancient remains unless it was important."

I sighed again. "I didn't know the remains were ancient. I thought they were relatively recent."

"Ah," she said. "Still, to pick up on a body twelve feet below-ground, that's impressive, Sundance."

I shook my head. "I'm not convinced that I did that, though."

"I'm not following."

I turned to her. "Robinson and Perez took me to feel out the ether at the bank down there," I said, pointing, "and I had this sense like something was off. I kept seeing my symbol for murder and the tug I felt was from outside the bank, so I followed it and it led me here. Then I swear I saw four unmarked graves right where those spotlights are, and there was a guy in a bulldozer about to run over the graves. I stopped him, we started digging, and the rest is ancient history."

"Let's go back to the four graves," Candice said.

I shivered with cold. What'd been a fairly mild day had turned chilly, and while the borrowed Windbreaker was helping, my feet and hands were so cold they were numb. "Okay," I said, my teeth chattering a little.

Candice seemed to notice, because she said, "But first, let's get you out of here, fed, and warmed up. Would you rather head back with me to the hotel for a shower and room service? Or to the nearest restaurant for something to eat?"

At the mention of food my stomach gurgled noisily. I hadn't eaten all damn day. I would've left hours before, in fact, but Robinson, Perez, and Rivera were all still there, along with several FBI crime-scene techs who'd been scanning the ground with some sort of X-ray gizmo that was able to detect human remains in the soil.

I guess Rivera had been so surprised and impressed that I'd been able to detect a skeleton twelve feet down that he'd given my earlier prediction of four murder victims a lot of credence, and he'd insisted on having his team fully survey the landscape to search for those bodies.

I hadn't had the courage to tell him I now didn't believe they were ever there. "I think I have to stay a little longer," I said miserably.

Candice looked from me to Rivera and the other two agents. "Screw that," she said. "Those guys are dressed for the conditions, Abby. I mean, girl . . . you're wearing *sandals*."

"I'm okay," I lied.

Candice shook her head and removed her arm from my shoulders. She then took me firmly by the hand and pulled me over to Rivera, who was speaking with some local senator or congressman that I'd heard had money in the development deal. He looked angry enough to choke a horse and he and Rivera had been going at it back and forth in short bursts for a lot of the day.

Of course, none of that mattered to my BFF, who strode right up to them with me in tow, stopped in front of Rivera, and said, "Hey! You the one in charge?"

He paused midsentence and turned a flinty eye to her. "I'm Special Agent in Charge Rivera. And you are?"

"Candice Fusco-Harrison. So nice to make your acquaintance, Agent Rivera." she said, with as fake a smile as you could imagine. "Listen, Abby's frozen to the bone. I'm going to take her out of here and get her something to eat. She needs to be fed, warmed up, and put to bed before she collapses."

"We're not done here," Rivera growled.

"I can see that, but nowhere in her consulting agreement does it state that she needs to be subjected to such conditions as starvation and hypothermia. I'm taking her. And if you have a problem with that, you can call—"

"You know what? Go!" Rivera snapped, cutting her off. "Take her away and get her warmed up. I'll be in touch tomorrow about this mess."

I gulped, and looked at Candice. She and I wouldn't be splitting any betting pool money, and I'd probably need to pack my things after my shower and room service meal. I'd be sent back to Austin with one small win, and one big FUBAR. I'd blown it.

"You don't want me to come in tomorrow, sir?" I asked him, just to be sure.

"No," he said angrily. "I definitely do not want you to come in, Cooper. Wait for my call in the morning. You're dismissed."

My lower lip trembled in spite of my best effort to keep my emotions in check. I don't know why it upset me so much to be sent packing, but it did. Clearing my throat, I turned away and Candice and I began to trudge through the dirt toward the bank parking lot.

"Hey!" I heard Rivera call when we'd gotten about fifteen feet away.

I turned almost hopefully back to him. "The jacket," he said, motioning to the one I was wearing. "Leave it."

Candice growled low in her throat. Rivera had meant to embarrass me by treating me like someone who was skulking off with government property—which I technically was, but I'd fully intended to give back the jacket the next day. I mean, it wasn't like Dutch didn't have three of the same Windbreakers in our closet at home.

My lower lip trembled a little more as I shrugged out of the Windbreaker and the cold breeze hit my chest hard, making me even more miserable. Angry now, I dropped the Windbreaker in the dirt and turned away from Rivera, itching to toss him the bird over my shoulder while I was at it.

Candice walked close to me and muttered, "He's such an asshole."

I would've verbally agreed with her if I could've worked my way past the lump in my throat.

The long car ride back to the hotel was made a little better by the fact that the first thing Candice did was stop at a local Starbucks in a strip mall with a Walgreens and, after leaving me in the car with the heater running, came back with a Venti caramel decaf latte, a pair of thick socks, and even a set of slippers she'd found at the drugstore. She also made me wear her coat until I stopped shivering.

"If I haven't told you lately that I love you," I said to her as we got under way again, "totally my bad. You're awesome and I love you."

She grinned while she drove. "Drink your coffee," was her only reply.

After a shower that should've been much longer were it not for the drought conditions in Southern California, I came out to a meal of a grilled cheese sandwich and a big bowl of cream of tomato soup. Sinking onto the bed after taking the first bite of the grilled cheese, I moaned with happiness. "Ohmigod," I said. "What kind of heaven *is* this sandwich?"

"It's got bacon, Granny Smith apple slices, and Gouda cheese."

"Holy freakballs, Candice," I moaned again after a second bite. "How are you not fighting me for the other half of this sandwich?"

"I'm using all my powers of restraint," she deadpanned. She then took the lid off her own dinner, which I noticed was nothing more than a small fillet of grilled salmon and some steamed veggies. Candice almost never eats junk food, which is ninety percent of my diet. I'll probably go before her, but at least I'll die happy—likely clutching a plate full of chili cheese fries.

We ate in silence for a bit—which I appreciated. I didn't want anything to distract me from the magnificence of that sandwich, made all the better by the most heavenly bowl of soup I'd ever tasted. It was more tomato bisque than soup.

But at last I sat back and patted my bulging stomach. "Thanks for that, Huckleberry."

"My pleasure. Now spill it."

Taking a deep breath (or as deep a breath as my stomach would allow), I told her everything. "I still don't know how I could've been so wrong," I said in conclusion. "I was *so* certain those girls were buried there."

"Did the medical examiner comment on the sex of the ancient remains?"

I shook my head. "He said he was leaving that up to the archaeologists. The skeleton is old enough that it's much smaller than modern people, so there's no way to really tell without doing some in-depth measurements of the pelvic bones, but my guess is that the skeleton is male."

"Why is that your guess?" she asked.

I shrugged. "It's what my gut says. Which means at some point we'll learn about it and my feelers are just out ahead retrieving information that's yet to come in."

That made Candice consider me curiously. "How do you know if something has happened in the past versus the future, Abs?"

"Sometimes I don't," I admitted. "I mean, sometimes it's hard to tell. Time is a tricky thing, but mostly I can tell it's the future because it *feels* in front of me, whereas the past *feels* behind me."

"Sort of like 'no' feels like a weight to you and 'yes' makes you feel a lightness?"

I pointed at her. "Yes, exactly like that."

"Okay, so what does the present feel like?"

I blinked at her. That stumped me. "Uh, I don't get what you mean."

"Well," she said, "you told me that when you came up that hill to that big stretch of cleared land, you saw those graves as if they were real, but now we know that they're not, right? And then you saw the sign for the new development and that looked alternately new and old to you, right?"

My brow furrowed. "Yes. Yes, that's true."

"So, my question to you is, did the graves themselves feel

like they were something from the past, something from the present, or something from the future?"

My jaw dropped when I realized where Candice was headed with her probing questions, and I thought back to that moment when I saw the graves. I then remembered distinctly feeling that pulling sensation at the center of my solar plexus, which I'd interpreted to mean that I should move forward and stop the bulldozer from rolling over them, but now I understood that in a completely different light. "Ohmigod," I said, rather stunned by the revelation. "The murders haven't happened yet. I was feeling pulled forward when I saw them. They're in the future."

Candice nodded. She'd been thinking the same thing too. "When you told me you saw the sign and it was new, then old, then new, then old again, I had a feeling the graves were connected to a time in the future."

I ran a hand through my damp hair. "With the discovery of the Native American skeleton, that land won't be built on for years!"

"See?" Candice said. "You didn't fail today, Abby. You simply picked up on a series of murders that haven't happened yet."

I nodded absently because my mind was filling with a whole new set of images that were quite disturbing. In my mind's eye I saw the sign for the development again, but now it was old and faded, and the four graves were once again there in the dirt; however, the last grave in the set now felt different. Before, I'd been convinced that the graves all belonged to young women, but the fourth grave was distinct in that it no longer felt feminine. I wondered if it was because of the ancient remains found just below it, but there was something else about the grave, a sort of new added mystery about how it felt to me.

I pulled back from focusing on it in my mind's eye and stared at Candice.

"What's happening, Abs?" she asked gently. She'd worked with me long enough to know when I was getting clues.

"I think there's more to this story, Candice. I think we're going to get involved in it somehow."

"You mean, solve the murders?" she asked me.

I shook my head. "No. I think we're going to try to stop them from ever happening."

"Okay," she said slowly. "Do you know when they'll take place?"

I concentrated. I felt warmth, and my symbol for the summer came into my mind, but it didn't feel like it'd be the following summer. It felt more distant than that. "About two years from now."

"Uh-huh," she said. "Do you know who will be targeted?"

"Three young girls," I said immediately. "But four victims."

"What does that mean?" she asked.

I shrugged. "One of them might be male."

"Any names come to mind?"

I stared at the image of the four graves in my mind's eye. The fourth grave, however, now had a cross erected over it. The cross was weird, though—the horizontal bar was higher up on the post than usual. I didn't know what that meant. "No clue."

"Okay, do you know where?"

I shook my head. "I don't think it's any one place. I think he strikes when he has the opportunity."

"Who is he?" she asked.

I closed my eyes and tried very hard to concentrate on that answer. But all I got back was a series of shadowy images. "I think he's a brunet," I said, working as hard as I could to pull even the tiniest descriptor out of the ether. "White. Male. Brown hair . . . Ugh. That's all I can see."

"Okay," she said to me. "That's not bad, but that's pretty general. What else can you give me about him?"

I focused again on trying to tease out another clue, but nothing came to me. It was so frustrating. "I can't see anything else really relevant about him. He's very careful to hide himself. I think he tries to blend in and not get noticed, but he's a pretty sick person."

Candice didn't say anything else, so I finally focused on her. She was looking at me like she didn't want to say what she was thinking. "What?"

"Sundance, I'm not quite sure how we're going to solve a series of murders that won't take place for two more years when we've got no names, a very general description, and no initial location to go looking."

"Damn," I said. "You're right. But, Candice, I wouldn't have pulled those clues out of the ether if I weren't supposed to get involved somehow." And then a thought struck me. "Oh, my God," I whispered. "It's because of me."

"What's because of you?"

I put my head in my hands. "I was the one who made the bulldozer driver dig down to those remains. If not for me, that site would've been developed, homes would've gone up, and the area wouldn't have lain fallow so that the girls could be buried there. I'm the catalyst, Candice. Me!"

"Hey," she said, reaching forward to grab my wrists, pulling my hands away from my face. "You are *not* the catalyst, Abby. If this guy is truly going to murder these girls, then where he buries them is irrelevant."

But I was shaking my head. "No," I said. "No. There's something about that site. Something that he wants to make a statement about. There's a reason he's burying them there."

"Like what?"

"I don't know," I admitted. "But it all ties together. The bank, the site, the graves, the delay in development."

"Whoa," Candice said. "Abs, you just said the bank ties in with all this. How does it tie in?"

I blinked, realizing she was right. But again I was coming up empty. My radar was drawing links between the bank, the cleared development site, and the four bodies buried there. "I can't tell," I said. "But I know it figures in."

"Do you think it could be four of the bank's employees?"

My eyes widened. Something about that felt right. "Maybe," I said. "But two years from now, who knows who'll be working there?"

"True," she said with a frown. Then she sat back and shook her head. "Honey, I'm just not sure how to go about solving this thing, and even if we do find out who this future killer is, what are we going to nail him on if he hasn't already committed murder?"

"I have no idea," I confessed, feeling like there was no way to win here. "So, what do we do?"

"What can we do?" she replied.

I rubbed my temples. I was starting to get a headache from trying to piece the clues together. "I don't want to go home yet," I said.

"You think Rivera is going to send you packing?"

"Yes."

"Damn," she said. "That new probie, York, is gonna win the office pool."

I rolled my eyes. "Sort of the least of our worries right now, Huckleberry."

"True," she said. "But I was hoping it'd get you to smile."

"I feel like a failure."

"You're hardly a failure, Abs. Seriously, you need to give yourself a little more credit. I mean, look at *all* the cases you've helped Brice and Dutch crack! Your numbers don't lie, kiddo. You're good at what you do. The fact that you just happened to pick up on a murder case that hasn't happened yet is irrelevant. You're good."

"Tell that to Agent Rivera."

"Oh, I will," she said.

I was quick to say, "Wait, don't tell him that. Let's just see what he says in the morning. Maybe he'll let me stay on and work the bank robberies."

"Why is it important to you to stay on and work that particular case?" she asked.

"Because right now these guys think I suck." My lower lip began quivering and I had to press my lips together hard and clear my throat to continue. "I need to prove to them that I don't, or Gaston, Brice, and Dutch are all going to end up looking like fools who've been duped by a con artist. I've got to work the robbery cases, solve them, prove my worth, then convince somebody over there at the L.A. bureau to keep an eye on that plot of land next to the bank. Something bad is gonna go down there, Candice. The summer after next, you mark my words, and I can't walk away without trying to convince these guys that I'm not full of shit and that they should listen to me. Especially when it might be my fault that the killer is going to use that place for his personal graveyard."

Candice played with the sash on her robe while she listened to me. "First of all," she said after a moment, "nothing that happened or happens up on that hill is your fault. All of the blame resides with those who mean to cause harm to others. Period.

"Second, I'm certain that Gaston has weathered harsher storms than the L.A. bureau not wanting to vote you prom queen. Third, our husbands don't give a rat's ass *what* anybody else thinks of them, but they do care what we think of ourselves, and I know that it would pain Dutch in particular if you came away from here thinking you'd somehow failed. Fourth, I haven't given up on winning the pool, so I will help you any way I can to stay."

My chest filled with warmth. Candice is one of those true friends that everyone should have, but almost no one does. I've long thanked my lucky stars for her, and now I had one more reason to feel so grateful. "I'd really appreciate it," I said.

"I know. So, let's figure out how to keep you on the team."

I blinked with heavy lids. My stomach was full and my body temp was back up to the comfort zone. I realized that I'd just passed the point of being able to focus on Candice and the issue at hand. Still, I gave it my best shot. "How're we going to do that?" I asked, trying to stifle a yawn.

"Well," she said, "by doing what you and I do best. Working together, under the radar, and seeing what we see. If we can dig up some useful stuff on these robbers, then Whitacre's crew won't have a choice but to invite you back to the table."

"Good plan," I said as another yawn snuck up on me. "Let's do that."

I closed my eyes just to rest them for a minute when I heard Candice say, "Hey."

Forcing my lids open again, I saw that Candice was up from her seat on the bed, where she'd eaten her meal, and was now retrieving her laptop from the desk. "You sleep. I'll look into these robberies."

I remember muttering something to her as I sank back into the pillow, but not the specifics. The only thing I do remember is how good that pillow felt and how very tired I was. Then, nothing else until the next morning.

*   *   *

Candice woke me at half past six. I sort of jolted awake when she shook my shoulder and called my name. "What?! Who?! When?!" I exclaimed, nimbly launching out of bed like a ninja. Well, mentally I launched out of bed like a ninja. My body sort of launched out like an abruptly awakened tree sloth and sprawled out on the floor in a tangle of bedsheets and pillows.

"Nice dismount," Candice said. "I'll give it an eight. You would've had an eight point five if you'd stuck the landing."

"I'll file that away under 'things I never need to worry about again,'" I muttered, picking my head up from the pillow I'd taken with me to the floor. For a few seconds all I did was stare blearily around the room, trying to get my bearings.

"You gonna get off the floor today, Sundance? Or should I check back with you tomorrow?"

Groaning, I pulled myself to my knees and looked up at her. There was a promising cup of steaming coffee in her hand. "That for me?"

"It is. If you'll get all the way up, that is."

I yawned and shook my head to get rid of the sleep cobwebs. With a few more groans I got to my feet and reached for the coffee. Candice withheld it for a moment to add, "I'm going to give this to you, but I'm going to ask something of you in return."

I sighed and sat down on the bed. "There's always a catch."

"Come for a run with me," she said.

I scowled. Candice is one of those women who *enjoys* physical exercise. Like, for reals she enjoys it. I've watched her from the comfort and safety of a lounge chair in her condo's gym, and she actually *smiles* through wall balls. For those of you who don't know (and I didn't until Candice explained it to me), a wall ball involves squatting low with a medicine ball weighing more than a toddler, and sort of jumping up to a standing position, where you then release said toddler-weighted ball to a target about a million feet up on a wall, then catch it when it descends with outstretched hands before dropping back down into the squat for round two. On a dare, Candice got me to do a set of thirty of them once. It was the most awful experience of my life, but Candice goes at them like a machine gun spitting out rounds of ammunition, all the while wearing a grin like wall balls are the most joyful thing she can do. And don't even get me started about what happens to her expression when she's swinging a forty-four-pound kettlebell from her knees to over her head.

I think she may need therapy.

Hell, after watching her destroy the ego of the guy in the condo next to her when he decided to take her on in a challenge that involved a sixty-five-pound barbell, hoisted overhead forty-five times, coupled with forty-five pull-ups in quick succession, *I* might need therapy. I know he'll never be the same . . . the poor bastard.

Anyway, by now I've learned my lesson. "Thanks," I told her, turning my face away from the delicious-smelling coffee offering. "I'll pass."

"It's a mocha latte," she sang.

In case you hadn't guessed, Candice is evil.

My mouth watered. "That's okay. I'll pass. Hey, where're my pants?"

Candice tossed a pair of running tights onto the bed next to me. It's like she didn't even care that I'd said no to the run. "I sent all your clothes to the laundry, and I bought those for you at the Dunham's next door to the Starbucks when I went to get you coffee."

I eyed her sideways. "You're a real pain in my ass, you know that?"

"And these," she said, ignoring my comment while bending down to pick up a pair of new running shoes, "were on sale."

"I'm not running with you."

"But the best part," she said, setting my coffee on the desk to retrieve something else from a bag, "is this!" Holding up a gorgeous coral-colored running tank, she added, "It's so your color."

I glared at her. Hard.

Candice wasn't exactly put off. In fact, I might've encouraged her, because she had that "challenge accepted" look in her eye. "I'll take you out for breakfast after," she said, tossing the shirt at me.

It hit me in the face. Much like the realization that my best friend wasn't about to give up coaxing me into breaking a sweat. I fell back on the bed dramatically. "Why can't you go by yourself and leave me and the latte in peace?"

"Because I'm worried you're getting soft."

I sat up again. Quick. "You're worried I'm getting . . . what, now?"

She pointed to my midsection. "Soft."

I've always been a thin girl. I come from a family of primarily skinny people, and my metabolism has been working like a champ these past thirty-seven years, even though I live mostly on carbs, sugar, more carbs, and, oh, yeah, sugar. So when Candice pointed an accusing finger at my midsection, I jumped to my feet like a Pop-Tart out of the toaster to spend the next several seconds staring down at my middle, which (dammit!) *was* a little more round and bloated than I remembered.

"And your butt's getting big," she said next.

I gasped. Loudly. Then spun around like a dog after its own tail. "IT IS NOT!"

Candice crossed her arms and refused to take it back. "Sorry, Sundance, but as your best friend, I feel obligated to inform you that you've definitely been carrying a little extra junk in that trunk. I think that skinny little body of yours is *finally* showing off your diet."

My upper lip curled into a snarl. She'd said that with a small hint of glee. "I don't like you very much right now," I told her.

"I know," she said sympathetically. "But I can take it. Come on, honey, you knew it was gonna happen sooner or later. A girl cannot consume that much junk food in a lifetime without it someday showing up on her ass."

"Is it really that bad?"

Candice shook her head and became serious. "No, of course not. And, truthfully, I don't really care what you look like, but I do care that you're healthy. Which, for as long as I've known you, you have never been. I think it's time we changed that."

I considered Candice for a long moment, taking in her gorgeously toned arms, tight stomach, slender hips, long, lean legs, and healthy glow. She held herself with such confidence, such cool athletic readiness. It was impressive. Even when she was relaxed, she was a force to be reckoned with. And then I caught the reflection of myself in the large mirror above the desk. I was kinda pale. My skin was a little dry. My posture a mess. My muscle tone nonexistent, and my stomach and butt had definitely each gained a size. "Crap on a cracker," I growled.

Candice smiled like the Cheshire cat. "We'll do a three-mile run-walk, then go for breakfast. I think a healthy bowl of oatmeal and some fruit will make you right as rain."

Hours later (okay, so maybe not hours—I swear the run had played with the time/space continuum to alter my perception of just how long it'd taken . . . i.e., *millennia*) we were sitting in a café and I was pushing around gray-looking gruel and unripened fruit like it was the swill they serve in prison. "This whole morning sucks," I said. "Seriously, it totally sucks!"

Candice nodded as if she understood my pain. After elegantly setting down her teacup, she said, "I figure you're going to be like this while your body goes through withdrawal."

"What does that even *mean*?" I snapped.

"It means that you've been used to a steady supply of sugary, fat-filled, carb-loaded grossness your whole life. One meal that isn't jam-packed with any of that and your brain gets denied its usual supply of dopamine, which'll put you into a free fall of crabbiness."

My jaw clenched and my temper flared, but why I couldn't really pinpoint. All I knew was that I was angry at Candice. Or maybe I was just hangry at her. It was hard to tell. "Maybe I'm crabby because my feet hurt, my calves are screaming, my quads are ready to strike, and this new top you bought me has chafed me so bad under my arms that I can't even raise one high enough to give you the finger."

Candice smiled winningly at me. "That's the spirit."

I shoved a grape into my mouth lest I say something (else) unkind. Taking a deep breath while chewing on the grape, I swallowed and said, "Did you find anything out about the robberies?"

"Oodles," she told me. "Lots of good stuff."

"Like?"

"I found video of the bank that was robbed next to the site where you found the ancient remains."

"Do tell."

Candice picked up her tea again. "It makes for some interesting viewing. I'd like to have you watch it, though, before I comment further on what I found."

Wadding up my napkin, I tossed it on the table, where it bounced right into Candice's teacup. It wasn't like I was aiming to do that, but it sure as hell brought a smile to my face. "I'm ready to go," I said. "You?"

Candice considered the soggy wad of paper product in her drink, then gazed up at me with half-lidded eyes. "Nice shot."

"Thanks. I've been practicing." For emphasis I offered Candice my most winning smile.

She countered by motioning to the waitress. "Could you bring us the check, please? My friend here is paying."

A bit later and after a short shower, I came out of the bathroom to find Candice hovering over my phone. "Worried it's going to explode?" I asked her.

She picked up the phone and offered it to me. "I think Rivera just called you."

My gaze darted to the clock radio on the nightstand. "It's not even nine yet."

"Best to listen to the voice mail," she said as the phone chirped with the notification.

I did, setting it on speaker so we could both hear. "Ms. Cooper," Rivera said. "It's Special Agent in Charge Rivera. I've updated Director Whitacre about yesterday's events and your role in them. We think it best if we terminate your services at this time. Please contact your bureau chief to arrange for a flight home. If you have any further questions, you should contact him."

The message ended there and I sat down heavily on the bed. "I've been fired before," I said. "And I knew it was coming, but shit. This blows."

"You're telling me," Candice said. "The pool was up to six fifty."

Ignoring her attempt at levity, I tossed the phone to the side and got up to blow-dry my hair. "Would you do me a favor and call your husband and tell him that we need two seats on the first available flight out? With any luck we'll be home by late tonight."

"No," she said.

I stopped in my tracks and turned to look back at her. "Oh, so I have to call him and deliver the bad news?" I asked, a little challenge in my voice. Candice makes me act the role of a grown-up more than anyone I know. It's totes annoying.

"No, I don't think either of us should call him."

I turned fully around and crossed my arms. "Explain."

"Nothing's really changed here," she began. "I mean, we sort of assumed Rivera was gonna cut you loose, and I did spend a lot of my sleeping time last night researching these bank robberies, and we have a series of murders that will take place at some point in the future to halt, so why should it matter if Rivera doesn't want us around? We can still work the cases and have you prove yourself by finding a clue that the FBI didn't have before you got involved."

I noticed that Candice didn't suggest we'd be the ones to solve it. I was betting she'd wanted to say that, but—amazeballs friend that she is—she didn't want to put any extra pressure on me. Suddenly, if Candice had suggested another run, or even a set of wall balls, I'd have been in. She always seemed to have that effect on me—she made the seriously difficult seem totally doable. "Okay," I told her.

She blinked. "What do you mean?"

I blinked at her. "What do you mean, what do I mean?"

"I mean, why aren't you protesting? Are you playing with me?"

I rolled my eyes. "Come on, I'm not that bad, am I? I'm in,

Candice. You're right; we don't need the L.A. bureau's permission to look into these cases. We can roust up some info on our own."

Candice eyed me critically for another couple of seconds, probably wondering if I'd say something like, "Gotcha! Now, let's get the hell outta here!" but when I didn't offer up any kind of counterargument, she said, "Okay, then. Good. Now, we just have to figure out what to tell Brice before he ca—"

My phone rang, interrupting her. I looked at the display, then held it up to Candice. "Too late."

"Dammit," she muttered, then took the phone to answer it. "Hey, babe. It's me. Abby's in the shower." She listened for a bit, then said, "I understand. She gave it her best shot, and there's no faulting her for it—not that she's letting herself off the hook or anything. . . . Yeah, I'm afraid she's taking it hard. She really wanted to do some good for these guys, but they weren't cutting her any breaks from the start. . . . Right, right. Okay, well, if it's all the same to you and Dutch, I think that a couple of days out here by the beach might do her a world of good. I'm going to drive us up the coast a little ways, check us in to a B and B, and force that girl to relax—take her mind off her troubles. You guys won't have a problem with that plan, will you?"

Candice winked at me while I gave her a thumbs-up.

"That's great, Brice, thanks. What's that? When do I think we'll be home? Uh . . . I don't know, maybe four or five days from now. I'm gonna play it by ear. The important thing is to just make Abby feel better about herself. Some beach therapy should be just the ticket. I'll have her clear it with Dutch, so don't say anything to him until I let you know, okay? . . . Great, sweetheart. Love you."

Candice then handed me the phone and I called Dutch, saying almost exactly what Candice had said to Brice, and playing up the pity party for myself. "Beach therapy sounds great, Edgar," he said sweetly. "You two have a good time together and relax. I'll hold down the fort here, and look forward to seeing your new tan lines."

I giggled at that. "Thanks for understanding," I told him, suddenly missing him very much.

After getting off the phone, I gave Candice a thumbs-up, then stepped into the bathroom again to dry my hair. The grin on my reflection in the mirror was huge.

Chapter Seven

. . .

A short time later, Candice and I watched the video of the La Cañada Flintridge bank robbery together, huddling around her laptop. Neither of us spoke until I'd replayed it a third time. The video depicted four robbers, wearing ninja costumes, which showed almost no skin except for the area around their foreheads. Their eyes were obscured by sunglasses, and their mouths were covered by the costume. They also wore gloves to prevent leaving any fingerprints.

The one thing I noticed was that they moved just like the assassins they'd dressed up as. They were each broad shouldered, narrow at the waist, like trim and fit athletes. They were also nimble, quick, and disciplined, without the telltale signs of anxiety or clumsiness I'd come to expect from all the robbery videos I'd seen.

Bank robbers on the whole tend to be nervous and stiff while in the process of robbing a bank. I've watched a lot of videos of them over the years, and even though many of the thieves attempt to project a sense of calm, they almost never succeed convincingly.

"Wow," I said after the video ended. "These guys are stone-cold smooth."

"Right?" Candice said, her arms crossed over her chest and her expression pulled down in a frown. "I mean, I know it's their fifth robbery, but no way should they be that good. Look at how fluid they are, like trained soldiers. Not a misstep or odd gesture among them."

"Yep," I agreed. "Nor are there any hands shaking or legs trembling in the mix. None of them seemed even remotely nervous. This looks practiced. Drilled down to the finest detail."

"Which is why they're so efficient," Candice pointed out. "They were in and out with fifty thousand dollars in a little over three minutes."

"Same amount from all the banks?" I asked her.

She shook her head. "This was the only bank that gave up the information about how much the thieves got away with. My guess, though, is that the other banks were hit up for similar amounts."

"They move so smoothly," I repeated, backing up the video again. "It's like they've had training in martial arts or dance or something."

"Probably martial arts," Candice said. "I mean, why else choose the ninja outfit?"

"Because it's a damn good outfit," I said. "It obscures anything that might lead to your identification in a lineup. And I'll bet the people in the bank were so scared they wouldn't even be able to tell you anything about the robbers that could've been seen up close."

"They're all of slight build. Lean, even," Candice noted. For emphasis she pointed to the two robbers closest to the doors.

"Yeah," I said. "I caught that too."

Next Candice pointed to one robber's hands. "They all wore

gloves, so no fingerprints, and no one was injured during the robbery, so no DNA left behind."

"What about the weapons?" I asked, tapping the screen where one robber wore an array of silver throwing stars at his belt.

"They all wore them, but nobody threw them," Candice said. "I checked online and there're no reports of anyone at any of the robbed banks getting injured. Or that any of the stars were ever thrown."

"Interesting weapon to bring to a bank robbery, wouldn't you say?" I asked.

"Wouldn't be my first choice," she confessed. "But they'd be effective if I were a teller and was asked to hand over the dough for fear of ending up with one of those between my eyes."

"Do you have a theory about why there were no dye packs used? I mean, fifty grand is a lot of money to just let walk out the door without trying to foil the plan, right?"

Candice smirked at me as if I'd said something cute. "For most banks, dye packs are a costly pain in the ass. The money they lose in the robbery gets covered in ink, and then they have to spend lots of their own man-hours accounting for all the serial numbers on each bill to have it replaced. It's easier on them to simply file a claim with the FDIC and let the FBI worry about catching the thieves."

"Would've made our jobs a little easier, though, huh?" I said.

"Who said there was any fun in easy, Sundance?" my best friend replied with a grin. "Anyway, all we have right now is this footage, so turn on that intuition of yours and tell me what's pinging off your radar."

I stared at the computer again and replayed the entire video for a fourth time. One of the robbers caught my attention and I focused on him. "This one," I said, pressing my finger to the image. "The guy by the door. He's the leader."

Candice squinted. "I would've pegged the guy at the counter."

I shook my head. "No. There's something about him that makes me think he's in charge. Don't quite know what it is yet, but he's the one to focus on. And there's also something about the way he moves. It's a little different from the others, right?"

Candice leaned forward while I rewound the footage a bit and let it play to show her what I was looking at. "He's . . . more confident," she said. "Which is saying a lot, as these four are by far the most confident bank robbers I've ever seen, but you're right, there is something he projects that the others are responding to."

"And that," I said, pausing the video to point again to the screen. "See his right hand? He's tapping his finger to his thigh. I think he's counting the seconds."

"Hmmm," Candice said. "Weird when there's a clock right on that far wall," she said, observing the slightly blurred image of the clock to the left of the door.

"Not really," I said, studying the ninja leader. "To watch the clock, he'd have to take his eyes off the people in the lobby, which would make him vulnerable. This way, he can watch everything that's going on and keep the gang on schedule."

We watched in silence to the end of the footage and then I swiveled slightly in my chair to face Candice and ask, "Where's the security guard in all this?"

"Don't know," Candice said. "But I'd like to."

"Do I smell a field trip back to the bank next on the agenda?"

She flashed me another grin and reached for her purse. "You do, my friend. You do."

*   *   *

We arrived back at the same bank I'd visited the day before with my good ol' buds Dumbledumb and Dumbledumber. I was in much better spirits now that I didn't have to worry about hurting their feelings.

Given the choice, one hundred percent of the time I'd rather investigate a case with Candice at my side. Unless of course we're getting shot at. Or attacked with knives. Or are falsely imprisoned, pulled into raging rivers, rammed off the edge of bridges, kidnapped, strangled, or strapped to a bomb, or are running from serial killers, the mob, the law, and/or our husbands . . .

pause . . .

pause . . .

Hmmm, allow me to amend. Given the choice, ten percent of the time I'd rather investigate any case with Candice at my side. The other ninety percent I'd rather be at the Taco Shack enjoying a giant wet burrito, but why split hairs? The point is that I was glad to be out from under the FBI'm-a-Dumbledumb's scrutiny, and advancing the case with my bestest bud at my side.

"Tomorrow I think we should pull you into the gym," Candice said casually as we exited the car. "A round of wall balls and kettlebell swings would do you some real good, Sundance."

Hmmm, allow me to amend *again*. One hundred percent of the time I'd rather not investigate anything for anyone anywhere ever again.

With a mean squint I said, "I don't much like you today."

"Ouch," she mocked. "How *will* I go on?"

"You'll be sorry tomorrow when I die under the weight of a wall ball."

"The kettlebells are the more serious threat," she warned as she held open the bank door for me.

"To you or to me?"

"Not sure yet," she said. "It could go either way."

"Good morning!" said a cheery voice, and we both turned to see a woman with dark blond hair, twisted into a pretty severe knot, approach us, wearing a dark blue suit and a white silk top. "Are either of you interested in one of our low, low interest rate credit cards today?"

Candice appeared to perk up a little at that. "How'd you know?" she asked the woman, who seemed honestly startled by the question. Turning to me, she added, "Hey, Abby, I think she's psychic!"

I didn't really know what was going on, so I just forced a smile and blinked in confusion.

For her part the woman blushed and said, "I'm not—I swear! But we are offering a great deal on all our credit cards. Would you like to come on over and fill out an application?"

"I would," Candice said happily. When the woman began to lead the way over to a desk, my BFF winked at me and mouthed, *Play along.*

As we were sitting down, the woman extended her hand to Candice first, then to me. "I'm Mary," she said.

We gave our first names to her and then she launched into a short lecture about all the financing options available at the bank. I wondered if Candice really intended to fill out the paperwork for a credit card; it seemed a lot to do just to get on a bank employee's good side, as I assumed she was doing only so she could pepper the woman with questions about the robbery.

Sure enough, as Candice pointed to one of the brochures

fanned out in Mary's hand at the end of the lecture, she said, "I like that second option with the reward points, Mary, but I'm a little nervous about sitting here to fill out the paperwork. I heard this bank was robbed a few weeks ago?"

Mary's winning smile faltered. "Oh, my," she said, covering her mouth and blushing like we'd just told her she had spinach in her teeth. "That wasn't really a big deal," she said. "Just some bad people who probably won't ever come here again."

Her voice rose a little at the end, and became slightly shrill. She blushed for a second time and quickly handed Candice the brochure. "It only takes a moment to fill out the application," she said. "We can have you approved and on your way in fifteen minutes!"

Candice took the brochure and the pen Mary eagerly offered her and began to scribble down her information. "Is it true you guys were robbed by *ninjas*?"

Mary cleared her throat, obviously uncomfortable about the fact that Candice wasn't letting it go. "We're not supposed to talk about it," she whispered.

Candice pressed her lips together like she couldn't believe poor Mary was being forced to keep all that terribleness bottled up inside. "Years ago," she said, "I was robbed at gunpoint."

Mary's eyes widened. "You were?"

"I was," she said. "I've never been more scared in my life! And do you know that I can't remember one single detail about the guy that mugged me? But I sure as hell can describe the barrel of his gun."

Mary nodded along like she knew exactly how that could happen.

"For weeks afterward I could hardly get out of bed—I was so scared," Candice went on. "I mean, I think I might've had a little of that PTSD, you know?"

Mary swallowed hard. "I'm having trouble sleeping," she confessed.

"Oh," I said, chiming in. "You poor thing."

"This is such a safe area!" Mary continued in a hushed voice. "It's why I've never worried about working in a bank, you know?"

"We do," Candice and I said in unison.

"And it wasn't really all that scary, to tell you the truth. None of the robbers even spoke a word. They just pointed and we got the message."

"Well, thank God no one was hurt," Candice told her softly, leaning in to further the impression of a small conspiracy between her, Mary, and me. "If you employees hadn't kept your cool and cooperated, who knows, right?"

Mary shuddered. "My mind keeps going through everything that could've happened that day," she said. "I try to remind myself that nothing bad happened to any of us. Well, except for Phil."

Candice put a hand to her mouth. "So, someone was hurt?"

Mary rolled her eyes. "No, no, it wasn't like that. He was our security guard. He'd been with us for about four years. He lost his job over the whole thing because he was in the men's room during the robbery."

"He was?" I asked. I didn't know security guards could take a break from watchdog duty, but then again, how could anyone deny a person a bathroom break?

"It really wasn't his fault," Mary said. "He ran into some stomach trouble and was in and out of the restroom all morning."

"And they fired him for that?" Candice said, shaking her head like she couldn't believe it.

"They did," she said, with a *tsk*. "But he landed on his feet, thank God. He's working over at Walgreens now. They give him a chair to sit in at the pharmacy counter at least. Here he had to stand on his feet all day."

"Aww," I said. "That's nice that Phil's story had a happy ending."

Mary sighed. "Yeah, he got lucky."

"Have you thought about leaving?" I asked her. As a reflex, I'd scanned her energy and noticed that a job change was definitely in her future.

She waved dismissively and said, "No! Where would I go?"

I smiled, because I knew she was lying. "Have you ever thought about real estate?"

Her head pulled back in surprise. "Real estate?" she said with a small, nervous laugh. "Oh, that's not my thing."

Yes, it was. "Ah," I said with a shrug. "I think you'd make a great real estate agent. You know all about property finance and you're super personable."

Mary blushed again. "Thank you, Abby," she said. "That's so sweet of you."

Candice then said, "You know, Mary, I really think you should do it. I think you should go look for another job. I mean, after I was mugged, I had to quit my job and look for another line of work too. It was the best thing I could've done, because it gave me something to focus on other than being afraid all the time."

Mary nodded. "I've been really on edge since it all happened," she said. "I know they won't come back—I mean, I know that logically—but emotionally I catch my breath every time that front door opens."

"Did you see them come in?" I asked.

"I did," she said. "I was sitting right here when the door opened and they filed in. The whole bank went deadly quiet as everyone caught sight of them, and then they fanned out and one of them approached the counter and handed Lucy a note. We all knew what was happening, but we were too scared to move."

"Don't you guys have a silent alarm under your desks or something?"

Again a blush tinged Mary's cheeks. "We do, and I pressed it, but I think I waited too long. The bank thief by the door was really mean-looking. He stared at me and shook his head like he knew I wanted to press the alarm and he'd hurt me if I did, so I waited until they began to leave to press it."

"You did the right thing," Candice told her. "Seriously, Mary. After all, it's not worth your life, right?"

Beads of sweat had broken out across Mary's forehead. The memory of the moment the leader of the gang of robbers had threatened her remained fresh and terrifying for her. I felt so bad for her. "Mary," I said gently. "I think you should go see a professional and tell her about what happened. I think it might help you to talk about it with someone who can help you."

"You mean like a therapist?"

I nodded.

She shrugged. "Maybe."

Candice handed her the brochure, which she'd completed. "Abby's right," she said. "You need a few sessions with someone who can help you cope with the fear. I know it helped me."

"It did?" she asked. "Really?"

"Really."

Mary blushed again and took the application from Candice. She then put all the information into her computer and we continued to chat amicably with her for the ten minutes it took for Candice to be approved for twenty thousand dollars. Her credit was good enough to qualify her for a triple platinum card—because double platinum wasn't enough, apparently.

We left the bank a little later and I wasn't sure we'd learned much other than the fact that Candice had an amazing FICO score.

After getting in the car, I said, "Interesting interview technique."

"Hey, I'd apply for a mortgage if it would get every witness to open up like Mary did."

"The poor woman," I mused. "I think you're right; she really does seem to have PTSD."

Looking at me, Candice asked, "You think she'll be okay?"

I felt out the ether and replied, "I do, but not for a little while. She's resistant to therapy, but willing to change careers, and that'll work to keep the night terrors away for a bit. Sometime next year, though, I think all that's happened to her is gonna creep back and she'll go get help."

"Good," Candice said, starting the engine. "Now, let's go find Phil."

"How're you going to find the security guard?" I asked. "We didn't even get his last name."

"We passed a Walgreens two lights down," Candice said reasonably. "I'll bet he works there."

"You think he'd stay in the same neighborhood?" I asked.

"Sure! I mean, he worked at the bank for at least four years, so I'd be willing to bet he also lives nearby and this is a short commute for him. You watch—he'll be there."

Candice was dead-on. We found Phil slouched in a chair at the pharmacy of the Walgreens, making sure nobody tried to rob the place of Sudafed or prescription painkillers. Of course, if someone was intent on robbing the place, the withered old geezer parked in the chair wearing a security uniform probably wasn't gonna be much of a deterrent.

"Phil!" Candice said, like she'd known him forever.

He jerked at the sound of his name and eyed her curiously. "Hey, there," he said, and it was obvious from his expression that he was trying to place where he knew her from. "How you been?"

"Great, Phil, just great," she said, stopping in front of him to reach out and squeeze his shoulder. "I'm surprised to see you here, though. Why aren't you over at the bank?"

Phil's brow rose slightly, as if he remembered that he must've known Candice from the bank. "Oh, I left that job. Too much time on my feet, you know? Here they give me a chair and a steady stream of pretty ladies to walk past."

He said that with a twinkle in his eye, like he was getting away with something. That made me like him a whole, whole lot.

Candice laughed and slapped his arm lightly. "You old dog. Actually, I'm so glad you're okay! I heard that the branch got robbed a couple of weeks ago."

Phil nodded, like that was some sorry business, all right. "Yeah," he said. "We got hit."

"Were you scared?" Candice asked him.

"Nah," he said with a chuckle. "I was in the bathroom the whole time." Patting his abdomen, he added, "Had a hell of a time that day. Caught some kind of nasty bug that ran right through me, if you get my drift."

"Yikes," Candice said. "That's awful, but still, I'm glad you weren't at your post or you could've been hurt by those robbers."

Phil waved his hand dismissively. "They got lucky," he said. "At the bank, they let me carry a gun. Here, all I get is pepper spray." For emphasis he tapped a small canister attached to his big black belt.

"So you never got a look at the robbers?" Candice said.

"Nope," he told her. "Not even a peep."

"Well, I hope you didn't get in trouble for being sick and away from your post," Candice said to him.

Phil scowled and added a shrug. "It probably would've been okay with the bank if the Feds hadn't made such a big stink about it."

"The Feds?" Candice said, as if she were suddenly alarmed at the mention of the FBI. "What kind of stink could they make about it? I mean, you were sick. What were you supposed to do?"

"They thought I might've been in on it," he admitted with a roll of his eyes. "I told 'em to go ahead and investigate me. I got nothin' to hide."

"Did they?" I asked, genuinely curious.

"Oh, yeah," he said, his eyes now wide. "They talked to everybody about me. My neighbors, my boss, the people at the bank . . . even the manager at Starbucks where I get my hot tea every morning!"

"You're kidding," I said, thinking Perez and Robinson were at least thorough.

"Nope," he replied, crossing his arms with another scowl. "They were trying to account for every minute of my day and back up my story that I was sick in the can during the robbery. Stupid waste of their time and my tax dollars if you ask me."

Candice reached out to squeeze Phil's shoulder again. "Well, I'm glad you're well again, Phil, and that nothing bad happened to you."

"Thanks," he said, patting her hand.

We left Phil then and headed back to the car. "Anything ring false from him?" Candice asked as we were buckling ourselves in.

"No," I said with a sigh. "There was nothing about his

energy that suggested he was lying or trying to hide anything. His story checks out, at least against my radar."

Candice tapped the steering wheel thoughtfully. "Which is weird, right?"

"You mean, in that it's a really odd coincidence that at the *exact* moment Phil is indisposed, the bank is robbed?"

"Yep," she said. "Makes me wonder where the guard was at the other four banks during the robberies."

"Only one way to find out," I said.

Candice reached back behind her to her iPad, which she'd apparently hidden in the backseat under her coat, and pulled it forward to consult it. After a minute she said, "Okay, there's a bank in Pasadena that looks promising and it's about a half hour away. It was the third bank hit."

I donned sunglasses and said, "Let's roll."

We arrived at the bank and Candice took about five minutes to work on her appearance. I watched her, curiously fascinated. First she brushed and smoothed out her hair, then swept it up into an easy chignon, pinning it with a few bobby pins located in a neat little pack in her purse. Next, she applied a deep burgundy lipstick, which made her pale skin and hazel eyes pop. Last, she shrugged out of her light jacket and unbuttoned her silk blouse down to her cleavage, exposing a bit of black lace bra and the foreheads of both "ladies."

Walking in, I also noted there was no security guard at the entrance, and coming into the lobby didn't produce sight of one either. By the time my attention returned to Candice, I realized she'd already completed the transformation she'd started in the car.

Now, I've known Candice for about seven years, and in that time I've seen her alter her appearance completely, simply by squaring her shoulders, changing her posture, and doing something like pursing her lips. She's remarkable in that way; it's sort of like how when you go to see a Meryl Streep movie, you're never quite seeing Meryl, but a different person entirely, even though nothing about her facial architecture has changed.

I recognized the personality currently projecting out of the body of my best friend—she'd donned her resting rich face. I nearly shivered with pleasure. This was a favorite persona of mine, as there was always a bit of a show to go with it. "I swear," she began in a tone loud enough to carry while popping one hip out and resting her bent elbow on it. "You can't find good help these days, Abigail. We've been standing here for an *hour* and no one has even greeted us yet!"

A man about our age appeared in front of us as if by magic. "Hello," he said, adopting a forced smile. "Welcome to Sun Coast Bank. Have you heard about our low-interest-rate credit cards?"

That line again? Gee, these bank people really liked to push the credit cards.

Candice stared at him up and down as if he were some offensive appetizer that she'd been offered on a tarnished platter. A sheen of sweat appeared on the poor man's brow. "Who's in charge here?" she asked, pulling down her Gucci sunglasses to look haughtily at him over the frame.

"I—I am, miss," he said, his voice catching a little.

She gave him that up-down again and I had to press my lips together to keep from smiling. Meanwhile the sheen of sweat on his brow began to bead a little. "You?" she said, as if she couldn't believe it.

"Yes, ma'am," he said with a vigorous nod. "Is there something I can help you with?"

Candice sighed dramatically. "I'm new to the area," she said, pulling her glasses off in that way that rich people do when they want you to see that it's annoying that they have to do it at all. "And I need to transfer a large quantity of funds from my bank in New York to an establishment here."

The bank manager bounced slightly. Candice had just sung his magic tune. Thrusting out his hand, he said, "I'm Sam Gabris, ma'am."

Candice eyed his hand and her upper lip curled a bit in distaste. Still, she extended her own and allowed him exactly one pump before she withdrew it. "Caroline Parker," she said. Making a wispy hand motion to me, she added, "This is my sister, Abigail."

Sam turned to me, sticking out his hand again, and I shook it without the lip curl.

"Won't you two come this way?" he said, his voice hitching again.

We followed him to an office, which was great, because I had a feeling Candice preferred some privacy when she outright lied about her identity. After we all took our seats, Sam said, "How much were you looking to transfer, Ms. Parker?"

"Mrs.," she corrected, making a show of setting her glasses in her handbag and placing it demurely at her feet.

"Sorry," he said, flushing a little. "Mrs. Parker, how much did you want to transfer over from your bank in New York?"

"Twenty million," she said.

I braced myself in case Sam's eyes popped out of their sockets to hit me in the face, which I swear they nearly did. "Dollars?" he gasped.

"Yes, dollars," she replied impatiently, then looked at me as if to say, *Can you believe I have to subject myself to this idiot?*

I rolled my eyes, but inwardly I thought, *Aw, poor Sam.*

For his part, the perspiration on Sam's brow, which had all but evaporated, reappeared with gusto. "I'm sorry," Sam said again. "It's just . . . that's a great deal of money to deposit into a bank. Not that I want to lose your business, Mrs. Parker, but wouldn't you be better served putting that into a portfolio of some kind?"

"It's for a real estate transaction," Candice said simply. "I'm acquiring a home here in Pasadena, but there's been a delay in the negotiations and I need to move those funds to a bank based here for reasons I'd rather not get into."

Sam's face fell. "Oh, Ms. Parker, I'm sorry, but are you saying that you're not a resident of California? In order to open an account here, you'd need to be a resident."

Candice shifted in her chair, a look of annoyance crossing her features; she then reached for her purse and began to pull out her checkbook. "No one said anything about not being a resident," she sniffed.

Sam gulped as a droplet of sweat trickled down his sideburn while his eyes stared unblinking at the emerging checkbook. "You'd need to prove that you were a resident, Ms. Parker. A driver's license and a utility bill is usually all we require."

Candice paused in the removal of her checkbook, then let it slip from her hand back into her purse and set that down. "I see," she said.

"It's company policy," Sam said weakly.

"Ah," Candice said, staring at him with a cold expression.

Another bead of sweat leaked down the side of Sam's face. "You know what?" he said, reaching for his office phone. "Let me just call the regional director and see if we can't make an exception for you—"

Candice held up her hand. "Before you do that," she said with a tight smile, "I'd like to ask you about your bank's security."

Sam's hand gripped the phone's receiver as he stared at her like a deer caught in headlights. "Our . . . security?" he said.

"Yes," she replied. "I've heard rumors."

"Rumors?"

"Yes, Sam. Rumors."

"What rumors?"

"That there've been a number of bank robberies in the area, and I want to make sure that not only will my money be safe, but that should I need to come into this establishment, *I* will be safe."

Sam swallowed audibly. "The area has a very low crime rate," he began, setting the receiver back into its cradle and looking anywhere but at Candice.

"Yes," Candice said, turning to glance out the window at the fancy neighborhood. "Which is why I feel confident investing in a new home here in Pasadena, but I often visit the bank when I'm in the mood for shopping, and I never use plastic; it's a personal thing. I'd hate to come here and be *involved* in some incident."

Sam nodded, still avoiding her gaze. "I completely understand. The safety of our customers is our utmost concern."

"And yet," Candice said, "I see no security guard posted anywhere within your establishment."

Sam finally lifted his gaze, which, oddly, seemed guilt-riddled. "We like to project a comfortable atmosphere for our customers, Mrs. Parker, and we find that the presence of a security guard can often make our clientele feel . . . uncomfortable."

"Ah," Candice said to him. It was impossible to tell by the tone if she approved of his response, or found him an idiot.

I decided to help Candice steer the conversation into the right direction. "Your bank has never been robbed, though, right, Sam?"

He wiped at his brow and appeared surprised and embarrassed that his hand came away wet. "Like I said, the safety of our clientele is the most important thing to us."

Candice and I traded a look. "He's avoiding answering that," I said to her.

"I noticed." Turning back to Sam, she said, "So, the rumors are true. You were one of the banks hit in that string of robberies."

"It was a minor incident," he said quickly. "And the police have assured us that it's very unlikely to ever happen again."

I squinted at him. "Kind of like lightning not striking twice in the same location?"

He pointed at me, probably sensing an ally. "Exactly!"

"I see," Candice said, tapping the arm of her chair. "That doesn't exactly reassure me, Sam."

"No one was hurt," he said quickly. "And the whole thing was over in about three minutes, Mrs. Parker. I know it sounds bad, but it really wasn't."

Candice considered him for a moment before speaking again. "Tell us what happened, Sam, and leave nothing out. I'll make a decision then about opening an account here."

"I'm not really supposed to talk about it," he confessed.

Candice reached down and grabbed the handle on her purse. "Fine. Let's go, Abigail," she said.

Sam held up a hand and said, "Wait, wait! I'm willing to make an exception for you, Mrs. Parker, if you'll promise me that nothing I tell you leaves this room."

Again Candice and I traded looks and she shrugged. "We promise. Now, what happened? And remember, I want details, so leave nothing out."

Sam cleared his throat and wiped at his brow again. "It was a few weeks ago, around four in the afternoon. We had only one customer in the lobby when the door opened and in came four men wearing all black. They stood in a U formation, and one of the men stepped up to the counter and presented my teller with a note. She complied with the directions, and as soon as she handed over the money, the thieves left. I swear it was over in less than three minutes."

"And no one was hurt?" Candice pressed.

"No, Mrs. Parker. No one."

"Were any of the patrons robbed?" she asked next.

"Not a one, ma'am," he replied.

"Were any weapons drawn?" I asked.

Sam shook his head vigorously. "None. They didn't really even have any weapons to draw from."

"What does that mean?" Candice asked.

Sam's face flushed again, like he'd been caught in a lie. "The robbers had these throwing stars tucked into their belts, but they never pulled them out. They just stood around, motioned for us to all hold still, which we did, and then they passed the note to my teller."

"That sounds frightful," Candice said with a shudder. "And I can't believe that your corporate office won't spring for a security guard!"

Sam tugged at his collar and his shoulders sagged. It was clear he was losing "Mrs. Parker" and her twenty-million-dollar deposit. I suddenly wondered if he would've gotten some kind of promotion or bonus for that amount of money showing up in his branch's accounts. "That might seem like a logical step, Mrs. Parker, but if you'll look up the FBI's crime statistics, banks where an armed security guard is present escalate into violence fifteen times more often than banks with no security presence. Sometimes it's just better to give the thieves what they want quickly and efficiently so that they can move out of the bank as soon as possible. Sun Coast Bank would never want to risk any escalation of violence to our staff or to our clientele."

Candice cocked her head thoughtfully at him. "Well," she said. "I suppose that does make some sense. But how do you know these same thieves won't be back?"

"Because they've hit other branches in the Pasadena area, and never the same bank twice. It's only a matter of time before they're caught, and meanwhile, I promise you they won't be back."

Candice picked up her purse and got to her feet. "I'm afraid I'm going to have to think about this, Sam."

He nodded like he fully understood. But still, he seemed really bummed, and my heart went out to him. "Please take my card," he said, pushing it at her. "Call me with any other questions you have."

Candice took the card and motioned to me. With that, we made like Elvis and left the building.

Chapter Eight

. . .

The rest of the day was mostly a repeat of the interview with Sam. None of the other banks had any kind of security posted on the day of the robbery, and it sort of quickly became clear why: All the rest of the banks were located in fancy-schmancy neighborhoods, where the presence of a security guard was likely to be seen as a cause for alarm rather than reassurance. I thought it was funny that these were probably the same kinds of people who wanted to live in gated communities with guards at the entrance, but not see one at their banks because that would make them wonder if the neighborhood was starting to become unsafe.

Oh, the irony.

Of course, it also could've been that Sun Coast's corporate office either was too cheap or couldn't afford a full-time guard at each of their establishments. I was thinking it was probably the former.

But then I had to wonder, why was there a guard at the last bank hit in La Cañada Flintridge? After I posed this same question to Candice over dinner, she came up with the answer.

"That branch was robbed before," she said, then turned to look at me and added, "Twice."

That surprised me. "Really?"

"Yep. Once nine years ago, and again about four years ago. The area was hit hard by the housing market debacle in two thousand seven. It didn't really start recovering until about three years ago, but I think the previous robberies at that bank were cases where the perp was desperate. And I think that particular branch could get away with staffing a guard without people being nervous about their neighborhood going to the dogs."

"Yeah, I could see that. Still, I'm not liking the coincidence of Phil being in the restroom while the robbery went down."

"I thought you said he was clean," Candice reminded me.

"I think he is, but I just can't buy that he's sick and out of the way on the day of that robbery. Especially since none of the other banks had guards."

"We could look into him a bit," Candice offered.

"You mean, do your PI thing where you snoop into his financials and see what comes up?"

"Yeah, something like that."

"Couldn't hurt," I said, doing my best to stifle a yawn. "God! Will I ever get used to this time change?"

Candice smiled. "Probably around the time we head home. Come on, Sundance. Let's pay the bill and get back to the hotel. You can hit the hay and I'll start snooping."

I fell asleep to the sound of Candice's perfectly trimmed nails clicking on the keyboard, but woke up around two thirty a.m. with the most nagging feeling. Sitting up, I looked around the room, which was dark, but not so dark that I couldn't see, thanks to the streetlight from the parking lot sending a golden glow through the partially drawn curtains.

I lay there for a little while hoping to go back to sleep, but after half an hour I knew it wasn't going to happen, so I got out of bed and tiptoed to the bathroom, where I took care of business, and while I was washing my hands, I eyed my reflection and considered that I looked extremely troubled.

Something in the ether was off. And it was a bad kind of off. Also, there was a sort of urgent thought that kept playing through my mind. I felt the need to head to the bank in La Cañada. And not wait until daylight. There was an important clue that I felt we'd overlooked, or that I might discover if I headed out there and snooped around a little. I shook my head at my reflection. No way was I going out alone to some bank's parking lot at three in the morning. . . .

My intuition chimed in again. I felt that if I wanted to solve the bank robberies, I needed to get my ass out there. Pronto.

"Crap on a cracker," I muttered as I swept my hair up into a ponytail and crept out of the room to slip into my sweats and running shoes. I hesitated for about ten seconds, wondering if I should wake Candice and beg her to come with me, but she looked so peaceful sleeping that I just didn't have the heart. Plus, I had no plans to get out of the car, so having her along was unnecessary. Probably.

I made it out of the room and over to La Cañada without issue. Pulling into the parking lot at the Sun Coast Bank made me completely reevaluate the decision, however. The place was creepy. And dark. And I also had to wonder if I might draw some attention sitting in my parked car at half past three with the engine running and the lights off.

But still, that nagging sensation of something being off remained. I shifted in the seat a few times, ready to bolt out of there and make it back to the hotel room before Candice woke up. I hadn't left her a note, and in hindsight that was probably stupid, but if she texted me to ask where the hell I was, I could text her right back.

"What?" I asked myself. "*What* is it that's off?"

I stared at the bank's windows for a good ten minutes. Nothing happened and no further clues emerged. "This is so stupid," I said to myself, and reached to put the car into reverse. No way was I gonna hang around here all night and hope that something resembling a clue jumped out at me.

As I glanced over my shoulder to back up the car, however, a flash of light caught my eye and I braked hard enough to make the car jolt. Staring out the rear window, I saw the light bob up and down slightly, and the direction of the beam was coming from the hilltop where I'd pinpointed the remains of the Tongva tribesman.

"Shit," I whispered. My gut was telling me to get out of the car and go investigate. But I seeeeeriously didn't want to do that. I mean, hello creepy setting, right?

I debated with myself for a good five more seconds; all the while the beam of light bounced along somewhere up over the ridge of the hill. "Dammit!" I swore again as I put the car in park and cut the engine. Thank God, Candice had finally taken the swear jar out of commission when she'd shown me a scientific study indicating that people who swear regularly are more creative, more open, more honest, and in some cases even smarter than those who don't. I took all of *that* to the bank, along with the money from the swear jar, and paid off my SUV.

As quietly as I could, I got out of the rental car and moved to the edge of the parking lot, glancing up the hill. The beam of light was fading—as if whoever was carrying it was getting farther away. Gripping my phone tightly, I climbed over the guardrail and made my way up the hill, ducking low as I got close to the top, lest I be spotted. I had no idea who was wielding the flashlight, but I knew he or she was relevant to that sinking feeling I had.

Just as I got up over the top of the hill, I saw a figure hunched down near the opening of the pit where the tribal remains were buried. The area around the excavation site was cordoned off by four stakes and yellow caution tape, but that hadn't stopped the figure wielding the flashlight from ducking under the tape and squatting at the edge of the large hole.

I still couldn't tell if it was a man or a woman, but he or she was now pointing the beam of the flashlight into the bottom of the pit, having a good look around, I thought.

I bit my lip, caught between the urge to yell at the figure for trespassing and the impulse to keep my presence there a secret.

What I noted was that my intuition was telling me to stay hidden, and not to make it known to the figure that I was there. Nearby in the surrounding trees, a twig broke and I jumped. I was creeped out by being here in the middle of the night, spying on some looky loo at the excavation site.

I questioned my radar again, because nothing I was seeing appeared to have anything to do with the robberies, but my intuition spoke differently. I felt there was something tangential about the figure at the excavation site and the bank behind me being robbed. I wondered if the figure could be one of the robbers, and then I really shuddered.

Still, I wasn't going to learn anything by turning away and hustling back down to the car, so I waited and watched while the figure remained squatting next to the pit, shining that flashlight down into the grave. And then, the stranger stood, and from the short hair and the somewhat broad set to his shoulders, I could tell that it was a male. He picked up a backpack I hadn't noticed was next to him, slung it over his shoulder, wiped his hands on his jeans, and began to move away from the pit.

Whoever it was was walking away from me, and while I didn't want to go stalking off after him, my radar wasn't giving up pushing me to follow along. "This is *such* a bad idea!" I whispered, getting up from my crouched position to hustle along to my right and come up in line right behind the stranger.

As I followed, I did my best to keep to the shadows, and not make any noise. The stranger never once looked back, thank God, so we made good time moving out of the clearing and to a street that bordered the cleared plot of land.

I was now about a half mile away from my rental car, and with every step I grew a little more anxious. I didn't like this, and yet, that compulsion in my gut to follow this person wouldn't subside.

So I kept going, never getting too close to the figure about two hundred yards ahead of me, and always keeping that beam of light in my sights. Finally we entered a neighborhood with nice-sized homes and well-kept landscaping, nestled in the foothills of the surrounding mountains. The terrain was quite hilly, and I was working up a good sweat even though the night was chilly and I didn't have a jacket on.

I was tempted at one point to use my phone to find out where we were exactly, but I didn't want to risk the light from the display calling attention to myself, so I did my best to simply remain patient and follow this through to the end.

At last, by my estimation a good two miles from the bank, the figure turned onto one of the driveways and approached the closed garage door. I stayed on the opposite side of the street and backed up into some bushes that bordered two houses, keeping my fingers crossed that no one saw me.

The figure shone the light onto a small panel at the side of the garage, and a moment later the door began to lift. The light from the garage came on, and I ducked even farther into the bushes, but kept my eyes on the stranger. When the door had lifted high enough, he stepped into the garage and over to the door leading into the house. I saw his profile in the light of the garage, noting that it wasn't a man I'd been following, but a boy of about fifteen or sixteen: tall with wispy black hair and pale skin. He was too far away for me to get a clear view of his face, which remained in profile, but my radar was pinging, so I knew he'd led me to the right place.

Seemingly unaware of my presence, the young man hit the button to the side of the interior entrance and the garage door began to reverse itself, slowly winding down with barely a squeak.

Once it'd closed completely, I sat perfectly still for several more moments, then moved forward out of the bushes and over to the mailbox of the house where the boy had gone inside. Looking up and down the street, I opened the mailbox and felt around inside, hoping the boy's parents hadn't gotten their mail that day. "Eureka," I whispered, pulling out one of several envelopes hidden inside, tucking it into my sweatshirt. I now had the boy's address, and once I got back to the hotel I could make a note of it and remail the letter without ever needing to open it.

Wasting no more time, I got the hell out of there and back to the car faster than I'd run the same distance with Candice.

When I arrived back at the hotel room, I found Candice awake, pacing the room. And she was *mad*. "What the hell are you doing out prowling around at four thirty in the goddamn morning, Abby?! I woke up twenty minutes ago and couldn't find you anywhere! I was about to call the police!"

I waved my phone at her. "I had my cell. You should've texted."

She glared at me. "I. Did."

Blinking, I pulled up the screen. Sure enough there were several texts from Candice, all demanding to know where I was. And that's when I realized that I'd had the phone's "Do not disturb" function on. The texts had never pinged because they'd all come in before seven a.m. "Oops," I said, offering her an apologetic shrug. "My bad."

"*Where* were you?!" she demanded, crossing her arms for effect.

By way of explanation, I pulled out the envelope I'd taken from the mailbox and handed it to her.

She stared at it without taking it. "What's that?"

I tossed the envelope on the table and moved to the bed to kick off my shoes and fall backward onto the mattress. "I don't know exactly," I said with a yawn. "I woke up and had this feeling like there was a clue to the robberies at the La Cañada branch, and I had this overwhelming urge to go check it out. When I got to the bank, there wasn't anything obvious, and about the time I was going to come back here, I saw someone using a flashlight at the top of the hill where the tribesman was buried. When I got to the top of the hill to check it out, someone was there, poking around the excavation site. I followed him and he led me to that address. I don't know what he has to do with all of this, but my intuition was pushing me the whole time to find out where he lived and bring back the address to you, so something is there that's connected to our investigation." With another big yawn, I pulled the covers up around myself. The adrenaline rush from earlier had completely worn off, and I'd struggled to keep my eyes open the last five miles of the ride back to the hotel.

"You're lucky I love you," Candice growled.

I thought it best to answer her by simply rolling over and going to sleep. I'm a true friend, I know.

Around seven a.m. I felt the mattress shift violently underneath me. "Earthquake!" Candice shouted, right in my ear.

I bolted out of bed like that ninja again, sprawling on the floor and crawling in the general direction of a doorframe. I'm deathly afraid of acts of God. Hurricanes, tsunamis, earthquakes, tornadoes, wildfires, the Four Horsemen of the Apocalypse . . . Fear of these things keep me up at night.

Okay, so maybe they don't exactly keep me up at night as much as they're a snarly little voice in the back of my brain that tells me that you can't ever get out of the way of an act of God if it's gunning for you.

"Do we stay? Do we go?" I shouted, bear crawling first toward the door, then back toward Candice. *"What do we do?"* I am woefully unprepared for an earthquake. All I know is that you're supposed to either stand in the space of a doorframe or bolt outside away from the building, but it depends on what kind of building you're in when the quake starts, and for the life of me I couldn't remember which option might afford me the ability not to get killed to death.

Belatedly I realized that Candice was laughing.

With a hammering heart, it finally dawned on me that she'd played a really good practical joke on me. "Aw, Sundance!" she said. "You should see your *face*!"

I shifted the bear-crawl stance to sit on my butt and glare up at her. "Why?" I demanded.

"Tit for tat," she told me. "Payback for last night."

I rubbed my face and had to consider that I might've had that coming. I mean, as I said, I hadn't left her a note and I hadn't replied to her texts. "Okay," I said. "We're even."

"Not by a long shot," she remarked. "Come on, get dressed and let's get to the gym. You owe me some wall balls."

I don't know what upset me more, the idea of being hit with an actual earthquake or being hit with a wall ball.

Scratch that. Give me the earthquake anytime. And I can say that because I got hit in the face with the wall ball at least a hundred times. Which is also the number of medicine balls that Candice made me toss against a stupid, unforgiving, aiming-for-my nose-hairs wall.

And I'm not kidding. That wall had it in for me; it's like it knew *exactly* where to toss back the ball for maximum punch. (There maaaaay have been a nosebleed involved.)

Still, because I hung in there and didn't overly complain (due to being punch-drunk), Candice "treated" me to a plate of piping hot pancakes. Gluten-free, vegan pancakes, that is.

"Deese taste like feet," I complained, my nose stuffed with cotton.

Candice was once again smirking at me over the rim of her teacup. "You've only had one bite. How about giving them a chance, Sundance?"

I glared at her. The smirk had quirked up a bit. "No points for rhyming."

"Can I help it if I'm a poet and don't know it?"

I pulled out the cotton from my nose and stabbed my fork into the center of the flapjacks, refusing to eat them. "Seriously, these suck."

Candice sighed. "They don't suck. They're just not loaded with fat, gluten, or processed sugars."

"Like I said, they suck."

"Abby, do me a favor and look down at your lap for a second."

"Why?" I said warily. If she was looking to sucker punch me, it wouldn't be that hard. My eyes were nearly swollen shut.

"Just do it, okay?"

With a scowl, I looked down at my lap. And braced myself. "Annnnnd?"

"What do you see?"

"What am I supposed to see?"

"Look at your stomach," she said.

It was my turn to sigh, but as my gaze was already pointing down, I took in my stomach. Which was flatter than it'd been the day before. Like . . . for real. It was actually flatter. "I'm less bloated," I said, kind of amazed.

"Mmmhmm," she said. "I've suspected that you were gluten intolerant for a while. And I also suspected you were lactose intolerant. One day without gluten or dairy and look at you, Sundance. You *already* look healthier."

I glanced back up at her. "Candice! *All* of my favorite foods come with gluten and dairy!"

"True," she said. "But maybe we can find you some new favorites."

I pointed to my plate. "You'll have to do better than foods that taste like feet."

Candice shoved her quiche toward me. "Fine. You win. Try this."

I eyed it skeptically. "What's in it?"

"Eggs, cream, cheese, spinach, sun-dried tomatoes, and sausage."

"Sausage?" I said, hopefully. "There's actual *sausage* in here?"

Candice nodded and I took a bite. It . . . was . . . delicious. "Oh, man," I told her. "That's the stuff." After devouring the quiche, I noticed that Candice still had that knowing smirk plastered onto her face. "What?"

Leaning forward, she said, "You just ate a quiche made with cashew cream instead of dairy cream, veggie cheese instead of real cheese, and soy sausage."

"Shut. Your. Mouth."

"It's true, Sundance. You just ate a healthy meal, and enjoyed it."

"I think I may be sick."

My bestie chuckled lightly. "Come on, let's pay the bill and get back to the hotel. I want to show you what I came up with on that address you handed me last night."

"When did you have time to research it?" I asked.

"Right about the time you did a face-plant into your pillow after coming back from investigating on your own in the middle of the freaking night, with no backup or anyone to save you should you have gotten into serious trouble."

"Ah," I said, thinking maybe I shouldn't instigate a revisit to the events of last night when I'd done my disappearing act. I mean, Candice is one tiger you definitely don't go poking without getting a hundred wall balls tossed in your face. Holding up my hand, I motioned to our waiter. "Check, please!"

We arrived back at the hotel and I waited while Candice got settled at the desk and pulled up a screen on her laptop. I noticed right away that it was the electronic version of a data sheet, which she usually kept for people she was investigating. "The house belonging to the address you gave me is owned by Samantha and Will Edwards. They have two children: a daughter named Emma—seventeen—and a son named Trace—fifteen. Will is an engineer for a company that makes high-tech drones for various military and domestic purposes, and his wife, Samantha, is a faculty advisor for UCLA.

"Emma is a gymnast, a cheerleader, and in love with her selfie stick. She's also *in love* with kittens, puppies, bunnies, Athletica leggings, which are like, *so* the best, and Liam Payne from One Direction."

"Who's that?" I interrupted.

Candice waved a dismissive hand. "It's not important. Emma's brother, Trace, has no online footprint that I can find. But that's probably typical of a boy his age."

"He's probably the kid I followed from the hill above the bank," I said.

Candice blinked. "The person you followed last night was a kid?"

"Yeah, didn't I explain?"

"No. No, you didn't. You were acutely absent of a good explanation, in fact."

"Really?" I said, all innocent-like. "My bad." When Candice cocked an eyebrow in the silence that ensued, I quickly gave her all the details I could remember from the night before.

At the end of my story, Candice scowled at me in that way that suggested I'd done something stupid. She looked at me like that a lot, actually. "Why didn't you wake me up?"

"Because when I left, I had no intention of getting out of the car."

"So why did you?"

"I don't know. I saw the beam of a flashlight and my radar pinged. I felt I *had* to go investigate it, and the trail led me to someone entering that house at around four in the morning, which, you gotta admit, for a fifteen-year-old to do that, it's a little suspicious, right?"

Candice rolled her eyes. "God, Abby, how long's it been since you were a teenager?" I had no reply for that . . . mostly because I was still trying to calculate the math when Candice continued with, "Maybe it was fairly innocent. Maybe Trace couldn't sleep and he wanted to check out the place where he'd seen so much police and FBI activity the day before. Maybe it wasn't even the Edwardses' kid, but Emma's boyfriend, who had to travel across the clearing to sneak into her house while her parents were sleeping. Or maybe you didn't actually see a kid, but Mr. Edwards when he couldn't sleep and was trying to get some fresh air. Or maybe—"

I held up my hand in a stop motion. "Okay, okay, I get it, I get it. You don't think following that kid back to his house has relevance to the case, but I'm telling you, it does."

Candice took a deep breath and lost the attitude. "Sorry," she said. "Of course I believe you. I just don't know what a fifteen-year-old boy could have to do with a series of bank robberies."

I tapped my lip with my index finger and thought about that. "What if he doesn't? I mean, what if he doesn't directly have anything to do with them?" I found myself trying to sort through a very murky ether. I felt the boy was in some way connected to the robberies, but the thread linking him to the crimes was thin and fragile as a single hair.

"What do you mean?" Candice asked.

"I mean, what if he somehow saw something or knows something that could be relevant to solving the case?"

"Like he witnessed something on the day of the robberies?"

I pointed at her. "Bingo! Yes, just like that." And then I thought of another angle. "Or maybe he's connected in another way. Like, what if it's less about him, and more about his dad!"

Candice drummed her fingertips on the laptop a few times.

"He seems pretty clean, Abs. I already checked both him and the wife out. There's no criminal history to speak of."

"Yeah, but didn't you say he was an engineer at a drone company?"

"Yes, so?"

"I don't trust people with drones."

"Why?"

"If I told you, I'd have to kill you." (True story.)

"Ha. Ha," Candice said haltingly. But then she added, "Fine, I'll vet him a little more."

"Good. I mean, couldn't he have used one of the drones to conduct surveillance on the banks?"

Candice ignored me in favor of switching windows and pulling up an app on her computer. She then typed very quickly and in a few moments a photo of a man with salt-and-pepper hair and a second chin popped up onto the screen. "Who's that?" I asked.

"Will Edwards," Candice said. She then opened up another window on her computer and I saw that it was the video from the bank robberies. After watching it for a few seconds, she pointed to Will's driver's license and said, "He's six-two and two hundred and ten pounds, Abs. No way is he one of the guys in the video."

I frowned. "Dammit," I said. "Why couldn't this be easy?" Candice simply shrugged. With a sigh I sat down on the bed and closed my eyes to better focus on what my radar was trying to tell me. The tricky thing about intuition is that it can speak to someone like me in a variety of ways. Sometimes it's through a series of images playing out in my mind's eye. Other times it's simply a "knowing." Some things I just know without understanding why I know them. That's called claircognizance, and it's very cool because it doesn't require a lot of work on my part. More often than not, however, it's my clairvoyance—the pictures-in-my-mind thingie—that's receiving and interpreting the most information. What's difficult about using clairvoyance is that there aren't any words to accompany the pictures, and sometimes the images are open to a whole lot of interpretation, which I usually get right, but not always.

Anyway, I was almost convinced that my claircognizance was telling me that Will Edwards was somehow connected to the robberies, but I needed my clairvoyance to confirm it. Thus, after sitting on the bed, I closed my eyes and took a few deep breaths, asking myself the question of just what that connection was.

The answer was a little odd. In my mind's eye I saw two ends of a broken chain lying on the floor. Then I saw a man's hands pick up each end of the chain, loop a new link through either end, and close it off to form one solid chain.

I felt I understood the metaphor, vague as it appeared. "Will Edwards is the missing link in solving the robbery cases," I said, after opening my eyes. "He's involved somehow, Candice. We just have to figure out how."

Candice had swiveled her chair around to face me. "Okay," she said, "but just to be clear, you're sure it's a connection to the robberies, and not to the girls who may get murdered, correct?"

Again I bounced that off my intuition and was surprised by the answer. In my mind the right half of the chain now appeared to have blood smeared on it, while the left part of the chain had a hundred-dollar bill stuffed into one of the links. "He's connected to both crimes."

Candice's eyes widened. "To both?"

I got up from the bed to pace the floor next to Candice. I went over the image in my mind's eye again, and knew I wasn't wrong. "Yes," I said at last. "Will Edwards is linked somehow to both crimes. He's the key."

Candice nodded. "Okay," she said. "Okay."

She then bent her head over her laptop and began snooping into Edwards's life. I took a shower, got dressed, and stepped out into the hallway to call my hubby.

"Abby," he said in that deep voice that makes a slow shiver inch pleasurably up my spine. "How's my baby doll?"

No one says "baby doll" like my husband. It rolls off his tongue as one word, smooth and seductive, like a tiger's purr. Another delicious shiver spread out across my shoulders.

"Hey, sweetie," I said. "Miss you."

"Do you?" he replied, a beckoning resonance in the question. "How much?"

I laughed throatily. "A lot. Like, a *lot*."

"Hmmm," he said. "Sounds promising. When're you coming home?"

I sighed. "Soon. I wish I could come back now, but there's . . . some stuff I gotta do out here."

There was a pause, then, "You and Candice are working the bank robbery cases off the books, right?"

"How'd you know?"

"You two are pretty predictable."

I smirked. "Does Brice know?"

Dutch chuckled. "Yep. Hell, Edgar, he knew even before the two of you did. Right after getting the call from Rivera telling him that you'd been tabled, he told me that he knew you and Candice were probably gonna come up with some trumped-up excuse to stay in L.A. and make everybody think you weren't working the cases, while you'd really be off on your own, working it off the grid."

I rolled my eyes. "Does anybody else know?"

"The office has a pool going on how long it'll be before you guys solve the case and take the credit away from the L.A. bureau."

I shook my head. "Did the money from the first pool roll into that one?"

"It did. It's up to two grand."

"What happened to Candice's money?"

"We threw it in. If you guys bring it home by next Saturday, the whole pot is hers. Although she may have to split it with Gaston, who's counting on you to come through and redeem his reputation. Of course, if you solve it by Friday, which is where I have my money, you and I can head to Bermuda."

It was my turn to laugh. "Second honeymoon?"

"Wouldn't know," he said sweetly. "I'm still on the first."

My eyes misted. Sometimes Dutch could simply level me with a beautifully romantic retort like that. I love him so much, but I'm also crazy *in* love with him too. He's just so manly, strong, and confident; like G.I. Joe, he makes me feel safe and protected the way he can simply take charge—even in the direst of circumstances, he always keeps his cool. And yet, there's this soft side to him too. He's Steve McQueen, Han Solo, and Paul Newman all rolled into one. Swear to God he's the perfect man. I mean, the guy even does *laundry*!

"Then I guess I'll have to solve this case by Friday, babe, so that the honeymoon can continue."

"Great," he said. "Anything I can do to help?"

"I'm not sure, but wouldn't that be cheating?"

"Maybe. If it means seeing you in a bikini on that pink sand in Bermuda, I'm willing to live with it."

"Good to know," I told him. We talked about other things for a bit, and he had Eggy and Tuttle—our two pups—bark for me so I could hear them, and then it was time for both of us to get back to doing our thing. I hung up feeling so homesick I could cry, and I thought about marching back into the hotel room to tell Candice that we were packing and catching the first flight home we could, but my conscience wouldn't let me. I was out here for a reason that had nothing to do with proving myself to a bunch of bureau boys. There was something much bigger at stake, like the lives of three . . . possibly four girls who might someday fall victim to a serial killer.

Their murders felt so certain, so destined, and that was unusual because the future is almost always malleable. I hoped I could change the path they were on, and stop a killer before he even got started, but how I was going to do that in a week and a half I had no idea.

"Abs?" I heard Candice call.

Turning, I saw her poking her head out of the room. Lifting my cell to wiggle it, I said, "Just hung up with the hubby."

"How's he doing?"

I smirked. "Devastated that I'm still here working the case."

"Ah. Does my husband know the truth about our beach-vacation ruse?"

"He does. In fact, he called it before we did."

She frowned. "Are we really that predictable?"

I shrugged. "Maybe when it comes to doing the right thing, we are."

Her frown turned into a smile. "You always know just what to say."

"It's part of my charm."

"Yeah, well, bring that charm along. We're gonna go stake out Will Edwards."

"We are?"

"Yep," she said, handing me my purse. "I wanna get a look at this guy up close."

"But what about lunch?" I was a little panicked, because when Candice began a stakeout, she tended not to budge for hours at a time. Not even to pee.

"We can eat after."

"But—"

"Sundance," she said sternly, "get in the car. I promise I have a plan that doesn't involve listening to your stomach rumble for three hours."

Grudgingly, I followed after her and we headed over to the corporate side of town.

Chapter Nine

• • •

Will Edwards worked in a big skyscraper that was nothing to write home about. After searching the parking garage beneath his office building for a good half hour, Candice managed to locate his car, which I thought was pretty remarkable on her part. The car itself was a silver Ford Fusion, and we watched it like a hawk for another half hour until a man approached fiddling with a key fob and his phone. "Is that him?" I asked.

Candice leaned forward, holding up her phone, where I saw that she had Edwards's photo on the screen. "That's him," she said.

The guy was big. Tall, heavy in the belly, and lumbering on two legs that looked stiff at the knees. I watched him using both my intuition and my ordinary observation. There was no grace to him; he sort of shuffled along, preoccupied by too many things and missing all the important stuff. I felt that he led a distracted life; his mind was always elsewhere. You could see it in his expression, in the way he fumbled with his phone and his key, never giving either his full attention. His gaze was also a little glazed, as if he didn't sleep well, and I wondered if the extra weight he carried was interrupting his sleep patterns. His energy seemed "thin" to me, which is what happens when people are under too much stress, don't sleep, and make poor food choices. They run on autopilot, and it's terrible for their health.

Will Edwards struck me as being in awful health. I could pick up his high cholesterol and high blood pressure from twenty feet away. "That guy's on a steady march to an early grave," I muttered.

"Yeah?" Candice asked.

"Yeah. He doesn't eat right, doesn't sleep, doesn't rest, doesn't stop, and his health is really suffering. I give him ten to fifteen years tops unless he turns it around."

"Funny," Candice said.

When she didn't comment further, I tore my attention away from Edwards to ask, "What's funny?"

"You can pick up someone else's bad health habits, but yours don't register."

I felt a flush hit my cheeks. She was right. I turned back to Edwards and had to wonder if my energy looked a little like his. Could another psychic pick up my poor eating habits and my nonexistent exercise plan?

It gave me pause, that's for sure. "Okay, so maybe tomorrow we'll go for another run."

"Atta girl," Candice said, elbowing me gently in the arm.

By now Edwards had made it to his car and had managed to unlock it and slip inside. We waited until he pulled out of the slot and moved toward the exit before we took up the tail.

Candice stuck closer to him than I think she normally would've when she was tailing a target. No way was Edwards going to realize he had a tail. He talked on his phone and drove three to ten miles under the speed limit the entire time.

At last he pulled into an In-N-Out Burger and headed to

the to-go window. "Want anything here?" Candice asked me, and it didn't take a rocket scientist to know she was testing me.

"Nah," I said. "I'm good for about another hour or so."

We waited in the parking lot near the exit and kept our eyes on the rearview and side mirrors. The line was pretty long, so we had to wait about ten minutes for Edwards to pass us on his way out. As we pulled into traffic behind him, I felt my hopes that he'd do something suspicious on his lunch hour fade. Clearly he was heading right back to the office with his lunch.

Except that as we approached his office building, he never put on his turn signal, or slowed down. A moment later he passed the building altogether.

"Running an errand?" I asked Candice.

"Maybe," she said.

We followed Edwards east all the way to a seedier part of town and then to a part where seedy would lock the car doors. "Well, this is getting interesting," I said.

"And a little concerning," Candice agreed.

Edwards pulled into the parking lot of a motel that definitely rented by the hour . . . if not the quarter hour. The asphalt in the parking lot was at war with sprouting grass and weeds, and so far, the foliage was winning. Of course, that was the scenic part of the place. The building itself had probably seen better days, likely immediately after it was built, but not a day since. Looking at it, I thought the motel could've been painted white at some point, but the paint was so decayed it was little more than the hint of a stain on the graying wood underneath. Doors to most of the rooms hung loosely, or didn't seem to want to close all the way. The sidewalks were so stained with dirt and crumbling that it was hard to tell they were sidewalks, and some of the windows were covered over with plywood or, if they were merely cracked, with duct tape.

As Candice edged to a spot well away from Edwards, I exclaimed, "Gee, Candice, maybe we should go back to our hotel, pack, and move our stuff over *here*!"

"We'd probably save a lot on the daily rate," she said with a chuckle. And then we both fell silent while we watched to see what Edwards would do next.

After parking, the man lumbered out of his car and headed toward the small shack-type structure attached to one end of the building, marked FFICE—the *o* was missing, or it'd been stolen, or sold to cover the electric bill, who knew?—and then emerged a few moments later with an orange plastic key. Heading to room number twelve, he let himself in and shut the door.

The blinds were drawn on the only window that looked in, so we had relatively little idea what he might be doing in there, or rather, maybe neither one of us wanted to *think* about what he was doing, but then, five minutes after he entered the room, someone approached.

I say *someone* because that's kind of the only way you can describe her. She was big for a girl—hell, she was big even for a man—and she walked toward the room like a performer heading into the spotlight. She had black, somewhat wild hair, ginormous boobs, and more makeup than Gene Simmons in full KISS face paint.

In fact, KISS might've been the inspiration for her whole look, because there sure was a lot of leather, metal studs, and exposed skin happening.

"Um . . . wow," I whispered.

"You said it," Candice agreed.

We continued to watch the woman saunter toward Edwards's room, then stop in front of it and lean a little against the door frame before rapping the wood casually with the backs of her knuckles.

The door opened immediately, and Edwards stood there in his dress shirt and droopy tighty-whities.

I wasn't sure what was harder on the eyes—his pasty legs in that diaper, or her, leaning up against the door, all *Come hither.*

I mean, you can't look at something like that and unsee it, or unimagine what nasty things they'd be doing for the next half hour. "I'm suddenly glad I didn't have lunch," I said.

Candice nodded, a look of shock and awe on her face.

We fell silent again as Edwards's "guest" walked into the room and he closed the door.

We didn't speak again until the door opened exactly one half hour later, and when that door opened, both of us gasped. Now we knew it was coming, but the sight of Edwards rumpled, disheveled, and barely dressed, his open shirt revealing a large belly smeared with makeup, was enough to make anybody suck in some air, and possibly gag it back out again.

For his part, Edwards looked like he'd be giving his guest a five-star rating on Yelp. He wore a contentedly bemused smile on his face, which was the most animated expression he'd worn since we'd first spotted him. The woman looked like she just wanted to get paid and head home to take a bath, or brush her teeth, or rinse her mouth out with bleach.

He said a few words with that goofy grin while he zipped up his pants and fished through the pockets, finally producing some cash, which he handed over. She snatched the money out of his hand, tickled him under his chin with one long nail on her index finger, then turned on her heel without so much as a "Well, this was fun!"

He didn't seem to mind the abrupt departure; he simply sighed, watched her backside for a few bounces, then quietly shut the door.

I looked to Candice, ready to ask her what we should do

next, when I saw that she was shifting her gaze back and forth between the closed door and the streetwalker. "What're you thinking?" I asked.

"I'm thinking that these two have gotten together before," she said, motioning with her chin toward the woman, who'd stepped off the sidewalk to walk over to Edwards's car solely for the purpose of running her finger along the trunk.

It was an interesting thing to do. The gesture spoke of both familiarity and an intimate connection. Granted, it probably didn't get much more intimate than what they'd just done, but this was different. This was bordering on something emotional.

Candice shifted the car into gear and waited for the prostitute to exit the parking lot before she pulled out of the space. "Where're we going?" I asked.

"We're following her," she said.

"We are? Why?"

"Because streetwalkers are a great source of information, and if Edwards has bragged to anybody about being involved in the bank robberies, it'd be to that woman."

"What if she tells Edwards we're checking up on him?"

"What if she does?" Candice said. "He's not gonna know who we are. Besides, I doubt she'll tell him."

"Why do you doubt she'll tell him?"

"Because I'm going to pay her not to."

By now we'd reached the streetwalker and Candice slowed the rental just enough to pull up alongside her. Rolling down my window, my partner nudged me and said, "Get her attention."

I looked at my best friend like she had to be kidding, but another (harder) nudge convinced me she was serious. "Fine, whatever," I said, leaning out to wave at the woman, who was doing a pretty good job of ignoring us. "Excuse me!" I called.

"If you're lost, sugar, I ain't gonna help you," she said, a distinct Southern lilt in the words.

"We're not lost. We're after some information."

"Do I look like four-one-one to you?"

"No," I said. "You look like a woman who expects to get paid for her time, and how that time is spent, either talking to us or . . . *entertaining* someone else, is entirely up to you."

She paused and finally considered me. "You a cop?"

"Nope," I said. When she eyed me doubtfully, I held up my little finger and added, "Pinkie swear."

A flash of annoyed impatience crossed her features. "I ain't got time for that shit," she told me, and went back to walking.

At that point Candice leaned forward and whistled sharply to get the woman's attention. "Yo! How about we take you for a bite to eat? We'll pay you for your time, and treat you to some lunch too."

That got the woman to cast an intrigued glance toward our car. "I am hungry," she said.

Candice nodded, looked quickly back at the street to make sure she didn't crash the car while inching forward to keep pace with the woman. "You look like you could use a good meal," she said seriously.

Finally the woman stopped again and after placing one hand on a hip, she said, "Do I get to pick the place?"

"You'd better," Candice said. "We don't have a clue about where to eat around here."

The woman frowned. "Cuz there ain't no good place round here." She then walked forward to the car and tugged on the handle. I tried to get the door unlocked before she did that, but I was a second too late and she glared at me until the lock clicked.

"Sorry," I told her after she'd gotten the door open.

She regarded me with half-lidded eyes. "Whatever." Once she was settled into the backseat, she said to Candice, "Head up to that light and take a left."

Candice proceeded to drive toward the light, but before she got there, I felt something against my right arm, resting on the window frame. Looking over, I noticed it was the woman's hand, tapping my arm. "My rate is sixty bucks an hour," she said. "Cash."

She'd caught me off guard, and I looked at Candice because I didn't know what to do. Candice mouthed, *Pay her!*

Digging into my purse, I pulled up some cash and handed our guest three twenties. She stuffed the bills into her bra and leaned back against the cloth seats to stare blankly ahead.

Thinking it might be polite to make conversation, I squirmed around in my seat and said, "I'm Abby. This is Candice."

Candice waved and eyed our passenger in the rearview mirror. "Flower," she said.

I pressed my lips together, unsure if she was pulling our leg, or if she was serious. "That's a pretty name," I tried.

Flower smoothed out a patch of hair on the side of her head. "It sure is," she said. Then she seemed to take note of the road ahead. "Get onto the highway," she told Candice. "Red Lobster is three exits down." Candice and I shared a subtle "Ooo, boy . . ." look while Flower continued. "Gonna have me some lobster today. And some all-you-can-eat shrimp. Mmm, *mmm!*"

A long and painful time later we sat amid the detritus of a shellfish massacre and I glared angrily at Candice. It'd been her idea to take Flower out to eat, after all.

"Here's your check," said our oh-so-not-happy waitress. I bit my lip. From the moment the poor girl had appeared at our table, Flower had set about running her ragged. The poor server had been like a ball in a pinball machine, no sooner setting down a ramekin of extra cocktail sauce than being sent for more tartar sauce. Then lemons. Then extra refills on Flower's soda. Then more shrimp, biscuits, salad dressing, extra napkins, and on, and on, and on. As a result, all of the other tables in the girl's section had been neglected, and I know at least one table had complained to the manager.

I tried to smile reassuringly at our waitress as she set the bill down in front of me, but she simply nodded curtly and walked away. Gulping, I looked at the tab. It was more than two hundred dollars.

I tried to get Candice's attention to get her to chip in for the bill (which, by the way, was all Flower; Candice and I had had nothing more than iced tea), but my partner in crime was currently picking small bits of crab shell out of her hair and patently ignoring me.

I sighed and pulled out my Amex card, setting it into the little pocket of the vinyl book the bill had come in. I'd take Candice's half of the check out of our winnings from the office pool.

The waitress appeared again at my elbow, and after she cashed us out on a little gizmo attached to what looked like a smartphone with the Red Lobster logo on it, I handed her two twenties and a ten, and said, "Thank you so much. You were great."

Our server took the cash, blushed a little, and finally smiled sweetly at me. "Have a nice afternoon," she said, leaving us alone again.

"All right, Flower," Candice said smoothly. "Now that you've had your fill of lobster, shrimp, and crab legs, how about we get down to brass tacks?"

Flower patted her belly and exclaimed, "Oooh! Sugar, after a meal as fine as that, I'll tell you anything you want to know."

"Awesome. My first question is, how long have you . . . uh . . . known Will Edwards?"

Flower squinted at Candice. It was obvious she hadn't been expecting a question about him. "Will? Hmmm, I've know him at least a decade or so."

I blinked rapidly, taking that in. It seemed unfathomable. "Ten years?"

"Give or take."

"So he's a regular," I said.

"He's not my oldest client, but he's probably the most loyal."

"You must know quite a bit about his personal life, then," I said next.

"Give or take," she repeated, and then the look in her eyes became slightly guarded. "Why don't you two tell me what you want with sweet Willy boy before I answer any more of your questions?"

"We're looking into a possible connection between him and a couple of bank robberies," Candice told her.

Flower's brow furrowed. "A couple of what?" she said. "Bank robberies? Girl, are you for real?"

"We are," she said.

Flower shook her head and started laughing. I didn't like it, and, by her expression, neither did Candice. "Well, now I know you two are crazy," she giggled. "Will Edwards ain't no bank robber!"

"We know he didn't do the actual robbery," I said, "but we still think there's a connection."

She rolled her eyes. "Honey, if that man had any hand in robbing anything bigger than a vending machine, he'd tell me. Hell, he'd even tell me about the vending machine."

"How can you be so sure?" I said.

"Because Willy likes to talk through the whole thing, if you get what I'm sayin'. He's a gabby one."

"What does he talk about?" Candice asked.

"Shit," Flower said. "What doesn't he talk about? His kids, the wife, the house, the neighbor's dog, the job, the boss, the diet, the doctor, his prostate . . . Nothing is off-limits with that man. He got his oil changed last week and he gabbed about it nonstop to me today."

"Really?" I asked. "An oil change?"

Flower shook her head and sighed. "He's a boring one—I'll give you that. But I'm the only one that listens to him, makes him feel like a man."

"You sure he's not just a gabby guy?" I asked.

"Positive. The first three times he called on me, he didn't say a single word. He was so nervous he got his business done before we could even put the condom on."

I made an involuntary *eww* face and tried to think of something other than what images that statement conjured up.

"Anyway," Flower continued, "to help him calm down, I started asking him about himself and he answered me with one or two words for about the next month or so, but slowly he started coming out of his shell, and now I can't get that man to shut his piehole."

Candice looked at me as if to ask if I had an angle to get some relevant info out of Flower. "What do you know about his job?" I asked, using my radar to pinpoint the direction I wanted to steer the conversation.

Flower shrugged. "I don't pay that much attention when he talks about his work, but I do know that he works with cameras."

"I thought he worked with drones," I said.

"Yeah, he does. The cameras go on the drones."

I nodded. "Ah, okay. So, does he ever talk about using one of his own camera drones to spy on someone or something else? Like a business?"

Flower shook her head and gazed at me with an amused smile. "Listen," she said. "I know you're looking to make Will out to be a bad guy, but I'm telling you, he doesn't have a bad bone in his beautiful body—"

Candice choked on the sip of her tea she'd just taken, interrupting Flower. "Sorry," she said, red-faced and coughing. "Went down the wrong pipe."

At the mention of Will's "beautiful" body, I'm pretty sure Candice's reaction was more gag reflex then improper inhalation.

"Anyway," Flower went on, "he ain't spying on nobody and he ain't no bank robber."

"Maybe you don't know Will as well as you think you do," Candice said, clearing her throat to get the words out. "Maybe he's hiding the bad side of himself from you."

Flower actually laughed. "Honey, nobody hides the bad parts of themselves to a girl like me."

I had to admit, she probably had a point there. If Will was keeping part of his personality or his life hidden, he was much more likely to hide it from his wife, kids, boss, et cetera. In fact, revealing himself was *exactly* what he was doing when he went to see Flower.

"And don't think I don't know a bad egg when I see one," Flower continued. "Most of my clients, they're not like Will. They're dealers, dopers, and thugs. And most of them is dumb. Will's not dumb. He's really smart. Hell, later on today I got a date with a man who's been asking me for two weeks if I know anybody who can help him unload a kilo of white china that the dumb fool spilled gas all over."

"What's white china?" I asked.

"Heroin," Candice said.

Flower nodded. "Ain't nobody wants to buy shit that smells

like a gas tank," she said. "Not even a junkie. But he keeps asking like I might know somebody who knows somebody dumb
enough to take it off his hands. Fool. All my dates are fools.
Except Will. He's smart. And he's . . ."

"What?" Candice prodded when Flower didn't continue.

"He's kind," she said with a sad smile. "You don't get that
a lot in my profession."

I looked around the table, which was still littered with bits
of crab shell and cocktail sauce stains, and felt bad for not having been a little kinder to Flower during the meal. "Sorry," I
said, both for her situation and for my attitude.

She shrugged, like she was used to it and it didn't matter,
except that I thought it maybe did. "Comes with the territory,"
she said. "But the point I'm trying to make here is that Will is
a good man deep down. Whatever you suspect him of, I doubt
he had anything to do with it."

Candice and I traded "What do you think?" looks and I shook
my head and so did she. There was nothing more that Flower
could tell us. But then I had one last thought.

"Flower," I said, "maybe Will is involved without *knowing*
he's involved. Maybe he's seen something or knows someone
who's involved with these robberies."

"Like who would he know?" she asked.

I thought about the ninjas at the bank, how in sync they'd
been, and how they'd operated with such precision under the
watchful eye of the leader who'd stood by the door. It was almost
like a military special ops team, but the four robbers had been
slight in both height and frame. No way were they U.S. military,
but maybe they were something else, like part of a gang. But
what felt off about that was the way they'd each individually
moved. There was something so fluid and light in their movements. They'd each been light on their toes like acrobats from

the circus. "Maybe he knows someone with a connection to a gang of acrobatic thieves," I said, rattling the thought off before I'd had a chance to really think about it.

"Gang of acro who?" she replied, with a hearty laugh. "Seriously, are you for real?"

"We're for real," Candice said, backing me up, which I thought was pretty nice.

Flower rolled her eyes, and I said, "I know it sounds crazy, Flower, but think—has Will ever mentioned knowing anybody connected to a troupe of acrobats or someone in the circus?"

"Not to me," she said. "He's not the type to be hanging out with a bunch of circus people." Flower's eyes suddenly sparked with recognition. "Wait a second," she said, snapping her fingers. "You ain't talkin' about those little ninja turtles pulling that heist out in La Cañada, are you?"

"How'd you know about that?' I asked.

"I saw it on the news," she said with a scowl, as if I'd judged her, which I hadn't meant to do.

"Okay, do you know of anybody who could be connected to that robbery?" I asked next. "I mean, you said the rest of your clients are dopers, drug dealers, and whatnot. Maybe you heard one of them bragging about being involved."

"No," she said. "No one's been bragging about that job. Least not to me." She then yawned and stretched in her seat. "Whoo! That meal made me tired, y'all. Do you two have any more questions, or can you drive me back to my spot so I can get a lil' nap before my next client?"

"We'll take you back," Candice said, gathering up her purse and her keys. Before we departed the booth, however, Candice took out a hundred-dollar bill and handed it to Flower. "Do us a favor and don't mention this little chat to Will, okay?"

Flower took the money and placed a finger to her lips to indicate they'd be sealed.

Once we dropped our guest off at a corner about three blocks from the hotel, which she said was her spot, I turned to Candice and plucked out a small piece of shell from her hair. "Man, she had that mallet flying all over those crab legs, didn't she?"

Candice laughed, and mimicked Flower wildly pounding on a steaming crustacean. *"Wham! Wham! Wham!"* she said.

We both laughed and then sobered. "It was entertaining, at least. And she got a nice meal out of it."

"I doubt any of her clients take her out to dinner," Candice said. "Glad we could."

"Still, I wish we could've gotten more info about Will out of her."

"We got plenty of info," Candice said, "just none of it very useful."

"Not to mention costly," I said.

"What was the tab?"

"A little over two."

Candice took a deep breath and said, "This trip is starting to add up for us, right?"

"It is, and right now I'm working off the books. I'll get paid for the two days I spent with the bureau, but that'll probably only cover the rest of our stay at the hotel."

"And if you throw in the cost of our daily expenses for fuel and meals, Abs, this is going to get pretty expensive. So, I have to ask you, Sundance, how bad do you want to stick with this case? I mean, we've got no leads other than some sort of a connection between Will Edwards and the robberies, but we don't know what that connection is, or even how to find it. This could get super costly really quick and it might not lead to anything useful or to any arrests."

I leaned back against the seat, feeling discouraged. I missed my husband, my dogs, my house, and even the guys at the Austin bureau. I wanted to go home in the worst way, and opened my mouth to tell Candice that we should pack it in and head back to Austin when, instead, what came out of my mouth was, "We're sticking with it."

Candice cocked her head slightly. "You sure?"

"No. Not at all sure. But those three or . . . possibly four girls need me, Candice. The *only* lead I've got is that the bank robberies are in some way connected to their impending murders. How that all factors in, I don't know, but in order to prevent their deaths, I'm positive we have to solve this bank robbery case."

Candice sighed. "Okay, then," she said, making a right to head toward the highway again. "Then we go with plan B."

"Plan B?" I asked.

"Yep."

"What's plan B?"

"Don't know yet," she confessed. "But I'm sure I'll think of something."

Chapter Ten

. . .

Plan B turned out to be pretty simple. We ended up just tailing Will Edwards for the next couple of days, waiting for him to do something suspicious. Or interesting. Of course, it was hard to top the seedy motel and the meet-up with Flower, but Edwards had surprised us once, so we were hopeful.

We followed him from home, to work, to lunch, to another hookup with Flower, and then back to the office and then home again. None of that led to *anything* useful. Or newly interesting.

By the third day of sitting in the car staring at the taillights of his silver sedan, the both of us were pretty cranky. "Christ!" I snapped. "I cannot watch this guy lumber into his office one more time."

"Well, Sundance," Candice said, "this is what surveillance work is. It's dull, and repetitive, and boring, but short of breaking into his office at night and hacking into his computer to look for evidence, I'm not sure what else we can do to try to find his connection to the thieves."

"What if we talked to him?" I asked. It was a desperate proposition, I knew, but my gut said that simply watching Edwards from afar wasn't gonna lead us anywhere.

Candice stared skeptically at me. "You want to just talk to him," she repeated.

"Yes."

"And say what?"

I shrugged. "I dunno, how about, 'Hi, we're investigating a series of crimes and we think that you might have some information for us,' or something to that effect?"

Candice's left brow arched. "And you think he's just gonna say, what? 'Cuff me, ladies who have no authority in the state of California. I confess'?"

I sighed heavily. "Candice, I don't know what he'll say, but if he says anything at all, then my radar can ping against it and check for lies. He might slip and tell us something relevant that we can follow up on."

"What makes you think he'll talk to us at all?" she said next. "The second we tell him we're investigating a crime, if he has any hand in the bank robberies, he'll know that we're fishing around about them, and since we're not the Feds, or cops, or even licensed PIs in this state, he can tell us to go pound sand."

I smiled wide. "And that's when *we* ask him if he'd like for us to bring his *wife* a bouquet of *flowers.*"

Candice's other brow joined its arched twin. "Ahh, blackmail. Why didn't I think of that?"

"You would've," I assured her. "Eventually."

"I would've," she agreed. "Still, that's good leverage. Okay, Sundance, when he comes out for lunch, we'll corner him and see what we see."

A few hours later Candice eased the nose of our car directly in front of Edwards's vehicle, blocking him in. He honked politely and we simply sat there, waiting.

He honked louder and we did nothing. He laid on his horn

for a good ten seconds, drawing the attention of another man walking to his car, but still we sat there with patient smiles on our faces.

Finally he opened his door and leaned out a little. The move was awkward given his large belly, but he managed it okay. He gave us that palms-up "What gives?" gesture, and we continued to sit and stare at him.

Getting out of his car, he approached us with balled fists, but I wasn't sensing anger so much as fear wafting off him, which was interesting. He knocked three times on Candice's window and she waited a beat before pressing the button to let the window down. "You guys want something?" he asked us.

"Yes, Mr. Edwards," Candice said. "We'd like to chat with you over lunch, if you're free?"

Edwards blinked in reaction to the fact that Candice had addressed him personally, and then he sort of looked back and forth between us for several seconds without speaking. Finally, he found his voice and said, "Why?"

"It's a personal matter," I said. "Please, Mr. Edwards? We mean you no harm and only want a few minutes of your time."

Edwards leaned down a little as I spoke so that he could see me and when I was finished speaking, he picked his head up and looked around the garage, unsure, I suspected, what to do. We waited patiently for him to decide we weren't a threat and then he said, "I usually go to In-N-Out Burger for lunch."

"Perfect," said Candice, easing her car away from his very slowly. "We'll follow you."

Edwards got into his car and pulled out of the slot and Candice kept on his tail but not too close to cause him to get spooked.

We made it to In-N-Out Burger and parked right next to Edwards, then moved as a group inside. We let him go first to order, and I stood near him while he waited for his food. Candice got us two tap waters, because there was absolutely nothing on the menu she'd let me eat. My stomach grumbled in protest.

We sat down with Edwards and he saw that we weren't eating and I think that made him even more nervous. "You guys on a diet?"

Candice smiled easily. "We are."

"Okay," he replied, opening the cardboard box his burger had come in. "So, who are you and what do you want?"

Candice tapped my leg and I said, "My name is Abby and this is Candice. We're investigators—"

"Cops?" he said, taking his eyes off the burger long enough to stare at us with some trepidation.

"No," I said. "Private investigators who often consult for various law enforcement communities."

He pursed his lips. "Law enforcement communities? Like who?"

"Like the FBI," I said.

That got his attention. "What're you investigating?" he asked, and I saw that his forehead was suddenly coated with a bright sheen.

Candice took a small pull from her straw. "A series of bank robberies."

His burger paused halfway to his mouth and he cocked his head at us. "Bank robberies?" The coat of sheen on his forehead glistened and began to show beads. "Why would a couple of PIs be investigating bank robberies? Isn't that up to the police?"

"It's actually the jurisdiction of the FBI," I told him. "And we were hired to bring a new approach to the investigation."

Edwards chewed thoughtfully, then wiped his mouth with his napkin before subtly reaching up to mop his brow. "I never heard of the FBI bringing in consultants."

"We like to keep a low profile," Candice said, leaning in to rest her elbows on the table.

Her proximity—the equivalent of getting into Edwards's face—made him sit back against the booth and the sweat on his brow broke out again. "So why're you guys interested in talking to me?"

"Because we think there's a connection between you and the robberies," I said bluntly.

Edwards set his half-eaten burger down and shook his head. "You two have the wrong guy. I never stole anything a day in my life."

My radar pinged loudly in my mind. "Liar, liar, pants on fire," I said.

His face registered confusion. "I'm not lying," he insisted. "I had nothing to do with any bank getting robbed."

"You know what I find curious?" Candice asked. When Edwards didn't answer, she continued anyway. "I think it's a little weird that you haven't asked us which banks were robbed and why we think there might be a connection back to you. I mean, if someone sat me down and said what we said to you here, my *first* question would be to ask if it was my bank that was robbed."

Edwards's mouth formed a thin line and he glared at her, unspeaking.

Candice pulled her phone out of her pocket and began tapping at it. "Maybe you'd like to see the banks that were robbed?" she said, then turned the phone toward Edwards. I caught a flash of the screen. It was an image of Edwards disheveled and smirking as he stood in the doorway of the motel right as Flower was lifting away the money from his hand.

I hadn't even known she'd taken the picture.

Judging by Edwards's expression as he took in the image, neither had he. The blood drained from his face and his eyes watered. "What is this?" he whispered, never lifting his gaze from the screen. "A shakedown?"

Candice tucked the phone back into her pocket. "Of sorts," she said. "What do you know about the robberies in Pasadena and La Cañada Flintridge?"

He pulled at his collar and his eyes darted back and forth while he stared at the tabletop. He was looking for a way out. I was hoping we hadn't given him one. "Listen," he said. "I have a wife and kids—"

"We know," Candice said, cutting him off. "And I'd hate to see that photo end up on anybody's Facebook page. Your wife is really into social media. She posts all the time."

Edwards looked up at her. "You can't," he said. "She'll kill me." Candice and I both frowned at him. "I'm serious," he insisted. "Like, she'll *actually* kill me."

"Hmm," I said, because I'd detected no lie or exaggeration in his statement. "Better not risk it. Now, tell us what you know."

He shook his head and pressed his lips together. "I can't," he said.

"Okay," Candice said with a shrug. "Come on, Abby, let's head back and send Mrs. Edwards a friend request."

"Wait!" Edwards said. "You don't understand."

"We're open to explanations," I told him.

Edwards pushed his half-eaten meal aside. It seemed he'd lost his appetite. "I signed an NDA," he said. "I can't talk about it or I could get sued into the ground."

I stared at him. So did Candice. Of all the possible responses, his admission of signing a nondisclosure agreement wasn't something I'd been expecting. "Nondisclosures don't apply if there's been a crime, Mr. Edwards," Candice said.

"If it's all the same to you, lady, I'd like for my lawyer to tell me that. And if you force me to talk to you about it under duress, then they can sue you too."

We were on tricky ground here and Candice and I knew it. Meanwhile, Edwards got up and took his lunch over to the trash can, where he threw out the uneaten portion, then placed his tray on the top and walked out of the restaurant.

Candice and I shared shocked expressions at his sudden departure. "What just happened?" I asked her.

"I think he left," she said, getting up.

I went with her to the door and peered out. Sure enough, Edwards had gotten in his car and was just pulling out of the slot. We dashed outside and hustled over to our car. I pulled on the handle while looking over my shoulder as Edwards exited onto the street. When I lifted up on the handle, it stayed locked, and after three tugs I glanced back toward Candice to see why she hadn't unlocked it yet. "Hey," I said, when I saw her looking down at something on the ground. "What gives?"

Without lifting her gaze, she motioned for me to come around to her side. I did and that's when I saw it; there was a huge gash in the left front tire, leaving it totally flat.

"He slashed our tire?!" I gasped.

"He did," Candice said, lifting her chin to look down the street toward Edwards's car as it slipped out of sight amid the other traffic.

"That son of a bitch!" I growled, shaking my fist in the direction he'd fled.

"Yep," Candice said. She then headed around to the trunk and popped the lid. Pulling out the spare and the jack, she came back to me and placed the lug wrench in my hands. "You work on those while I hoist the car."

I glanced down at myself. I was wearing camel slacks and a

light blue silk top. No way was I staying clean through this. "Great," I muttered. "Just great."

Ten minutes later we were back on the road. I'd had to wash my hands several times to get the grease from the lug nuts off, and there was a slight smear of black grime on the knee of my pants, and my shirt was now very wrinkled, but overall it wasn't too bad.

Candice, as usual, looked perfect with nary a hair out of place. "Do you *ever* look rumpled? Disheveled? Or unkempt?" I asked.

"Have you ever seen me look rumpled, disheveled, or unkempt?"

"Not really," I said.

"Then there's your answer."

"Sometimes I hate that about you."

"I'm okay with that," she said.

"So, where're we going?"

"The airport."

I pulled my chin back in alarm. "The airport? Why? We're leaving?"

"No, Sundance, we're not leaving. We're going to trade this car for another one with four good wheels and something Edwards won't recognize tailing him."

"I still can't believe he just got up and ditched us," I said.

"Yeah, that was pretty unexpected. He's got more balls than I would've guessed."

"And what'd he use to slash our tire, anyway?" I asked.

"A very sharp knife," she said. "Given that he heads to Flower's neck of the woods on a regular basis, it's not really surprising to me that he's armed with a knife."

"Do you think he went back to work?" I asked.

"Maybe. But it's more likely he headed off to either warn an accomplice or to ditch some evidence."

"Ditch some evidence? You now think he was involved?"

"Don't you?"

I played her question against my radar, and I had to admit that there did seem to be some sort of actual involvement on Edwards's behalf, which was odd, because before we'd confronted him, I could've sworn he was innocent of participating in the robberies. "I do now," I told Candice. "He seemed super nervous when we started talking about the robberies, right?"

"He did, and he broke out in a sweat like that in front of two PIs. We aren't the Feds or the cops and he was shaking in his boots. He's feeling super guilty or nervous about something."

"I really have to wonder what his role in all this is, though," I said. "I mean, what was that crap about signing an NDA?"

Candice shook her head. "I've been mulling that comment over too. It's a really odd thing to say. Like, what the hell does a criminal worry about breaching an NDA for, and what possible nondisclosure could spell out the terms of a bank robbery? You can't form a valid contract over a crime. No one could sue him for talking about it."

"Do you think he knows that?"

"How could he not? I mean, Abby, how dumb or naive would you have to be?"

"He strikes me as neither dumb nor naive, but maybe just a little too disconnected from the world."

She nodded. "That's him exactly. He wears that faraway gaze all the time and you think he's not so smart, but there's something in his eyes when you get his attention."

"Riiiiiight?" I agreed. I knew exactly what she meant. Edwards had been a surprise. I'd clearly underestimated him based on his appearance and demeanor. It was something I vowed not to do again.

We traded out cars and had to file some paperwork about the slashed tire, which took a little while. By the time we got back on the road, I was good and hangry. "There's a place," I said, pointing to anything along the road that even looked like it served something to eat.

"Would you stop?" Candice snapped.

"Would you?" I snapped back.

Hmmm, maybe we were both hangry. Candice gripped the wheel a little tighter and drove for just a bit before pulling into a Jamba Juice.

The second she parked, I turned to her and said, "You're kidding, right?"

She rolled her eyes, clearly tired of my whiny self, and exited the car, leaving me sitting there in my famished misery. I pouted in my seat, considering my options. Looking left, I spotted a pizza joint within walking distance. Trouble was, if I went for it, Candice could simply ditch me and let me find my own way back to the hotel.

Of course, it might be worth it to get a piece of the carbs I'd been craving.

But then I glanced down at my waist and had to admit that the bloat I'd been carrying for several months was greatly reduced. Candice really might be on to something with that whole gluten- and lactose-intolerance stuff. With a groan I got out and followed after her inside.

To my surprise Candice had already ordered for both of us, and she was just slipping the cashier some bills when I sidled up next to her. She handed me something light chocolate colored and said, "Drink."

I took a tentative sip. It was amazeballs. "Holy mother of all that is good and delicious!" I moaned. "What *is* this?"

"My private recipe," Candice said, pocketing the change and taking the other drink.

I followed her back out of the shop like a dutiful puppy, sipping and slurping and moaning with happiness.

I could taste bananas, and peanuts, and almonds, and cocoa, and maybe even a hint of vanilla. We sat in her car in silence for a little while, sucking down our smoothies and I suppose waiting for our glucose levels to rise and bring us back to being congenial. "Sorry I got snippy with you," Candice said.

"Me too. Wanna go back to the hotel and braid each other's hair?"

She laughed with relish, and I delighted in the richness of the sound of it. Candice had a great laugh. It was a shame we so seldom heard it. "How about we check to see if Edwards went back to work, and if he did, we'll stake him out until he heads home, and then we'll call it a night."

"That sounds like all sorts of fun," I said drily.

"I know, but he's the only lead we have, so I think we should stick close for a while."

"Okay," I said, wishing there was more in the ether for me to dig up about that connection between Edwards and the robberies. "Candice," I said when my intuition hit on something new. "Maybe you should look into Edwards's work history."

"His work history?"

"Yeah. I feel like there's a hint to the past that's related to his work that might help us."

She nodded. "I can do that once we get back to the hotel."

Our plans were foiled when we drove to the parking structure where Edwards typically parked and we couldn't find any sign of his car. Candice even drove all around the surrounding neighborhood, checking to make sure he wasn't trying to give us the slip by parking someplace on the street, but his car was not to be found.

That worried both of us, because it suggested not only that Edwards was probably hiding from us, but that he might be hiding evidence from us too.

Around four thirty we turned away from the bland office building and drove to a spot just down from Edwards's house, but his car wasn't in sight, which didn't really mean anything because he usually parked it in the garage. But then, right around five fifteen we got lucky when a minivan belonging to the missus pulled into the drive and the garage door swung up.

Edwards's silver sedan wasn't inside, so wherever he'd gone when he ditched us, it didn't appear to be home.

We waited some more until close to six thirty and Candice finally called it a day. "Let's pick his trail back up in the morning," she said.

"Can we go to dinner now?" I asked.

"You're hungry again already?"

"No. I need a cocktail and going to dinner is the best pretense for indulging in something to take the edge off this crappy day."

"Agreed. But there's one stop I want to make beforehand."

"Where?"

"Best Buy," she said. "There's one on the way back."

I discovered why Candice wanted to stop at the big electronics superstore shortly afterward when she purchased a vehicle-tracking device. "I should've tacked this sucker to Edwards's car from the get-go," she said. "We would've been able to see his trail even with the slashed tire."

"Hindsight," I said. "Next time we'll be smarter."

We got back to the hotel, ditched our work clothes, and changed into jeans and sweaters. We both agreed that sticking close to the hotel was the way to go; we'd already spent way too much time in the car.

As I was sprucing up my hair one final time before going to dinner, there was a knock on the door.

I poked my head out of the bathroom to find Candice staring questioningly first at the door, then at me. I shrugged. I had no idea who it could be.

"Who is it?" Candice called.

"Special Agent Hart," came the reply.

"Oh!" I said, and hurried to the door. "Hey!" I said when I saw her. "What's up?"

"I could ask you the same thing, Abby," she said. "Rivera found out today you were still here, and asking questions of the former security guard at the La Cañada bank. He's on the warpath."

I made a face. "Shit."

"Hi," Candice said from behind me while sticking her arm past mine to extend it toward Agent Hart. "Candice Fusco. I've heard a lot about you."

"Hello, Ms. Fusco. I've heard a great deal about you too." The two shook hands cordially, but there was a wariness to both of their stances. I found it amusing as hell.

"We were just going to dinner, Kelsey. How about you come along?" Behind me, Candice coughed into her hand. I ignored that and added, "Really, we'd love to have you."

Hart looked from me to Candice and back to me again. "I wouldn't want to impose," she said.

"It's no imposition," I told her, then backed up to grab my purse, pat Candice on the arm, and add, "It'll be fun!"

Candice turned her face away from Hart to show me that she thought it'd be anything but fun.

I just grinned bigger and led the way out the door.

Chapter Eleven

. . .

We made polite conversation until the martinis arrived. Two sips in, Hart dropped the pretenses and got down to business. "So, why're you two still here?" she asked.

"We love L.A.," Candice said tartly. "The people, the weather, the surf. Can't get enough."

"Right," Hart said. "That's believable."

"This is bigger than just the bank robberies," I said, dispensing with the snark and going for honest. I trusted Hart, and I thought telling her couldn't do us any harm. We weren't really getting too far on our own after all. "I think there's going to be a series of murders from a sicko who will then bury them at the top of that hill in La Cañada Flintridge."

Hart considered me curiously. "The graves you said you saw?"

"Yes. When I was first drawn to the spot, it wasn't because of some ancient buried remains. It was because there's something in the ether pointing to a series of murders, and I intend to stop them before they happen."

Hart shuddered slightly. "That's like something out of that movie, *Minority Report*."

"I agree it sounds freaky," I told her. "But I'm convinced

that if we don't solve the bank robberies, then those murders are going to happen."

"Why?" she asked next. "What's the connection?"

I shook my head. "I wish I knew. So far we're very much in the dark and I'm operating on gut instinct alone."

"Doesn't your ability allow you to see more information?"

"Not this time," I admitted. "The ether can be a murky place. It's like navigating through an early-morning fog— sometimes you hit a patch that's impossible to see more than a few feet ahead, and other times you can see several streets over. This is one of the thicker patches."

"Then how can you be so sure that these future murders will take place?"

I sighed. "It's really hard to put into words what I feel intuitively. Mostly because no words exist to aptly describe what it is that I know to be true. But I *do* know that at least three, possibly four girls will be murdered. And they'll be buried up on that hill. Who does it and why, I can't tell you, but the only way to stop this guy is to identify him, and I believe that he's connected to the robberies."

"It's not that I doubt you," Kelsey said. "It's just unlikely that a bank robber would make the jump to serial killer. The pathology is quite different."

"I know," I agreed. "Really, I do. I've been consulting with the bureau long enough to recognize that the mind of a socio-path differs widely from the mind of a thief, but there *is* a connection. I just don't know how. Yet."

"What do you guys have so far?" she asked.

I glanced at Candice, who shrugged one shoulder and said, "Not a lot. Abby thinks there's a man who could be at the center of all this and we've been tailing him for a couple of days."

"Who?"

I answered. "A guy named Will Edwards. He lives in the subdivision that borders the lot where we found the remains."

"Have you checked him out other than tailing him?" she asked.

Now, I knew that we really shouldn't be doing any background checks on anyone here in California, as we weren't licensed in the state, and admitting to a federal officer that we had in fact done that could land us in hot water, but I figured we were already in for a penny, so I told her the truth. "We have. There's nothing. On paper he's clean."

"Bank records?" Kelsey asked next.

"No," Candice said firmly. There were lines even she didn't cross.

"Good. I can't access them without a warrant, but I wanted to make sure you two weren't skirting the law."

"We're not," I said. It didn't mean we wouldn't—it just meant that, so far, we were being perfect little Girl Scouts.

"Okay," Kelsey said, and I knew she believed us. "Anyway, like I said, Rivera is on the warpath. He's pissed that you're still investigating the case when he told you to go home. He's worried you'll kick up some dust that'll come back on him, which is typical. He's a political animal and he's always looking to toss one of us under the bus when things go south. So I'm giving you the heads-up that you should expect a call from your director pretty soon. Rivera won't let this go until you two are back in Austin."

Candice sipped her martini and adopted a nonchalant expression. "So what?" she said. "We're not representing ourselves as licensed PIs or linking ourselves with the bureau. We're just a couple of citizens asking questions."

"Oh, I get it," Kelsey said with a bit of a grin. "I figure you have your own reputations to protect, which is why you're still here, and also why I want to help."

"You want to help us?" I said, perking up.

"I do," she said. "After all, you helped me out. Big-time. I think I owe you."

"I thought this was some other agents' case?" Candice said.

"It is," Kelsey admitted. "But I've been briefed on it, and know where the investigation is at the moment."

"Where is it?" I asked.

"Dead in the water," she said with a wink. "The truth of the matter is that we've got no leads and nothing else to follow up on. The case has gone nowhere, and until the robbers strike again or we get lucky, we're not likely to solve it. I think we need you."

"Cool," I said, feeling myself smile. "So, what can you tell us about the case that Perez and Robinson haven't?"

"What'd they tell you?"

"Nothing other than that there were five robberies in and around the Pasadena/La Cañada Flintridge area all by the same gang."

Kelsey looked like she was waiting for me to say more, and when I didn't, she said, "That's it?"

"That's it."

"Did they show you the video?"

"No," I said, "but Candice found one of the robbery videos online. It might be helpful if we could see the other tapes."

Kelsey scoffed. "That's the *only* video we have."

"Wait, what?" Candice said. "What do you mean the only video? How could that be?"

Kelsey put her palms up. "The bank had their entire video surveillance system run through a central server off-site at another facility. Apparently, someone hacked into the mainframe, inserted a virus that took all of the video recordings from every branch, and deleted them in real time. Because the cameras were working, no one noticed that the recordings were being erased. For whatever reason, it took them several weeks to get the network of cameras up and recording again, just in time to capture the last robbery."

"Well, *that* can't be a coincidence!" I said. "How long before the first robbery did the camera system go down?"

"Weeks," Kelsey said. "Perez checked. The two incidents are unrelated."

"But what was the point?" I asked.

"What do you mean?" Kelsey said.

"What was the point of hacking into the system and inserting that virus if someone wasn't going to take advantage of it?"

Kelsey shook her head. "The virus came from Russia. We traced it to a known ring of teenage hackers who like to mess around with video surveillance systems. To our knowledge, they have no boots on the ground here."

"But what if someone knew about the hack and took advantage of it?" Candice asked.

Kelsey nodded. "That's what we think too, but so far, we're unable to find proof that anyone here knew about it until after the breach had been detected."

"Why'd it take so long for the bank to get their surveillance recordings back up and running?"

"I don't know," Kelsey said. "Perez was going to track down someone at the corporate office to get that answered, but these guys have been less than forthcoming."

"What do you mean they've been less than forthcoming?" Candice pressed.

"I mean that three of the bank robberies occurred before the corporate office admitted to us that they didn't have any of the footage. They kept trying to stall—people were out sick, or on vacation, or having trouble with the file—that kind of thing. From what I remember, it got pretty tense for Perez and Robinson, and it took a visit from them to the corporate office to finally get the story about the hack."

"But why would they want to keep that a secret?" I asked. "I mean, their banks were being systematically robbed. Wouldn't they want to do whatever they could to cooperate?"

"You'd think they would," Kelsey said. "But we're seeing more and more companies try to cover up the fact that they've been hacked, due to how the news of it will affect their stock values, not to mention the willingness of the public to abandon institutions they perceive as being unable to protect their money or their personal information."

I was quiet for a few moments while Candice asked some additional questions about the robberies. My mind was humming with little gossamer-thin tendrils of intuitive information. There was something about the hack that was definitely connected to the robberies. Someone knew about it. Someone who used it to their advantage. It led me to ask my next question.

"Kelsey, is it possible for another hacker to see the work of these hackers?"

"What do you mean?"

"I mean, if someone got into the bank's mainframe and started nosing around and saw that the video surveillance equipment wasn't working, maybe they used that to their advantage. Maybe they organized a small gang and started hitting up the banks."

Kelsey seemed to consider that for a moment before she shrugged and said, "I suppose it's possible, but probably unlikely. The second hacker would have to know what they were looking for. This virus was pretty well hidden, from what I understand."

"Well, someone knew about it," Candice said.

Kelsey nodded, but I knew she wasn't convinced.

We ordered and moved on to other topics. As the night wore on, it was nice to see that Candice and Kelsey gradually began to let their guard down. They both relaxed the set of their shoulders and laughed when the other told a joke. What had been a tense first hour talking with each other became a rather fun girls' night out.

Around ten o'clock I started to yawn and couldn't stop. "You look bushed," Kelsey remarked.

"I am." I then motioned to Candice with my thumb. "This one had me up early for kettlebell swings."

"Sounds painful," Kelsey said.

"It was," Candice teased. "Maybe more for me than for her."

They both laughed at my expense, but I didn't mind. Hell, it was probably true, as I'm a world-class complainer, especially during exercise. No matter how out of breath I get, I can usually gasp out one additional whine before collapsing on the floor. Besides being psychic, it's my best superpower.

After paying the bill, we walked out to the lobby and parted ways with Kelsey. "Call me if you need my help with something you turn up," she said.

"We will," I promised. Even though I figured Candice and I would probably end up handling this whole case on our own, it was nice to know that Kelsey was willing to discreetly back us up should we need it.

Fifteen minutes later, I sank down onto the pillow and was asleep within seconds, and I don't remember a thing until bolting upright around two in the morning. I'd come awake from a very vivid dream, which I felt was strongly prophetic.

In it I'd been sitting in a bathtub, feeling the warmth of the water soothe and relax my tense muscles. While I sat there, the faucet on the tub began to sprout a vine that wove its way out of the fixture and climbed up the wall, sprouting leaves made of hundred-dollar bills as it went. When it reached the top of the wall, it clung to the ceiling and spread out there too.

Looking at it, I wasn't alarmed, just fascinated and curious, but then something bad happened. The bottom of the vine somehow became severed and it began to bleed. Red blood dripped into the tub of water and I shrank back away from the droplets, clambering out of the tub to get away from the scene. It was as I was climbing out that I startled awake, and was left to blink in confusion for a minute until I came fully awake.

The room was dim, but not so dark that I couldn't see. "Candice?" I whispered. She stirred, but only slightly. "Yoo-hoo," I called softly. "Caaaaandice."

"What's the matter?"

"Oh, you're awake?"

She sat up and sighed heavily. "I am now. What's going on, Sundance?"

"I'm not sure."

"You're not sure."

"No. But I have a gut feeling and I think we need to go."

"Where?"

"To Edwards's house."

Candice nodded and without another word got out of bed to head to the dresser where she'd stored her clothes.

I watched her in mild surprise. "That's it?" I asked. "You're not even going to ask me why?"

She didn't pause as she slipped a sweater over her head. "I've known you long enough to know that when your gut tells you to do something, we should do it."

"Huh," I said. "Cool." I got out of bed too and dressed

quickly. We were out of the hotel and headed north only five minutes after waking up.

There was relatively little traffic and we arrived at the Edwards home in no time. Candice eased the rental SUV—a totally different color and model from what we'd had before—to the curb across and slightly down from the house.

I was surprised to see so many lights on inside. Glancing at the dashboard clock, I said, "They're up late. Even for a Friday."

"They are," Candice said.

No sooner had she gotten those words out than a car approached. We ducked down as the lights hit us and to both our surprise, the garage door to the Edwards house opened and the car slipped inside.

"That's Edwards's car," I said, peeking over the dash.

"It is," Candice agreed. "He's back at an odd hour."

The car parked and I sat up straighter, leaning forward to squint into the light of the garage. "His car looks dirty. Like he's been somewhere dusty."

Candice looked from Edwards's car to the direction he'd come from. "Looks almost like he spent time in the San Gabriel Mountains," she said.

The door to the garage was still open as Edwards got out of his car. He looked weary and worried. I knew we were part of the reason why. At that moment a woman opened the door from the house and stepped out to greet him with crossed arms and an angry expression. She pointed a finger at him and said something that looked like an accusation. He hung his head and began to shuffle toward her and the door. She stopped him by shoving him in the shoulders and started yelling—like, *yelling*.

Candice rolled down the window and we could hear Mrs. Edwards shouting obscenities at her husband, but there wasn't any real context for the diatribe, other than maybe he'd gotten home at two thirty in the morning.

For his part, Will passed his wife without comment, lifting his eyes only once to push the button for the garage door to close it again. "Well, they seem like a nice couple," I said when they were blocked from view.

Candice snorted. "Now I know what he sees in Flower."

"Well, at least we know that he's definitely a person of interest."

"Yeah," she said. "The plot has definitely thickened."

We continued to watch the house for a bit—I'm not sure why, as I didn't think either of us expected Edwards to come back out and leave again. I was about to say, "Let's go," when I caught movement from our left and turned to see a young man in a hoodie pass very close to our car. I ducked down out of reflex and tugged on Candice's arm. She followed suit and we waited for the kid in the hoodie to continue on down the street, but he didn't.

He approached the Edwards house right up to the lawn and paused to stare at the lights on inside. I had a feeling the couple was still arguing, because none of the lights had been turned off even though it was now almost three a.m.

The kid stood there mysteriously for a bit; then he walked toward the driveway. I thought he was going to go inside the garage, but instead he crept around to the back of the house and disappeared.

"Edwards's son?" I asked.

"Could be," she said. We continued to watch the house to see if the kid would come around to the front again, but he didn't. Instead, a light upstairs went on briefly, then winked out. He'd made it inside.

"That is one weird family," I said.

"Agreed."

Finally, fifteen minutes later, one by one the lights in the house began to turn off until just two were visible upstairs. As Candice started the car, one of those two even went out, leaving only one light on at the far right end of the house.

I couldn't say why, but I had the impression that Will Edwards was sitting in that room with the light on. It made me think of him as a sad, lonely character, someone with too many secrets, one of which I was determined to reveal.

The next day Candice and I slept in. Or tried to. Director Gaston called my cell around eight a.m. I looked at the display, considered letting it go to voice mail, then thought better of it. Gaston wasn't someone you pushed to voice mail. "Hello, sir," I said, sitting up to answer the call.

"Good morning," he said warmly. "You sound like I've just woken you up."

I cleared my throat. My greeting had sounded a little rough. "No, sir. It's fine. How're you?"

"I'm well, Abigail," he said smoothly. "I trust you're still in L.A.?"

Crap. He'd asked me point-blank, and if there was one person I wasn't going to lie to, it was Bill Gaston. (Okay, so maybe he was also the *only* person I would never lie to, but why split hairs over semantics?) "Yes, sir," I said, hoping that my rather short answer would be enough.

"Taking in the sights?" he asked next.

I gulped. Gaston was never coy. Snide, sardonic, sarcastic, perhaps—but never coy. Still, I thought to counter with, "A few sights, sir."

"Excellent. Say, if you come across a group of bank robbers, would you call me and let me know the details before you contact any other member of the bureau?"

My jaw dropped. Was Gaston saying what I thought he was saying? Was he actually granting us permission to proceed even though Rivera probably wanted to run us out of town? "Umm . . . sure, sir. Of course."

"Excellent," he said smugly. "Have a good time, Abigail. My money's on you."

I couldn't see him, of course, but I swear he probably winked as he added that last line.

After I hung up, Candice stared at me. She'd woken up when I answered the call. "Gaston?" she said.

I nodded.

"He want us to come home?"

"No," I said, still a little stunned. "He wants us to enjoy ourselves."

"I don't get it," she said.

"Me either."

Candice stared at me like she was waiting for me to explain, but I could only shrug. "Okay," she said, getting out of bed to stretch. "If he's not calling us in, then we should get to work."

"On what?" I asked. "Candice, we've got nothing. If Edwards did hide some evidence last night, which—let's face it—is highly likely given the late hour of his return and the fact that he gave us the slip at lunch to go God knows where to do God knows what, we're never going to be able to find it."

"True," she said, moving to the dresser to pull out some teeny tiny shorts and a sports bra. "But maybe there's another angle we can work."

"What angle?"

"You mentioned it yesterday, don't you remember?"

"No," I said, watching her warily and hoping that whatever

kind of workout required her to don so little in the way of clothing didn't also involve me.

"You said that I needed to look into his work history. I was thinking about that last night after we got back from their house. Don't you think it's interesting that Edwards works on camera systems for his current employer and the banks all had issues with their video surveillance systems?"

"You think he was the other hacker?" I asked. "The one that saw the virus from the Russian kids and maybe took advantage of it?"

"Maybe," she said. "But it's something to go on."

"Good," I said, slipping out of bed to edge closer to the bathroom. If I could just keep her talking until I got inside and locked the door, she might go off and do her workout without me. "You should definitely follow up on that, then. I'm gonna take a shower and get—"

"You're showering before we work out?" she interrupted.

I stopped three feet from the bathroom. Dammit. "I was sorta thinking that you could work out on your own this morning. I mean, I only slow you down, and that's gotta be a pain for you, right?"

"Wrong," she said, moving over to loop her arm through mine, twirl me in a circle, and send me spinning back toward the room. "Now go change and meet me down in the gym in ten minutes. For every minute you're late beyond that, I'm going to make you do an extra quarter mile."

"You. Are. The. Devil!" I yelled as she flounced out the door.

Chapter Twelve

. . .

Around nine thirty I decided that Candice was on a mission to *kill* me. She put me through a series of box jumps, squats, kettlebell swings, wall balls, push-ups, leg pistols, and pull-ups that would've made Arnold Schwarzenegger cry uncle.

Mostly, I just cried.

Finally, when my legs gave out and I crumpled to the floor, she gave me a reprieve and let me crawl to the locker room to throw up. (True story.) When I emerged on quaking legs, she handed me a bottled water and said, "You're starting to look good, Sundance."

"Shut it, Huckleberry," I groused, snatching the water bottle from her hands. After taking a big gulp, I wiped my mouth with the back of my arm and added, "I hate you."

For some reason this delighted Candice, and she chuckled. "Come on," she said. "Let me buy you breakfast."

I wanted to grumble and complain some more, but honestly I was barely able to move. Everything hurt. Then we had breakfast—healthy of course—and the oddest thing happened. I felt great. Like, *great.*

Granted, I was seeeeriously sore, but there was something

going on in my brain that was telling me life was wonderful! People were awesome! Exercise was fun!

Clearly, Candice had ruined me.

And I totes would've told her so, except I felt too happy, bubbly, and full of energy to waste time on any of that.

I did manage to say, however, "I don't know what's happening to me, Candice. I feel like I could hug you, and I'm actually looking forward to what we might do in the gym tomorrow."

She grinned and lifted her teacup. "Welcome to the endorphins, Sundance. Enjoy the high."

Later, after I'd showered and changed, I left Candice hovered over her computer and went out to get a much-needed pedicure.

If there is anything I believe in, it's that pedicures are one of the best things ever invented. For me it's less about the well-manicured toes and soft, smooth feet, and more about the fact that for an hour I'm being pampered in one of the best little ways possible. I mean, that foot massage alone . . . right?

Lucky me, after consulting Yelp, I found a place that came highly recommended just a few exits up the highway.

Unlucky me, L.A. drivers are a totally unforgiving lot, and no one would let me over to take the exit, so I ended up getting seriously lost and finally managed to barrel myself over to an exit and pulled into a large parking lot for an open-air mall. When my heart stopped pounding from the ordeal on the highway, I looked around. The place was really charming, and I wondered if there was a nail salon nearby. After consulting my phone again, I did a little *whoop-whoop* when I discovered one located directly in the mall.

After navigating the pedestrian traffic to the center of the shopping plaza, I looked up the salon's location and found it just ten steps away. "Score!" I said as I moseyed on over to the salon.

After entering, I stood near the door and waited for a mother and daughter to be shown to a pair of twin chairs with footbaths before stepping up to the counter. "Hi," I said to the woman behind the counter. "I'd like a pedicure, please?"

"You have an appointment?" she asked.

"Um, no," I admitted. "Do I need one?"

She smiled tightly. "We prefer it, but I think we can squeeze you in. Sign in here." Pushing a clipboard toward me with a sign-in sheet attached, she added, "Pick out a color and take a seat over there. We'll call you as soon as we have a nail tech available."

I surveyed the rows of nail polish and finally selected a gorgeous deep blue gel polish, then took a seat to wait.

The place wasn't crowded, but all the nail techs seemed to be busy. It appeared I was going to have to wait a little while, so I leaned my head back and closed my eyes.

For some reason, the dream I'd had the night before came back into my mind. It'd been a very odd dream as they go, but my intuitive brain so often speaks in pictures that it was probably worth spending a little time trying to figure it out.

I thought about the bathtub setting first. Being in warm soothing waters in dreams is often a symbol for the womb and being surrounded by a protective motherly energy. My own mother is a narcissistic sociopath (yes, I said it; don't judge— she fits the psychological definition to a T), so I doubted that the tub represented her, and yet, I wondered about it because it felt like I should be getting the symbolism.

"Creation, maybe?" I muttered to myself.

That didn't feel right either, so I moved on to some of the other elements. The vine growing out of the faucet was interesting, and that it had money for leaves was quite mysterious. Money on trees would be more obvious, but this was definitely a vine. My mind drew a blank as to the meaning, especially when the vine was severed at the base and it began to bleed into the water.

After several minutes of trying to puzzle it out, I frowned and opened my eyes again. I couldn't seem to tweeze out anything meaningful that made sense to me about the literal meaning of the dream.

And the urge to solve its riddle was intense. I couldn't seem to let it go.

Frustrated, I got up and paced a little in the small waiting area. Right around the time I was going to sit down again, the woman at the counter called my name and showed me to a foot-bath next to the mother and daughter who'd come in just ahead of me.

Grateful for the distraction, I shook off my sandals and took up my seat, placing my bare feet in the tub and relishing the warm bubbly water that began to fill the basin.

The woman who'd shown me to the chair turned on the chair's back massager and I leaned into it and moaned, "Yeah, that's the stuff."

The woman next to me chuckled. "These massage chairs are the best, right?"

"They're heaven," I said, looking over to smile at her. She was a lovely-looking woman: tan and blond with bright blue eyes that sparkled when she smiled. Trying to make conversation, I took note of her toes, which were colored a deep burgundy. "Oh, wow, that's a gorgeous shade."

She wiggled them and said, "Thank you. My daughter"—she paused to motion with her head toward the teenager next to her—"thinks it's a shade that old ladies wear, but I like it."

"I think it's perfect," I told her. "I'm going for blue today."

"Blue is the new black," she said. "Next year I hear it'll be all about the browns."

I made a face. "Brown nail polish?"

"That's what I read in *Cosmo*. It'll be lots of bronzes and coppers and chocolates mixed in for variety."

"A nice bronze would be cool," I said, rethinking my position on brown nail polish.

"With your skin tone, it'd look great on you." The friendly stranger then took note of the time on her phone and said, "Oh, gosh, I've got to go. I have to get to the bank and then the grocery store, and I'm a little nervous about going to the bank. It was robbed a couple of weeks ago in broad daylight!"

"No way!" I said, shocked that she'd mentioned the very robbery I was investigating. In the back of my mind I felt my radar give a tiny ping.

"It was," she said, nodding for emphasis. "Criminals are so bold these days. Well, have a great time wearing your cool new shade."

"Thanks," I said. "You too!"

She began to get up, pausing only long enough to glance over at her daughter, who was too distracted by her phone to notice what was going on around her. "Come on, Ivy. We have to go."

My radar went, *PING! PING!*

And just as I was trying to put the pieces together, the woman knocked the little pedicure table with her heel, and her burgundy nail polish tipped over, hit the floor, and broke into pieces, sending droplets of burgundy flying.

"Oh, my God!" she cried. "Oh! I'm so sorry!"

Three nail techs rushed over and *literally* within seconds they had helped the woman away from the broken glass and had most of the nail polish swept up.

Meanwhile I was processing everything in seeming slow motion, and just when the woman and her daughter were leaving, I happened to glance down at the water and noticed several burgundy droplets of nail polish in my footbath.

"Holy . . . ," I whispered.

"Hello," said one of the nail techs, sitting down in front of me, pulling on a set of latex gloves. "Is that the color you'd like to wear today?"

"I . . . ," I said, looking from the door where the mother and daughter had just left, back to the nail tech, then down at my shoes and purse. "I . . . I have to go!"

"You do?" she asked.

I picked my feet up out of the water and tried to fumble for my shoes, but they were too far away. Glancing back toward the glass door, I could no longer see the mom and the girl. "Shit!" I said, hopping fully out of the bath and grabbing my sandals and purse. Not even pausing to put them on, I sort of hopped my way to the door. "Miss!" someone behind me called, but I didn't slow down. As I got my hand on the door, however, I thought of something. "Damn," I whispered, and turned quickly around to grab the clipboard on the counter, yank out the top sheet with all the names, and bolt out the door.

There was a squawk behind me as the woman behind the counter realized what I'd just done, but I certainly wasn't going to slow down and explain myself now. Hopping along, I tried to put on my shoes and find the woman and daughter duo at the same time. This didn't work well, so I took two seconds to shove my feet into the sandals, then take off in the direction the pair had gone in.

Luck was with me and I spotted them just entering a department store. I hustled myself closer, then hung back slightly to make sure they didn't spot me tailing them.

Luck was with me again when they emerged from the department store into the very same parking lot that I'd parked in. Their car was one row over from mine, and as soon as I saw which vehicle they were headed toward, I bolted over to the rental SUV, started the engine, and hauled ass out of the slot.

I caught sight of the mother and daughter again near the top of the lot, and hung back again to see which way they'd go.

They turned left onto a busy street, which presented a few tense moments for me because I had to wait for an opening in traffic to follow them, but at last I was able to zip into a lane and weave my way forward to tail the pair all the way to the bank.

Just as I'd suspected, it ended up being one of the branches on the list that'd been hit by the burglars. What these two could possibly have to do with the bank robberies I didn't know, but there was no way my dream could mean anything else. The water bath, the girl named "Ivy," the burgundy droplets that resembled blood in the water. My dream was about them, and I had to follow them to figure out why my intuition was pushing me in their direction.

I waited in my car while the mom pulled around the back of the bank to use the drive-through teller. There was only one exit out of the bank, so I wasn't worried I'd lose her, and I took that time to glance at the sign-in sheet.

It appeared that the mom's name was Cindy, and she and her daughter, Ivy, shared the last name of Clawson. At the very least I had their last names and if nothing came of following them around for a bit, then I could have Candice look them up and see what was what.

And that's sort of what happened. They came out of the bank, took a right, and drove north until they landed in the lot of a grocery store. I continued to keep my discreet distance from them, and waited a little impatiently for the pair to come out of the store, trying not to give in to the urge to leave the car in search of a restroom.

At last I spotted the Clawsons coming out of the entrance with a grocery cart full of bags and I breathed a sigh of relief. They'd go straight home, especially if they had anything perishable in their bags, which of course they would have.

As they neared their car, however, another woman approached and they stopped to chat with her. I was a little annoyed (I had to pee), but then I realized that the woman they were speaking to looked very familiar. I sat forward and stared out the windshield at the trio. "Holy freakballs," I said softly. "That's Mrs. Edwards!"

Sure enough, the woman Candice and I had seen yelling at her husband the night before was busy chatting it up with Mrs. Clawson and her daughter. As I looked on, however, I could see nothing sinister in their meeting. There wasn't anything covert or obviously suspicious—no furious glances to the side to see who might be around or listening—just two suburban moms chatting happily away.

For her part Ivy looked bored to tears—so . . . normal for a girl her age—and while her mom and Mrs. Edwards gabbed on, she pulled out her phone and did that double-thumb texting thing that teenagers are so good at. (I'm a one-finger tapper when it comes to texting, but I still manage to get the job done.)

At last the women parted and for a moment I was caught wondering which one to follow. Should I stick with the Clawsons, or wait to see where Mrs. Edwards might take me?

In the end, I chose the Clawsons. I mean, I'd followed them this far.

After loading their groceries, they made their way to the main road, then took a turn into a subdivision, and I followed, all the while trying to hang back a little in case Mrs. Clawson caught on that she had a tail.

She never gave any indication that she did, though, and soon she pulled into the driveway of a modest two-story house with a tile roof and camel-colored stucco. A large palm tree graced the front yard, and as discreetly as I could, I took a photo of the place while driving by; then I stopped at the end of the street to pull up the map app on my phone. Pinning the Clawsons' address, I made my way around the block and tried to figure out how to get out of the sub. I hadn't really paid a lot of attention to the way in, as I was too focused on staying back a ways and avoiding Mrs. Clawson's suspicions.

I should've consulted the map, because within two more turns I realized I was pretty lost, and muttered an expletive while I tried to find an inconspicuous place to pull over and look at the map function again. I made one more turn and that's when I hit the brakes. There, in front of me, was the clearing above the La Cañada Flintridge Sun Coast Bank branch.

"No *way!*" I said.

Unsure what to make of it all, I wound my way down from the hilltop and back onto a road I recognized. I wasted no more time after that getting the hell back to the hotel room.

I found Candice on the phone, curled up on her bed and twirling a strand of hair. No doubt the person on the other end was Brice. She only gets soft and gushy over him.

She held up a finger to let me know she'd be off in a minute, and I waved to her to take her time, ducking into the bathroom while she finished up her call.

After taking care of business, I came out and saw that she was still on the phone, and while I was anxious to tell her everything that'd happened since leaving the room, I also recognize how important it is to stay connected with your hubby. So I grabbed the hotel's complimentary notepad, and left her to some privacy and her call.

I would've sat down right outside in the hallway, but housekeeping was coming through with their big carts and I didn't want to get in their way. Skipping the stairwell (my quads were on fire), I used the elevator to get to the lobby, and sat there for ten minutes jotting notes to myself about what I'd discovered. Then I drew a sketch of my dream with the vine and the bathtub. After I was finished, I had to admire my handiwork; the sketch had come out better than expected.

"Hey," Candice said, and my head jerked up.

"Hi! I didn't expect you to come down here. I would've come back up."

"Don't sweat it," she said. "Housekeeping is cleaning the room and I needed a break."

"Did you leave a tip?" I asked. I *always* tip the hotel maids. I mean, I can't even imagine some of the disgusting things they clean up after on a daily basis.

"Yes," she said, rolling her eyes. "Only assholes don't tip housekeeping."

I smiled and patted the chair next to me. "Come. Sit. I have much to tell."

Candice sat down and cocked a curious eyebrow. "You have much to tell from a pedicure?" Then she glanced down at my toes. "I'm guessing you got sidetracked, because those toes do not look pampered."

"They're not," I said, and quickly explained what'd happened from the time I'd missed my exit, got lost, and found another nail salon, which had fortuitously put me smack-dab next to the Clawsons.

Candice shook her head at the end of my tale like she couldn't believe it. "How bizarre is it that you ended up next to the people represented in your dream? That's seriously freaky. Even for you that's seriously freaky."

"I know, right? I swear, someone from my crew really wants me to solve this case and they put me in the right spot at the right time." My "crew" is the word I use to describe the various spirit guides and deceased relatives who every so often give me a little intuitive guidance.

"Your crew?" Candice repeated. "Hell, why don't you just ask them who robbed the bank, since they're being so helpful?"

I smirked. "It doesn't work like that."

Candice crossed her arms. "How come every time we could really use some specific and direct help from them, you say, 'It doesn't work like that'?"

I shrugged. "Because it just doesn't. I mean, I'd love to have all the answers, but life is meant to be a challenge. We're meant to work at things and try to figure them out. If the answers all came easy, no way would we learn nearly as much as we need to."

Candice didn't look appeased by my answer. "Even when it comes to innocent lives being taken? Even then they're not going to help us?"

It was my turn to roll my eyes. "They *are* helping us, Candice. They planted the imagery in my dream last night, and put me right where I needed to be to find the next clue."

"Which is?"

"Well," I said, adjusting the sketch in my hands so she could see it better. "That's what we have to figure out."

Candice sighed and let her arms fall to her sides. "Okay, so what does this sketch mean?"

"What do you mean, what does it mean?" I said, thinking

it was obvious. "It means that I needed to be on the lookout for the Clawsons. They've got to have something to do with all this."

Candice pursed her lips and pointed to where the severed section of the vine was dripping blood. She said, "That's the part that I find really unnerving."

"Yeah," I agreed. "For me too."

"What if the vine is Ivy?" Candice said.

"Of course it's Ivy," I said. "That's what got me to really pay attention when Mrs. Clawson said her daughter's name, then dropped the nail polish and it splashed into my footbath."

Candice expelled a small sigh. "Yeah, but what if it's more than that, Abby? What if the vine bleeding into the water is about the nail polish *and* it also represents Ivy's murder?"

I gasped. "Holy shit, you're right! I didn't even make that connection."

Candice looked like she was surprised I'd agreed with her. "So you think that could actually be true? You think she could be one of the girls that gets murdered in the future?"

I thought back to the girl I'd seen at the salon and in the parking lot of the grocery store. She'd looked very typical for a teenager—bored with the conversations of the adults around her and very into texting with her friends. She'd been disconnected from the world around her, and I suddenly saw how easy a target she'd make. Even a year and a half from now, she'd probably be no less withdrawn from the world around her. It made me very afraid for her, and the shudder that crept along my shoulder blades seemed to confirm that she could be one of the girls targeted by the killer who would someday bury her near the excavation site. "Yes," I said to Candice. "Yes, I think she's destined to be one of the victims."

Candice pointed to my sketch again. "So maybe your dream

wasn't about the robberies at all. Maybe it's about the future murders."

I shook my head. "No," I said, tapping the leaves on the vine. "It's about both. They're connected in some way. They have someone or something in common."

"Okay . . . ," Candice said, her brow furrowed in thought. "What could link Ivy's murder to the robberies other than maybe the killer?"

I thought about the warm water of the bathtub in my dream again, and wondered if I'd actually been right about the first metaphor I'd come up with for it. "Mrs. Clawson," I said with a snap of my fingers. "Ivy's mother. She was talking to Mrs. Edwards and they seem to be friends, and we're pretty convinced that Will Edwards is connected to the robberies in some way."

"Are you sure he's not the killer?" Candice asked. "I mean, he did slash our tire. At the very least the guy is armed with a knife."

I reflected on that for a minute before I shook my head. "I just can't see that big, sluggish man with a preference for an even bigger woman suddenly developing a liking for murdering young girls. And the knife is probably just what you said about it yesterday, that he uses it for protection because Flower works in one of the seediest neighborhoods we've ever been to. Which is saying something, since we both grew up near Detroit."

Candice nodded. "True that," she said. "So, Mrs. Clawson and Will Edwards are connected to the bank robberies?"

I nodded, then shook my head, then nodded again. "Yes? Maybe? I don't know. Maybe we should review the video again and see if there's any footage of her at the bank. I mean, it's possible she could've been there at the time, posing as a customer, and helping out with the lookout, right?"

"There was no female customer in the bank at the time," she

said. "Just a guy in what looked like construction attire, and another gentleman who was maybe in his late sixties or early seventies."

I vaguely remembered seeing both those men on the footage. And then I had another thought. "Candice," I said. "Was there any footage of the robbers from outside the bank?" I wondered if perhaps someone like Mrs. Clawson wasn't standing guard outside to warn the others should the cops roll up, and also possibly to drive the getaway car.

"Yes," she said. "But it only shows the entrance and sides of the building. You see the four guys entering and leaving, but where they go after filing straight out isn't available. At least, not in any of the video links I've seen posted." She paused a moment to tap her lip and added, "Maybe we should call Kelsey and see if she has access to that. Maybe there's an angle that shows the parking lot of the bank that the Feds have managed to keep under wraps, away from the public."

"I'll send her a text," I vowed. "Did you get anything more on Edwards?"

"Maybe," she said. "I'm not sure yet."

"What's that mean?"

"About six years ago he began working for a company that produced video surveillance systems. The company was bought out by a larger conglomerate two years ago and he left shortly after the merger, probably because he didn't like the new management. I haven't been able to determine if the camera system sold to the bank came from either the original company or from the larger conglomerate, but there might be a lead there if it did—and if Edwards knew about, or had a hand in creating, the system."

"If he did, that'd be a big connection, right?"

Candice smiled. "It would, but it's difficult to tell if he worked on the camera system or not, and what role he had in creating it. I'll have to tread carefully when I dig for information, because companies that deal in security of any kind tend to be pretty tight-lipped about who worked on what and when. The fact that the camera system itself was hacked into won't make anyone any more forthcoming either."

My radar pinged and I just felt that looking further into Will Edwards's connection to the origin of the camera system was going to be worthwhile, no matter what the hurdles. "Keep digging," I told Candice. "There's something there."

Candice rubbed her eyes and yawned. "I'm on it," she said before trying to stifle yet another yawn. I realized suddenly how tired she looked. I also knew that, like me, she'd gotten only a few hours' sleep, but unlike me, she'd been staring at a computer screen for a couple of hours while I bounced around town tailing a mother and daughter. My energy was driven by adrenaline. Hers was driven by sheer willpower.

"Why don't you take a nap?" I told her. "You look beat."

She offered me a slanted smile. "I'm fine."

I waved my hand in front of her. "Your aura says otherwise. You need a nap, Huckleberry."

Candice's lids drooped and she made an attempt to widen them and shrug off her fatigue. I cocked a skeptical eyebrow and that made her smile again. "Okay," she relented. "Maybe just a quick one."

We went back up to the room and while Candice lay down, I sent Kelsey a text and asked her to call me, then went back down to the lobby in search of a snack and to hopefully await her call.

My phone rang just as I was polishing off a banana. (I know, you're reeling in shock right now that I didn't go for the Snickers, right? It was a shock to me too.) "Hi, Kelsey," I said when I picked up the line. "Thanks for calling me."

"What's going on?" she asked. "You have some info to pass on?"

"Maybe," I said. "First, I need to ask if you guys have looked for any surveillance footage from other businesses in the area of the robbers leaving the bank."

There was a pause, then, "We have, but so far we haven't managed to recover anything useable. We did find footage of the robbers both coming and going from two of the robberies, from a surveillance camera located outside of a liquor store and another at a gas station, but the footage is grainy and it appears that all four robbers came on foot from different locations and also left headed in different directions. So far there's no evidence of a getaway car or if they met up at a later location."

"Wow, really?" I said. "You'd think that there'd be some kind of useable footage somewhere."

"If there is, we haven't found it," Kelsey said. "I think the robbers planned which branches to hit very carefully. All five branches are well away from other businesses that could've recorded the thieves. It's really been a frustrating investigation for Perez and Robinson."

"Poor boys," I said, my voice dripping with sarcasm.

Kelsey laughed. "Okay, so what's this information you have to share with me?"

"Well," I said, thinking about how to best phrase my request. "Candice is pretty exhausted right now, so I need someone to look into the background of a woman named Cindy Clawson who lives at the following address—"

"Whoa," Kelsey interrupted. "Abby, I can't just go digging into somebody's background without probable cause. What evidence do you have to suspect this woman?"

I blinked. I had nothing but my gut and the dream from the night before. "I don't. But trust me, she's involved. Can't you just sort of do a little snooping without crossing any lines?"

She laughed softly. "It's not that simple. I'd need to get Rivera to sign off on an administrative subpoena to look into any of her digital records, and there's no way he's going to grant me that without knowing why I'm looking into her background. The second I tell him it's for the robbery cases, he'll have me in his office for a dressing-down like you wouldn't believe."

"So don't tell him it's for the robbery cases," I said, crossing my fingers.

"It'd have to be attached to something, Abby," she said. "Something that was assigned to *me*."

The way she emphasized that last word let me know she was trying to point me in the right direction. Lucky her, I'm not that slow on the uptake. "Oh, wait, Kelsey! My bad. You thought I was talking about the *robbery* cases? No way! I switched subjects and didn't tell you. My bad. I need you to look into Cindy Clawson for the *Grecco* case. I think she may have purchased some wine from him . . . or some artwork . . . or something. You feel me?"

"I do," she said right away. "And since you're a trusted source on that case, I feel compelled to follow up on your hunch. Okay, I'll get the sign-off from Rivera, but you should know that this could come back to bite me in the ass if it goes south, so we'll both tread carefully here with Mrs. Clawson, okay?"

"Deal," I said, happy as a clam that I'd successfully enlisted her help. To be sure I was covering all the bases, I added, "And you might want to look into her husband, Mr. Clawson, too, just to make sure she didn't try to hide anything under his name."

"Is that another hunch?" she asked.

"For sure," I said, even though it wasn't quite true.

After hanging up with Kelsey, I moseyed on over to the hotel pool and got a good dose of vitamin D. It was a little chilly out, but the sun was shining and I was in good spirits. Leaning back in the lounge chair, I closed my eyes and sighed happily.

The next thing I knew, someone had me by the shoulder and was gently shaking me awake. *"Who? What? Where?"* I exclaimed, sitting bolt upright with hands ready to karate chop anything threatening.

"Whoa, Sundance," Candice said, stepping out of harm's way. "Better put those away before you poke an eye out."

I holstered the karate hands and shook my head a little to get the sleepiness out. "What's going on?"

Candice held up my phone. "I came looking for you and saw you out here. Your phone was ringing when I walked up, so I checked the display and answered it. Kelsey called. She needs to see us. Right away."

I shook my head again, trying to catch up to everything Candice had just said. "Why?" I finally managed.

"They found something mixed in with the ancient remains you helped dig up. It's putting a whole new spin on things."

I had a sinking feeling in the pit of my stomach. "Did she say what it was?"

"No. She wouldn't tell me over the phone, and that can only mean that it's something bad."

"Shit," I said. "I was afraid of that."

Chapter Thirteen

• • •

We met Kelsey at a Starbucks midway between our hotel and the bureau offices. She was already there when we arrived, and the look on her face was . . . tense.

"What's happened?" I asked when we sat down, not even wasting time on the hellos.

"Perez and Robinson got a call an hour and a half ago," she began. "The archaeologist, Dr. Acuna, who was hired by the Tongva tribe to inspect and catalog the ancient remains discovered a few extra pieces."

"Extra *pieces*?" Candice repeated.

"Yes. Extra bones. A femur, a piece of the spine, the left half of the pelvis, and a jawbone. The teeth on the jawbone appear to have had some dental work."

"I didn't know the ancestors of the Tongva tribe had a dental plan," Candice said.

"They definitely didn't," Kelsey confirmed. "Anyway, given the fact that there were fillings in the teeth on the jawbone, Dr. Acuna called in one of our county's medical examiners, Dr. Catalpa, whom I know personally, as he's helped out with a few of our cases in the past. He's who we call when decomp is so bad that all we have left is a skeleton."

"Let me guess," I said. "The additional bones were from someone who died recently."

"Yes. Dr. Catalpa says they've been in the ground no more than a year. Two at the most."

"Whoa," I said, my mind racing to try to figure out how this new twist could figure into the cases we were working on.

Before I could draw any conclusions or hypotheses, Candice said, "How'd they get buried so deep? And, for that matter, how did someone know where to dig to put them next to a set of ancient remains when no living person could've known those remains were down there in the first place?"

"They didn't," Kelsey said. "Dr. Catalpa and Dr. Acuna examined photos of the remains taken immediately after the bulldozer dug them up. The extra pieces weren't there."

"So how'd they get mixed in with the tribesman's remains?" Candice asked.

"The tribesman's bones took a few days to be dug up, and each day they were photographed to make sure the process was well documented. The photos on the third day of the dig show the extra bones scattered among the skeleton of the tribesman. No one noticed until the photos were carefully screened by Dr. Catalpa and Dr. Acuna."

I felt a chill go through me and the memory of the Edwards kid walking away from the dig site went through my mind. But that had been the night immediately after my discovery of the tribesman. The bones hadn't appeared for two more days. We'd seen for ourselves that the young teen liked to sneak out of his house and patrol the neighborhood in the middle of the night. It could've been purely innocent. The kid could've merely been curious what all the fuss was about at the edge of his hood and wanted to see the dig site up close.

And yet, it was another one of those coincidences that bothered me, especially as it looped back to the Edwardses.

"What do they know about the victim?" Candice asked next. "I mean, I know it's only a leg bone and some extra parts, but is there anything that can point you guys to identifying who it was?"

Kelsey nodded. "The victim was young. The growth plates hadn't completely sealed on the leg bone. Dr. Catalpa is estimating that the victim was between twelve and fourteen. Maybe a little older or younger depending on the individual development. He also believes the victim was a male."

"Male?" Candice and I both said together. "You sure?" I asked.

"I'm not," Kelsey said. "But Dr. Catalpa said that the pelvis is more consistent with a prepubescent male rather than a female. The leg bone is also a bit heavier than most female adolescent leg bones, and the jawbone is also slightly heavier than most young females'. He says he's eighty percent certain they belong to an adolescent male. He'll need more time for analysis to determine race and solidify gender, and we can get a DNA sample from some tissue left on the pelvis, but it's highly unlikely this kid would be in the system, so the DNA would have to be strictly for profiling. We could also use it to identify the victim, if the dental records aren't available for some reason, for comparison to his parents' DNA, assuming we can offer up a possible name for the victim."

"I'm betting there're lots of missing young men his age in the area, though, right?" I said. The runaways alone would likely number in the dozens, if not hundreds.

"Well over six thousand young males between twelve and sixteen have gone missing from L.A. County in the last year alone," Kelsey said. "That's for a population of about ten million."

My jaw dropped. "You've got to be kidding me." I had no idea the number was so high.

Kelsey shook her head sadly. "No, not kidding. The vast majority of those cases, however, are either kids who've run away from home or who've been kidnapped by an alienated parent, who then either takes them across the border or to another state under an assumed name."

My heart hurt for all the parents who never got to know what became of their children.

"Still," Kelsey continued, "we estimate that at least five percent of those missing have met some sort of violent end."

The table fell silent as Candice and I absorbed that.

"Sweet Jesus," Candice finally said. "That's three hundred kids! A year!"

"It is," Kelsey said. "And it's heartbreaking."

I shook my head. Sometimes, no matter how many hours we put in helping the FBI with their cases, it was hard to think we were making any kind of real difference at all. "I hate statistics like that," I said.

"Me too," Kelsey agreed. "But if we're really lucky, maybe we can help bring closure to one family whose young child was murdered and tossed away like garbage."

Candice and I traded a look. We'd do whatever we could to help with that. "It explains why you couldn't identify the fourth victim from the graves you had a vision of," Candice said to me. "Remember? You were waffling back and forth between it being a male or a female. If the bones come back as a young boy, then we'll know why it was hard for you to pin down."

"That's true," I said. "I hate that it's true, but you're right."

And then I just couldn't get the thing with the Edwards kid at the grave site out of my mind, so I said to Kelsey, "You know, I saw Will Edwards's son nosing around the excavation site the other night around three a.m."

Her brow rose. "Will Edwards? The guy you've been tailing for the past couple of days?"

"Yep."

"And you're sure it was his kid?"

"I'm sure."

"What night was that exactly?"

"The night after I discovered the remains of the Tongva tribesman."

"You're sure it wasn't two nights later?" she asked.

"Positive."

"Do we know how old this kid is?"

I looked at Candice and she answered for me. "He just turned fifteen."

"And did you see him do anything suspicious other than snoop, Abby?"

I frowned. "No."

"Hmmm," she said, drumming her fingers on her coffee cup. "I'll give you that it's a really odd coincidence that you believe Will Edwards is connected to the bank robberies, and now his son is caught sniffing around the site where some bones belonging to a possible murder victim were found, but we've had reports of quite a few people from the neighborhood ducking under the yellow tape to take a look. Perez and Robinson are out there and they suggested that there're far too many footprints from too many different pairs of shoes to even begin to track them all."

I nodded. I'd figured that merely spotting the young man at the site wasn't enough to raise a red flag of suspicion, but something about seeing him there that late at night and trolling the neighborhoods on at least one night afterward bugged me. I didn't know if he had anything to do with the appearance of the extra bones at the burial site . . . but I didn't know that he was completely innocent either.

Candice said, "How can we help, Kelsey? I mean, I'm assuming you're telling us all this for a reason."

Hart's expression turned slightly smug. "You would be right, Candice. Rivera called me into his office when all of this came to light. He doesn't know what to make of it, but he's a little spooked that Abby mentioned there would be remains discovered on that hill and now two sets have actually been found. He wanted me to find you, Abby, and talk to you—get your impressions as to what we're really dealing with."

My mouth fell open. "You're kidding."

"Nope," she said, lifting her coffee cup to offer me a little victory toast.

I wanted to revel in smug satisfaction, but it all felt so hollow. Rivera was only trying to cover his ass, and a young man's remains had been tossed away like trash. It was too disturbing to feel good about. "I don't know what I can offer," I said honestly. "I mean, other than what I already have."

"Nothing on the boy?" she pressed.

I glanced at Candice, because Kelsey was putting me on the spot. Candice made a motion with her hand, like I should offer up something if I could. Taking a deep breath, I focused on the ether surrounding the newly discovered remains, and to my surprise, the image of the cross at the grave site came to mind, only now I could see that the cross wasn't a cross at all—but a *T*. And then, floating up from the depths of my intuition came a name. Crystal clear, it played in my mind like a familiar song. "*T* for

Trevor," I said. It just rolled out of my mouth and it seemed to shock both Candice and Kelsey.

"You got a name?" Candice asked with wide eyes.

She had reason to be surprised. I never get names. Well, maybe not *never*, but it's *super* rare for me. But this boy's spirit was restless. He wanted me to discover his identity. I could feel it. Closing my eyes, I tried to call up his image. It was very nebulous, but I felt strongly like he had dark hair, dark eyes, and long gangly limbs. At least when he was alive.

"Yes," I said. "His name was Trevor."

"Trevor what?" Kelsey asked, and I opened my eyes to see her scribbling herself a note.

"I don't know," I said. "All I'm getting is the name Trevor. It could be his first name, or it could be his last. If it helps, I think he had brown hair and brown eyes, but I don't think he was Latino or Native American. He feels Caucasian to me."

"Age?" Kelsey tried.

I frowned. I wasn't some database with all the right answers— "Fourteen," I said, when it just popped into my mind. The information was so clear it was a bit startling. "He died in the area," I added. "His remains feel close to where he lived."

"So, La Cañada Flintridge or Pasadena," Candice said.

"Yeah, I think so."

"Can you tell us how he died?"

"No clue," I said. Then in my mind's eye I saw a smoking gun—which didn't necessarily mean he'd been shot. It was simply my symbol for murder. "He was murdered," I said. "But exactly how, I'm not sure."

"Any idea by whom?" Kelsey asked next.

Her questions were starting to annoy me. I understood that she was simply naive about how my intuitive brain worked, but being pressed for details like this can feel almost like an invasion, or rather, like someone trying to take over my radar. By simply being asked a question, my radar will respond with an answer, bypassing my free will. I shrugged off the annoyance, however, and said, "By someone he knew. And possibly trusted."

"Anything else you can tell me?" Kelsey asked.

I waited to see if more information about Trevor would come to me, but nothing did. "No. I think you've got enough to go on for now. If I get anything else, I'll call you."

"Thanks, Abby," Kelsey said. "I'll go back to Rivera with this and we'll look into it."

As she gathered up her things to go, I put a hand out to stop her and said, "Did you get anything on Cindy Clawson?"

Candice looked sharply at me. I might've forgotten to mention to her that I'd asked Kelsey to dig up any dirt she could.

"No," she said. "But I only got Rivera to sign off on the subpoena right before I called you. I was in his office talking to him about it when Perez and Robinson called in with the news about the extra remains in the grave."

"Okay," I said, pulling my hand back. "Let me know if you find out anything."

"I will," she said.

After she'd gone, Candice turned to me. "I didn't know we were farming out our investigations to her now."

My cheeks filled with heat. I should've told Candice that I'd asked Kelsey to look into Cindy Clawson. "You were napping," I said.

"Really?" Candice replied. "That's your excuse for sidestepping me?"

"Sorry. You're right. I should've asked and/or told you about it."

"Yep."

"Can we be best friends again?"

Candice rolled her eyes, but the edges of her mouth quirked. "Fine," she said. "But you owe me dinner or something."

"Oh, man!" I said, lifting my phone to look at the time. "I can't believe it's almost four! We skipped lunch, Candice! And I didn't even *notice*."

"Let's grab something and talk about all this, okay? None of it is making a hell of a lot of sense to me right now, and I want to get a handle on it."

"Deal," I said, and we left in search of good grub.

A bit later I sat happily in front of a plate of perfectly grilled sea scallops on a mound of polenta that was so rich and creamy you'd think you'd died and gone to heaven. "How does this not have dairy in it?" I said with a small moan of pleasure.

"I'm telling you," Candice said, pointing her fork at me as she tucked into her Alaskan sea bass, "L.A. has all the best restaurants for healthy eaters."

"We should move here," I said, not at all serious.

"We should," she agreed, and winked.

After we'd finished eating, we both ordered coffee and got down to discussing everything we'd learned so far. "You're sure the robberies and the future murders are connected, right?"

"I am," I said. "There *is* a connection between them, but I can't really decide what it could be."

"And what about Trevor? Do you think his murder figures into this?"

I really wanted to say no, mostly because I didn't want to head down yet another rabbit hole, but something told me that his murder was another link in this very complicated chain. "He figures into this too," I said.

Candice made a face. "What about the ancient remains belonging to the tribesman? Does *he* figure into this?"

I let out a small laugh. "No. But he's pretty much the only one that doesn't."

"So we've got a bank-robbing gang of thugs who also could be serial killers?"

"No," I said. "That's not it. It's one killer and four robbers."

"That we know of."

"Come again?" I said.

"We only know of four because that's all the video shows. There could be others orchestrating the robberies who never actually appear at the bank."

"True."

"And we're still pretty sure that Edwards fits into this somehow, right?"

"He didn't get all sweaty and ditch us at the In-N-Out Burger for nothing," I said.

"True," Candice agreed. "The most perplexing clue you've turned up so far is Cindy Clawson. I'd be curious to see how she fits into all this."

I sighed and looked at the table. None of this made sense. "Me too," I agreed. "She seemed really nice, but if my interpretation of the dream I had is correct, she's linked to all this somehow. And I'm also pretty sure her daughter could end up being one of the murder victims someday."

"That's what's really bothering me," Candice said. "I have this urgent desire to look her up and warn her."

"Without sounding crazy?" I said. "Or freaking out a young girl a year and a half before she'll really be in danger? Good luck."

"You're right, but, Abs, if we're not successful and can't solve this one, then I am going to find a way to warn her."

I grinned at Candice. "You'll have to beat me to it. Anyway, the one clue that I'm actually bothered by is the old guy from the bank. I just find it too much of a coincidence that he was indisposed at the time of the robberies."

"You mean Phil the security guard?"

"Yeah."

"You want to go have another talk with him?"

"I do," I said. "Right now if possible."

Candice eyed her watch. "If he's even working today, he's probably on an eight-hour shift, so we'd have to hustle."

I pulled out my wallet and motioned to the waitress. "Let's hustle, then."

We arrived at the pharmacy just as Phil was putting on his jacket, ready to leave. Candice waved at him to get his attention and he brightened at the sight of her. "Well, hello, pretty lady. Nice to see you again."

"You too, Phil," she said. "I was wondering if you had time for a little chat."

He cocked his head at her. "I was just on my way out, but I'm only going home, so I got time. What can I do you for?"

Candice took a deep breath and dove right in. Nodding to me, she said, "My partner and I are investigators, working for a private citizen who's interested in helping solve the La Cañada and Pasadena robberies." Phil pulled back his head slightly and he looked on the edge of getting pissy, so Candice was quick to add, "We don't think you were involved, Phil."

"I wasn't," he said firmly.

"Yes, yes," she said sweetly. "But maybe you told someone you didn't feel well on the morning of the robbery, or even when you took your lunch, and maybe they took advantage of that information somehow?"

He scowled. "I felt fine that morning," he said. "I had my tea and some banana nut bread, read my paper, and felt my usual self. It wasn't until about six or seven hours later that I started to have some issues, and I don't usually take a lunch. I just snack a little on crackers during the day and have a big meal at dinner."

"And you never told any of the customers that you weren't feeling well?" I asked.

Phil scratched his head. "No," he said. "It came on really sudden. Well, the gurgling started a little earlier I guess, and then I just had to bolt for the bathroom. God, it was awful."

"You threw up, huh?" I asked.

Phil's face reddened. "No. It was the other kind. You know. The trots."

I was sorry I asked, but Candice was eyeing Phil curiously. "You said it was six or seven hours after you had your tea, Phil?"

"Yeah," he said.

"What kind of tea?"

"I don't know," he said. "It was some peppermint blend— really intense on the peppermint. The new girl at Starbucks talked me into it."

"The new girl?" Candice said.

"Yeah. She was a sweet young thing. Said it was her first day there and they were telling her to push the herbal teas, so I cut her a break and tried it. I didn't much like it, though. It was too frou-frou. I like the hard stuff. Their Royal English tea is the best."

Candice nodded and then she said, "Do you remember the name of the girl who served you, Phil?"

He scratched his head again. "Nah," he said. "Sorry."

"Have you seen her since?" Candice pressed.

"No," he said. "I think maybe she quit."

"And where do you get your morning tea from exactly?"

"The Starbucks on Verdugo Boulevard, why?"

Instead of answering him, Candice squeezed his shoulder and said, "You've been awesome, Phil. Thank you so much."

He looked a little stunned at the abrupt end of the conversation, and frankly I was too. I wasn't sure what Candice was on to, but as she'd already turned away, I decided to wave to Phil and follow her. "What's going on?"

Candice wound her way through the aisles until she arrived at the herbal remedy section of the pharmacy. "Eureka," she said, holding up a box with a purple label. I squinted at the lettering.

"Smooth Move tea," I said, and then it all clicked. "Holy shit!"

"Yep," Candice said. "Phil said the tea was strong. She probably hit him with a double dose."

I looked back toward where we'd spoken to Phil. "That poor guy," I said. "Whoever that girl was, she set him up and cost him his job."

"She did. The hard part is going to be proving it."

"She could be the girlfriend of one of the robbers," I said.

"That's what I was thinking," Candice replied.

"I take it we're now heading to Starbucks?"

Candice put the tea back on the shelf. "Wow, it's like you're psychic," she deadpanned.

I rolled my eyes and led the way out of the pharmacy.

The Starbucks was only three blocks over from the Sun Coast Bank branch where Phil used to work. We walked in and Candice asked to speak to the manager. A kid—who couldn't have been older than nineteen—came out from the back. "Hi!" he said after one of the baristas pointed to us. "What's up?"

I smirked at the informal greeting and thought, *This should be easy.* I then let Candice do the talking. "Hello," she said. "My name is Candice Fusco. I'm a private investigator out of Texas, here in California investigating a civil suit about to be brought against your establishment."

The kid in the green apron blinked behind his big-framed glasses. *"Really?"* he said, like he couldn't believe it.

"Yes, really," Candice said. "My client, who was here on vacation and visited your establishment approximately three weeks ago, was slipped something in his herbal tea that caused him significant gastrointestinal distress, and we believe one of your baristas purposely poisoned him with intent to cause great bodily harm. I'd like to speak with her and get her side of the story before I recommend to my client whether to file the suit."

My own eyes widened at the end of Candice's speech. She'd laid on the ruse pretty thick, and I hoped the kid didn't freak out and start making a lot of phone calls.

"Holy crap!" he said, loud enough for everyone in the place to hear him. And then he put up his hands and said, "Ummm, you know what? Let me call my dad. He's a criminal defense attorney and he'll know what I should do."

Candice realized her mistake immediately. "It's not necessary to get any lawyers involved," she said quickly. "All we need is the name of one of your former employees. A girl who worked here on the morning of—" But it was too late. The kid was already moving away from her like she had big, lawsuity cooties.

"Sherlock!" the kid called.

Another young man in a green apron popped up from behind the counter. "Yeah?"

"You're in charge out here for a minute. I gotta go call my dad."

Sherlock looked from his manager to us and back again like he didn't really understand the problem, but he'd be fine on his own. After receiving a nod from Sherlock, the manager bolted for the back.

"Shit," Candice muttered under her breath.

I couldn't have agreed more.

We turned as one and walked out the door, because there was no way we were getting any information out of that kid . . . ever.

After we got back into the car, Candice made a little sound of irritation. "I went in too hard. I never should've mentioned a lawsuit."

"I thought it was clever," I said, even though I privately agreed that she should've eased off the legal threats.

Candice turned the car on, then sighed heavily. "His dad will tell him to alert everyone with a pay grade above his, and before you know it, there'll be a wall of corporate lawyers surrounding the place and keeping any info out of reach, unless someone actually filed suit or came in with a warrant."

"We could tell Kelsey about what we suspect happened to Phil and have her follow up on it. She'll probably get a lot further if she flashes that badge."

Candice sighed again. "No, I blew it, Abby. By tomorrow morning any official who calls will be forwarded to the corporate office attorney, who's gonna ask for a warrant if we want a peek at their employee records."

Candice and I stared out the front window of the car while it idled. Neither one of us seemed to know what to do or where to go next. "This case sucks," I said, leaning my head back against the seat to close my eyes.

"Yep," Candice agreed. "I wish we could come up with one solid piece of evidence to solve even one part of this case."

"Me too."

"At least you were able to give Kelsey a name for the missing boy's remains."

I frowned. "Only a first name. There might be half a dozen Trevors who've gone missing out of six thousand kids," I said.

"Now, *that* was a depressing statistic."

"It really was. You have to wonder how many of those teens are runaways, living on the streets. They're probably close to home but unable to turn back, you know?"

"I do," she said. "And you gotta believe it's something that affects the whole community when a youth goes missing. I mean, not just the parents, but the kid's friends and teachers too."

My eyes popped open and I sat forward. "Whoa," I said.

"What's 'whoa'?"

"What if Trevor *was* a local?"

"You mean a kid from around here?"

"Yeah."

"Then he shouldn't be too hard to track down," she said.

"You're right. And I know just how."

"How?"

I pointed across the street to the library. "Right there."

We walked into the library and over to the help desk. I inquired about where I could find the La Cañada Flintridge school yearbooks, and the resource librarian motioned me to follow her. Candice came along, of course.

Heading over to a section void of other people, the librarian took us down a row of stacked books to the end and pointed to a lower shelf. "The elementary schools start on the left, the middle schools are in the middle, and the high schools are on the shelf above."

We thanked her and she left us to it.

I started with the La Cañada seventh- and eighth-grade yearbooks and Candice got busy with the high school. We took two volumes each, one from the previous year and another from the year before that, and headed to a table to sift through them.

I found Trevor four minutes into the search. "Here," I said, swiveling the book around so that she could see the photo I was pointing to.

Candice leaned over to look at him. "Trevor Hodges. You're sure he's the one?"

"He's the only Trevor dead on this page," I said. One of my rather unique talents is that when I look at a photo of someone who's passed away, he or she appears sort of flat and two-dimensional to my eye. It's subtle, but the dead person always stands out, especially when there are other people in the photo who are still alive.

"He fits the description you gave to Kelsey too," she said.

I brought the yearbook back around toward myself to really look at the image. The young man was a cutie-pie. He had the brightest smile, lots of freckles, front teeth that were too big for his mouth, and collarbones that poked painfully out of his shirt collar. He'd been thin and wiry—perhaps in the middle of a growth spurt at the time the photo was taken. "Poor guy," I said, smoothing my hand over his image. "What happened to you, huh?"

Candice took out her phone and typed in Trevor's name. She pressed her lips together when she hit on something and turned the screen toward me. The headline read, "La Cañada Youth Missing." The date on the article was a year and a half ago.

"I should call Kelsey," I said.

"We should," Candice said, taking the responsibility off just me.

"His poor parents," I whispered. "I can't even imagine what they must be going through after all this time."

Candice got up and put a hand on my shoulder. I was still staring sadly at Trevor's photo. So much promise in a face like that. It was hard to believe such a bright future had been extinguished so brutally. "You stay here," she said softly. "I'll go outside to make the call."

Candice left me alone and while she was outside trying to

reach Kelsey, I flipped through the pages of the yearbook to see if there were any other images of Trevor.

I found two more photos of him: one where he was up at bat for the baseball team, and another when he was singing in the chorus of some musical production put on for the parents.

I was about to put the book away when I flipped one final page without even thinking and felt my heartbeat tick up when I spotted the image there.

A young man with the most sinister eyes I'd ever seen stared into the camera, a wicked and—dare I say it?—cruel smile on his face. There was something about this kid, something that sent a solid shiver down my spine. And I mean, it was almost ridiculous, because it was only a photograph and who's to say that the lighting wasn't casting dark shadows in exactly the right way to make him appear sinister? . . . But I've been working with law enforcement for nearly a decade and I've stared directly into the eyes of more than my fair share of violent psychopaths, so I know one when I see one. Especially this kid. It was more than the predatory look in his eyes. Close up, his image projected a single intuitive note into the ether, one that made me catch my breath. He'd killed before. And he was hungry to do it again.

Now, I know that may sound crazy, but that clairsentient sense of mine wasn't just whispering it to me—it was practically shouting it. Glancing down at the name of the young man pictured there, I nearly fell out of my chair.

"Trace Edwards," I whispered. Every hair on my forearms and the back of my neck stood up on end. I remembered the young man I'd seen shining a flashlight into the pit of the excavation site. He'd been too far away for me to have a good look at him, and I hadn't really thought to project my feelers out to his energy while he was hunched over the excavation site. I'd been more concerned about not being seen, and then keeping up with him as he led me to his home. If I'd had my wits about me then, I might've assessed him intuitively and could've seen what I was getting off his image now. That he was a born killer.

But had he had anything to do with Trevor's murder? One look to the side of the photo hinted at a clue. Photo credit for the image of Trace Edwards was given to none other than Trevor Hodges . . . who, along with being in the chorus and on the baseball team, was also a member of the yearbook staff.

"Son of a bitch," I said, as if that settled it.

"Sundance?" Candice said. My head whipped up. She was just coming back to the table. "You okay?"

I turned the yearbook toward her and waited for her to get close enough to look at it. "Whoa, who's the creepy-looking kid?"

"Trace Edwards."

Candice's brow rose. "Yikes. I mean, seriously, that glint in his eye. The kid looks like something out of *The Shining.*" Then she glanced at me and added, "You followed *him* home in the dark?"

"Yes, but that's not the important part; look at who took the picture."

"Fuck," she breathed.

"I saw him poking around the excavation site the night the tribesman's remains were discovered, Candice," I said. "I think he was scouting out the pit as a dump site for Trevor's bones."

Candice took a step back to look at me in shock. "Whoa, you're thinking that, at the age of thirteen or barely fourteen, Trace killed Trevor?"

I eyed the image of Trace Edwards again. "When I look at him intuitively, I can tell that he's killed before."

"Wait, what? He's killed before?"

"Yes."

"Killed what?"

"What do you mean, what?"

Candice took that step forward again and pulled out a chair to sit down. "Can you tell if he's killed a person, or a thing, like an animal?"

"I . . ." For a moment I felt stumped. Candice's question was really valid. I was absolutely positive that the vibe coming off Trace Edwards was that of a psychopath, but as to whether he'd had anything to do with Trevor Hodges's murder, or perhaps that of a defenseless animal, I couldn't be sure until I focused my radar on that specific question.

So I closed my eyes and let whatever image was going to come to give me the answer form in my mind's eye. What I saw was a grave with the cross, or rather the *T*, at the head of it, and next to it I saw a black backpack with a bone sticking out of it and I had my answer. "Trace did it," I said. "He carried the bones from the original grave site in his backpack and tossed them into the pit on one of his nightly prowls."

"You're positive," Candice pressed.

"I'm interpreting what I see in the ether," I said carefully, "but do I know I'm right about that interpretation? Yes. I know I'm right."

Candice put her elbows on the table and laced her fingers together. "I'm inclined to believe you, but I don't know that anybody else will if we can't prove it."

I shuddered to try to shake the shivers. It almost worked. "He's taunting the authorities by placing a few of Trevor's bones in the pit. He wants to see if we're smart enough to even figure out who they belong to. As to proving that he did it, I don't know how we'll be able to do that. No one's connected him to Trevor's disappearance so far, and no one has stepped forward now to say that they saw him throwing the bones into the pit. I think he's going to get away with it."

"There has to be a way to link him to the crime," Candice said. I both liked and appreciated that she didn't add, "assuming he did it." She was taking my word for it, and maybe she was one of only two or three people in the world who would in a case like this.

"We saw him walking back to his house last night," I said. "He was probably checking to see if the bones had been collected."

"That'd be my guess."

And then something else occurred to me. The way the graves had first appeared in my mind's eye: four graves, three of them occupied by young girls and the fourth feeling less defined . . . That all made sense to me now. I knew that my intuition was trying to point me to Trace as the killer of all four. But why he was linked with the robberies I still couldn't be sure. "Candice," I said. "I think Trace is the future killer of those three other girls. I think he's got his sights set on murdering again, especially now that he thinks he's gotten away with Trevor's murder, and I think he'll make a ritual out of their deaths. He'll bury them next to where he put Trevor's remains."

Most psychopathic serial killers develop rituals for their murders. The style in which they kill their victims, how they pose them, where they bury or leave the remains—these can all become ritualized. Something about the pathology makes them gravitate to repeating patterns in a specific sequence, and I didn't think that Trace was going to deviate from that mold.

Candice wore a deep frown as she considered what I'd just said. "If that's true, with the fact that nobody's going to build on the site for at least a few years, he's got the whole area to play with. It's cleared land, elevated above the road below and surrounded by trees on almost all three sides. It'd be easy to dig a grave in the middle of the night, cover it up, and get out of there before anyone sees."

My shoulders slumped. "I handed him that patch of land on a silver platter."

"Or," Candice was quick to say, "you made it easy for us to figure out that the subdivision has a serial killer in the making. Abby, we've got to find a way to stop him. Can your radar point to how we do that?"

I started to shake my head but then stopped. My mind's eye held an image of the video of the bank robbery and refused to let it go. I had the distinct feeling that the way to deal with Trace was to solve the robberies. "He could've been involved with the bank robberies," I said.

Candice's brow furrowed and she pulled the yearbook close, flipping to the index page and scrolling down with her finger. She then moved to a page toward the front and scanned it before pointing out Trace among a group of other eighth graders. "He's thin enough and short enough to have been one of the robbers," she said. "The masks covering the lower half of their faces could've hidden his features too."

"So, who were the others?" I said.

We both looked again at the photo of Trace with a group of students, but it was obvious even in that photo that he was the interloper. The other kids all had their arms slung over one another's shoulders, and there was an obvious camaraderie between them, and yet Trace stood to the side, looking bored and disdainful. How he'd ended up in the photo of the group was a mystery. My guess was that he'd been passing by when he was stopped and asked by the person taking the picture to stand near the group. At least, to me that's what the image said was happening. Trace just didn't look like he fit in, or wanted to, or like anyone else wanted him to either.

"I can't see this kid leading three others in a crime spree like this," Candice said, voicing what I was thinking too. "Plus, Abs, the robberies were sophisticated. The robbers moved with a fair amount of synchronicity. No one missed a step. It was almost like a well-orchestrated dance, and I just don't see this kid able to pull that off."

"I agree," I said, with a sigh. Then I remembered where Candice had just been. "Did you get ahold of Kelsey?"

"I did. She got caught up in something for the Grecco case, and hadn't had a chance to look into the missing kid named Trevor, so she was very happy that we've done some legwork for her. She's going to walk the info in to Rivera and get back to us as soon as she can."

My radar pinged and I pointed to her phone. "Three, two, one . . ." Candice's phone rang.

She started and eyed me keenly. "I love when you do that."

I bounced my eyebrows and got up from the table, grabbing the yearbooks, as Candice spoke to Kelsey in hushed tones. I then headed toward the exit, not even bothering to see if Candice was following. I knew she was.

When we got to the car, I said, "I need to stop for coffee before we head into the bureau offices, and not at the Starbucks we just left either."

Candice smirked. "You knew she'd ask us to come in, huh?"

"I did."

"Okay, but caffeine is probably not a good idea this close to bedtime, Sundance."

"I'll get something decaf. It's not really that I want the coffee. It's that I want to make a point."

"What point is that?" she asked as she started the car and I buckled up.

"That I always get my way in the end," I told her, adding a wicked snicker.

I walked into the bureau offices feeling really full of myself, and with my puffed-out chest and giant-sized cup of coffee, pretty much everyone knew it. Perez and Robinson especially knew it—mostly because I made sure to take a BIG slurp of the coffee before sitting down at the conference table.

So what if I burned my tongue? Worth. It.

"Thanks for coming in," Rivera said to me when we were all seated.

I put a hand on the back of Candice's chair just to let him know that she was with me on this and no way was he gonna get my cooperation if he chose to ban her from the building again. "I didn't come in for you, Agent Rivera," I said. "I came in because Agent Hart asked me politely . . . and I actually *like* her."

Okay, so maybe I was a bit bitter about the whole being-asked-to-leave thing.

Rivera smiled tightly at me, while Kelsey ducked her chin to hide a smile. "Dr. Catalpa is comparing the jawbone to the X-rays supplied by Trevor's dentist," he said.

Candice pulled her chin back. "You got his dental records that fast?"

"Agent Hart called Trevor's parents. Mrs. Hodges's brother was Trevor's dentist. He e-mailed the X-rays to Dr. Catalpa ten minutes after Hart hung up with Mrs. Hodges. The X-ray comparison to the lower jaw removed from the pit shouldn't take long."

My radar pinged and I sat up straight and pointed to Rivera. "Is your phone on?"

His brow furrowed. "Yes."

I grinned. "Three . . . two . . . one . . . ," I said, then pointed at him. The moment I pointed, his phone chirped and he startled just like Candice had.

Pulling up his phone, he looked at the display, his eyes going wide. He answered with, "Dr. Catalpa. Do you have the results?"

I shifted my gaze to Robinson and Perez, who were doing their level best not to seem surprised. With a smug smile I took another loud slurp of the coffee and smacked my lips. "Mmmmm," I said, rubbing it in. Candice snickered and they glared.

Rivera was oblivious to our shenanigans; he was too focused on the call. "Thank you, Doctor," he said, then set his cell down to consider me. "Catalpa is convinced of the identity," he said. "We'll do a DNA test on the other bones to make sure they're from him as well, but it looks like the jawbone is definitely a match to Trevor Hodges."

"Duh," I told him. I was being snarky for sure, but I figured he had it coming.

Rivera didn't seem to like the snark. "Ms. Cooper, I've asked you here as a courtesy. . . ."

Hmmm. Seems I'd gotten his dander up. "You asked me here because I delivered for you, Agent Rivera. Even without your requesting it, I still delivered you a win. After all, *you're* the one who'll get to take credit for identifying Trevor within hours of discovering his remains—not me. The FBI doesn't publicly admit that they consult with psychics, now, do they?"

Rivera drummed his fingers on the conference table. I knew I was causing him to be pretty conflicted. He looked very much like he was considering kicking me out again, and that's exactly what I wanted. If he was going to ask me to come back and work for him, he'd have to eat a little crow to do it. If not, then screw him. So far, Candice and I were doing pretty well working this case on our own.

As Rivera and I were silently glaring at each other, Agent Hart leaned forward and said, "Sir, if it's all right by you, I'd like to take up the investigation into how Trevor's bones ended up at the excavation site."

Rivera's gaze slid to Hart. "LAPD will want to loop in on this, Hart. The bones were probably moved there by Trevor's killer."

"Understood, sir. And I'd also like to enlist the help of Ms. Cooper and Ms. Fusco. After all, they've been instrumental in helping us identify the young man."

"Aren't you wrapped up with the Grecco case?" Perez said. I wanted to slap him.

"I am," she said. "But we've collected enough evidence to keep the crime techs busy for a while. I can take a few days off that case to do a preliminary investigation into this one."

Hart was going out on a limb here, for sure. No way did she really have room in her schedule to work on Trevor's case, but she was doing it anyway, and it didn't take a genius to understand that she was doing it to act as a buffer between me and Rivera, Perez, and Robinson. It made me like her all the more, and it also made me ease back on the attitude. "We'd be happy to help," I said.

"We would," Candice agreed.

Rivera inhaled deeply and turned to Perez and Robinson, as if to ask them what they thought. "If they want to take it on," Robinson said, "let them."

Perez nodded and Rivera turned back to us. "Fine. But this is the only case you work, Cooper. Understood?"

I thought Rivera had a lot of gall, but I kept myself in check.

"Perfectly understood," I said sweetly. I then got up without being excused, lifted my coffee cup in toast to Agent Hart, and said, "Call me."

"I will," she said.

I left with Candice in tow, feeling rather smug.

Chapter Fourteen

. . .

Hart called the next day to say that she had some family stuff to take care of, and as it was a Sunday, there wasn't a lot that we could accomplish on the case anyway, so she suggested we take the day off.

I took her advice, because I really needed a break, and headed down to the pool. Candice, meanwhile, spent much of the day on her laptop searching for a new lead that she could follow up on.

She dug into Cindy Clawson's background and came up empty. She dug into Trace's online footprint, but the kid had one Instagram photo of some not-so-funny GIF, and that was it.

She tried to find out any information she could on Will Edwards's connection to the cameras used in the banks, and couldn't reach anybody who might know anything about it.

Finally, she headed out for a "quick run" of 13.1 miles, followed by a stint down in the hotel gym using free weights that left her sore and achy the rest of the afternoon.

Meanwhile I took my frustrations out on a bag of potato chips that I snuck out of the vending machine. (Okay, so maybe it was *two* bags. Or six. Whatever.)

We then got to bed early that night, vowing to each other to start fresh Monday morning.

When the next morning came, Candice got up first and donned running shorts and a tank top, and I reluctantly did the same. But only because I was feeling so guilty about the chips.

Still, to my surprise, as I was lacing up my shoes, Candice sat down on the bed opposite mine and said, "We need to talk."

"Sounds serious."

"It could be," she said. "I was up most of the night thinking about the case—"

"Which one?" I interrupted.

"All of them, collectively," she said. "The robberies, Trevor Hodges, the girls . . ."

"Okay," I said.

"Abby, we've got nothing to go on. I spent all day yesterday trying to find a new lead to follow, and after I blew that one on Saturday at the Starbucks where we suspect Phil was treated to a tea bag of constipation relief, I'm not sure where else to look for a clue."

I nodded. I'd tossed and turned a lot the night before, thinking much the same thing. I was out of ideas on where to dig up the next relevant clue too.

"There's got to be something we haven't looked at," I said, thinking that maybe Candice was suggesting we should give up and head home. I wasn't ready to do that, and I was afraid that Candice might be.

"There is," she said.

"What?"

"The inside of the Edwards home."

My mouth fell open. "How're you going to weasel your way in there?" I asked. "Will already knows us, and he'd recognize us on the spot, and I don't think Mrs. Edwards is just going to let you come in and snoop around. Plus, you definitely don't want to go have a look around when that kid is there."

"You're absolutely right," she said. "Which is why I think we should snoop around when no one's home."

My eyes widened to their maximum capacity. "You want to *break in*?"

"Yes."

"Are you kidding?"

"No."

"Why aren't you kidding?" I demanded. On rare occasions, Candice and I had perhaps pushed the envelope a little where the law was concerned. . . . Okay, so maaaaaybe we'd actually, on occasion, when we were desperate and being chased by bad guys, broken a *few* laws here and there (including B and E), but this was a little different. No one was chasing us, and to my knowledge we were not currently in danger for our lives.

Candice rubbed the back of her neck and bit her lip. The decision hadn't come easy to her, I could tell. "I don't know how to find out what we need to know if we don't get into that house and look around, Abby. There has to be a clue hidden there. A clue linking Trace to Trevor's death, or a clue linking Will to the robberies. Either thing will get us a trail to follow or hand to Kelsey so that she can issue a search warrant and discover the clue for herself. I'm not talking about disturbing or taking anything out of that house. I'm merely talking about going inside and having a look around. I'd be in and out in five or ten minutes. Tops."

I sat with that for a long time, but I wasn't convinced. "Maybe Kelsey can come up with something by looking into Will Edwards's online records?" I said.

"We could ask her, but I'm worried that with all that's currently on Kelsey's plate, adding one more thing for her to chase while we sit around may not be an effective use of time. Plus, even after she obtains the subpoena, it'll be a while before she gets access to Will's online information. My point is that time isn't something we have the luxury to waste. We can't stay out here for weeks and weeks, Abby. We don't live here and very soon we'll have to get back to our lives. If these cases aren't resolved by then, well . . . then four bank robbers go free and a psychopathic kid gets to grow older, stronger, craftier, and work on getting away with murder."

"But, Candice, we could get *caught*. And then what? I mean, it's not just you and I who'd get into trouble. Brice and Dutch are sure to catch hell if this blows up in our faces. Not to mention the hot water Director Gaston would be in, and if it's all the same to you, I'd rather not cause Gaston any giant-sized headaches."

"How can we get caught if you're using your eyes, ears, and that radar of yours to keep a lookout?" Candice asked.

"You're kidding, right?" I said.

"Nope. I'm still not kidding. I want to do this. I know we're taking a chance on this, but I think it might be worth the risk."

I didn't say anything. I just took that all in. It was hard for me, because in many ways Candice was a kind of moral compass for me, and when she pulled stuff like this, stuff that wasn't quite morally right or wrong but somewhere in the gray area, I was always a little lost about how I might feel about it.

While I was mulling it over, however, she said, "Can you at least look into the ether and tell me if we would get caught if we got in there and snooped around?"

My intuition immediately gave me the feeling that we'd be okay, as long as we were very careful and didn't take any unnecessary risks. I think that's what decided it for me. It was the fact that we could honestly get away with it and no one would ever have to know, if we were very, very, very careful. I said as much to Candice and she said, "Good. Then let's come up with a plan."

Candice and I spent the next hour or so coming up with a plan that of course involved the running gear. After she'd run a half marathon the day before, I didn't think she'd be so keen to get back out on the pavement, but Candice has always used exercise as a grounding technique, and since she was the one taking all the risk today, I decided not to complain and simply follow along.

Once we were sure about the plan of action, we headed over to the bank in La Cañada Flintridge, parking in the lot before making our way up the hill to the clearing. There was now yellow tape all around the area that'd been excavated, but how that would stop any truly curious soul from taking a peek was beyond me. Still, we didn't go beyond the tape, but took up the run that I'd mapped out on my phone, beginning at the back of the clearing and working our way over to the Edwards house. It took us less than twenty minutes.

As expected, at quarter to eleven on a Monday, none of the Edwards family appeared to be home. Mr. and Mrs. had probably gone to work, and the kiddos were no doubt off at school, so eleven a.m. was likely the perfect time for a break-in.

And if you're wondering how Candice was going to manage to gain access to the inside of the Edwards home, she'd been the one to notice the very large tree in their backyard, which she suspected Trace had climbed to get in through the window to his bedroom upstairs. As a backup, she also carried a sophisticated set of lockpicks, but I hoped she didn't have to use those, because picking a lock takes a good chunk of time.

When we were just about ready, Candice looked to me and I focused my radar on the house. "It's clear," I said.

"Okay," she said, "you head up the street to the end and sprint down like you're doing wind sprints. Keep an eye out to alert me if I need to hustle out of there."

"Okay," I said, nervous now that we were actually doing this.

As Candice nonchalantly strolled up the drive to the back of the house, where she was then going to find a way inside, I turned away to jog up the street. Cruising up to my starting point, I had to admit that I thought it was good that I could work out some of the adrenaline on the runs up and down the street, even though I could barely get my legs to move faster than the jog, and then of course I had to pay attention to any traffic on the street and keep my radar up in case one of the Edwardses came home.

By the sixth slow plod up the street, I was seriously wondering what was taking Candice so long. My lungs were on fire, my legs rubber, my mouth dry and begging for water. Why hadn't I brought water?

After looking at my phone, I realized that I'd only been doing the sprints for about four and a half minutes. "Sweet Jesus," I wheezed, stopping to bend at the waist and let my lungs heave. Walking stiffly to the stop sign at the end of the street, I stood for a few moments, hand on my hip, slightly bent, hoping I didn't die before Candice made it back out of the house.

One thing about exercise—it ain't for the weak.

As I was getting ready to start my next "dash" (and I'm using that term loosely), I felt a little *ping!* in the ether.

"Uh-oh," I said. Bringing up my phone, I texted Candice to get the hell out of the house.

She didn't reply back and I ground my teeth together. Had she gotten the text?

Biting my lip, I looked down the street. I didn't see anyone walking toward the Edwards house—hell, I didn't see anyone, period. No cars, no pedestrians, no neighbors outside gathering up the paper. Just an empty, quiet street.

But my radar was pinging again and I felt a strong sense of urgency, so I texted Candice a second time and hopped in place anxiously.

At the opposite end of the street I saw a car pull onto the road and begin to cruise toward me. To make myself look less suspicious, I started jogging nice and slow toward the car, keeping my expression neutral and trying to avoid staring at the vehicle.

Just as I feared, the car pulled into the Edwards driveway, parking, and out hopped a group of girls in cheerleading uniforms.

"Dammit!" I swore, lifting my phone to text Candice for the third time.

One of the girls moved up to the panel at the side of the garage and punched in the security code, leading the others inside. I turned my head right and left, looking anxiously for Candice, but she hadn't yet appeared.

"Son of a bitch, Candice!" I muttered. "Get out of there!"

The garage door closed as I came abreast of the house, and I paused to jog in place for a few beats, trying to decide what to do.

I was caught between whether to flee to the car, because standing around looking suspicious wasn't going to help any, or to wait for Candice, wherever she might be.

After a thorough internal debate, I decided to wait for her, and paced only a few yards away before turning around and jogging back. I kept stopping to check my phone, though, but there was no message from her there either.

"Candice Fusco!" I growled as I began to type out a fourth text. "I swear to God I'm gonna—!"

"What?" she said from right behind me.

I screamed.

"Hey!" she said, reaching for my shoulder and drawing me close. "Sundance, chill out, okay?"

My hand was at my chest and my heart was racing. "Where did you come from?" I demanded.

"I got your text and snuck around the block," she explained. She didn't even look sorry. Hell, she looked amused.

"It's not funny!"

She took me by the hand and dragged me forward several yards away from the Edwards place. "Let's keep it moving, okay?" she said. Then she eyed me critically. "There's some water back at the car. We should get you some."

"I'll get *you* some!" I snarled.

Huh. Apparently, dehydrated-me is as charming as hangry-me.

Candice chuckled. "What does that even mean?"

I wiped my brow and felt my face. My skin was crazy hot, and my thoughts were becoming muddled now that the adrenaline was wearing off. "I need to sit down," I announced. And without further ado, I did just that.

Candice stopped as well and considered me with a slightly worried expression. I thought she might even look a bit guilty. "You need water, Abs," she said. "I'm going to get the car. You stay here and I'll pick you up. I'll be back as soon as I can."

I waved weakly at her and pulled my knees up to rest my elbows on them. "Go," I managed.

Candice took off at an impressive sprint, and I watched her stride away, confident, strong, fit, and gloriously beautiful.

"Bitch," I said softly to her retreating form. But I meant it with love.

Looking around, I got up to hobble over to a tree to lean against and keep in the shade. A few cars drove by, but no one stopped to ask if I was okay or to offer me water. I was about four houses away from the Edwards place, and I didn't even care if anyone inside looked out the window and saw me.

Around the time I caught sight of a buzzard circling high overhead, I noticed someone walking toward me from the opposite direction. I wondered if I should get up and just start moving on down the street, but the person didn't seem to take note of me. It looked like a man, and then, as he got closer, I realized it was a young man.

The adrenaline coursed through me again and I knew without even seeing his face up close that it was Trace Edwards. He walked with his head down and a pair of earbuds in his ears.

He turned up his drive and I saw him pause at the back of the car in the driveway. He looked from there to the house, tilting his head as if he was looking at one of the second-story windows. And then his whole demeanor shifted and he moved toward the panel at the side of the garage and let himself inside.

The vibe I had from pointing my radar at him while watching what he did caused me to involuntarily shudder. That kid was bad news. Like, seriously bad news.

I've been in the crime-solving business for a few years now, and I've seen enough to know that some people are just born evil. It may be that the gene that was supposed to deliver them a conscience got mutated into something else, but some people are, at their core, incredibly frighteningly dangerous, villainous human beings. There's no therapy or drug that's going to work on them. No environment that's going to shape them into someone good. No mother's or father's love that's going to touch them. They're beyond help and hope from the moment of their birth.

The energy I touched on when I focused my radar at Trace was that of just such an individual. I knew it as certainly as I knew my own name. He was seriously disturbed, and given the chance, he'd continue to grow up and do evil things.

I watched the house anxiously, but I couldn't tell you why. I didn't like that he was in there with his sister and her friends. It unsettled and upset me and I wanted so much to march up to that house and do something to get him out.

And as if Trace's sister (what was her name?) had the same bad vibe that I did about her brother, two minutes after he went inside, the garage door opened yet again and the girls came out. Quickly. Two of them peeking over their shoulders even.

Trace's sister opened the passenger's side door of the car, but before getting in, she looked back angrily at the house, then shook her head and motioned to the other girls, and within a few moments they were in the car and zipping away, leaving Trace alone.

I glanced up at the second story and saw the curtains part as the girls drove away. It gave me the shivers.

Almost at that exact moment, Candice pulled up and leaned over to open my door. I got up stiffly and hobbled over to the car.

Even before I had the seat belt on, she handed me a water bottle. "It's a little warm," she said. "But drink as much as you can. I think you got overheated, Sundance."

I took a huge swallow. It was warm, but it was heaven. "Thanks," I told her. "Let's get out of here."

We made our way to a smoothie shop and Candice told me to sit tight while she went inside and brought out that awesome banana/peanut butter delight. I wanted to tell her about Trace, but she told me to shut up and focus on replenishing my glucose levels, so I did that for a bit.

"Can I talk now?" I asked when I was feeling almost normal.

"Yes," she said.

"I saw Trace Edwards this morning."

"Where?"

"He came home from somewhere—I don't know where."

"The kids can leave campus for lunch," Candice said. "I wish we'd thought about that before we came up this way."

"You didn't get caught, did you?"

She shook her head. "No. I was climbing back down the tree when I heard the car pull into the driveway."

"So, that's how you got in, huh? The tree up to the second story?"

"Yep," she said with a wicked smile. "Trace has nailed a couple of handholds into the trunk to make the climb up and down easier. It was child's play."

Thinking about him returned me to my earlier point. "His sister and her friends don't like him."

Candice's face pulled down in a frown. "If he was your brother, would you?"

"No," I said, shuddering again. "That kid is so damn creepy, Candice."

"Especially if he really did kill Trevor," she said. Then she eyed me sideways and added, "You should see his room."

"What's it like?"

"The walls are black, along with the curtains, bedspread, and area rugs. For light he's got a black lightbulb in the only lamp in the room, but to make things a little homier, he's decorated with small collectible torture devices like thumbscrews and tongue clamps, and put an impressive collection of Japanese swords on the wall.

"And don't even get me started about what's on his hard drive. The kid has a fascination with executions and carnage. His Web browser's history is disgusting. He likes beheadings the most, the aftermath of bloody car crashes second, and an assortment of other gruesome photos and history."

"Wow," I said flatly. "He sounds like someone you'd want to bring home to Daddy."

"The kid's a sick fucker," Candice said.

My eyes widened. Candice didn't roll out the f-bomb unless she was good and disgusted. Or pissed off. Or a little of both.

"By contrast, Emma's room is amazing," she continued. "That girl has more trophies and awards than most high school trophy cases. She's Mensa smart, a National Merit Scholarship recipient, led a team of other teens who won some huge robotics award for a robot that can actually swim underwater, and she's already been accepted into Stanford."

I squinted at Candice. "The cheerleader?"

Candice nodded. "The *captain* of the cheerleading squad. And the debate team. And the gymnastics team. And the senior class treasurer. And the Model UN. And she volunteers at a local animal shelter. The girl is everywhere achieving every*thing*."

"Huh," I said. "That must be an interesting dynamic at the dinner table."

"Well, you can see how it must be," Candice said. "The mom probably dotes on the daughter, and the dad is completely disconnected, and so the son—who, as I said, is already a sick fucker—resents the hell out of Emma getting all the attention and praise, so he stalks and kills Trevor Hodges just to make himself feel powerful."

I thought about seeing Trace approach his house just a short time ago, and how his entire demeanor had changed when he saw the car belonging to his sister's friend. But then, I also felt that even if Trace had been showered with attention, he would've turned out the same way. He was born demented. It wafted off him through the ether like the scent of decay, foul and abhorrent to my intuitive senses.

"We have to figure out how to get him out of society," I said. "We have to take him off the streets."

Candice gripped the steering wheel a little tighter—a determined look on her face. "We'll find a way," she said. "And we'll find a way to solve the bank heists too. I poked around in Edwards's home office. I'm pretty sure he's short one computer."

"Really?" I asked. "What makes you think that?"

"It's his workstation," Candice said. "The man's a slob. I don't think he's dusted his home office in years, and on his desk there's a rectangle free of dust, in exactly the size of a small laptop."

"What if that's his work computer and he takes that to the office every day?" I asked.

Candice shook her head. "Nope. The guy has three desks arranged in a U. His primary desk has a twenty-seven-inch Mac. The one on the left is where he keeps his work laptop—there's a docking station and cables to pull up the screen on the big monitor, and that desk is fairly free of dust, mostly because I think he uses it quite a bit. The workstation on the right, that's the one that has the most dust, so it's been used the least, and now that computer is gone."

"Candice, he could have that with him," I said, but then I felt my radar sort of home in on what she was trying to tell me. That the sudden absence of the computer was somehow connected to the bank heists.

"He could have it with him," she said. "Or he could've ditched it because there was evidence of his involvement with the bank heists on the hard drive."

"You think he would've thrown away a perfectly good computer?" I asked, just to play devil's advocate. "Couldn't he have simply deleted the files?"

"I think that anybody who knows anything about computers

knows that evidence is very, very difficult to delete completely from a system's hard drive. If Edwards was worried after our visit, then he'd be smart to have raced home, unplugged the computer, and tossed it somewhere in the mountains in a place where no hiker was likely to find it."

"That would explain the dirty car the other night," I said.

"It would."

"So what do you think was on the computer?"

"Evidence," she said.

"So how're we going to nail him for the bank heists?"

"Well," she said, in that way that indicated that she'd done something sneaky. "I'm sort of hoping that he and the wife talk about it. They had one hell of an argument the other night, and maybe Mrs. Edwards will bring that up again."

"How're we going to know what they discuss?"

Candice took a hand off the steering wheel to hold up her phone and wiggled it. "I set up a bug," she said.

"A bug," I repeated. "You mean, like a bug to eavesdrop in on their conversations?"

"Yep."

"That's kind of genius, but totally illegal," I warned.

"Said the girl who was my lookout for today's B and E."

"Hey, that was against my better judgment."

"And yet, you agreed that it was our best option to dig up more evidence to bring to Hart," she said.

I made a face. "Okay, so you've got me there. I guess I'm not looking forward to spending all my free time listening to the Edwards family, hoping our boy Will says something incriminating."

"We don't have to waste any of our free time, Abs," Candice said. "The bug I planted comes with an algorithm to record all of the conversations in the kitchen, and send an alert to an app on my phone anytime somebody says the word 'bank,' or 'heist,' or 'hit,' or even 'robbery.'"

"Really?" I said hopefully.

"Really. Apps like that make my job so much easier."

"Huh," I said. "Technology is so cool. But even if Edwards does blurt out that he was involved in the heists, it's not like we can use that, or even give it to the Feds. Kelsey would have a cow if she knew we'd bugged their house."

"Kelsey doesn't have to know," Candice said with a stern look at me. "If Edwards talks about the robberies, he might drop a hint about where the missing computer is, or point us to a name that we can use. Like one of the robbers. Hell, he might even get a call from one of them and we can then follow the trail from there."

"It's still pretty unlikely that Edwards is going to talk about the heists, though," I said, feeling so frustrated. I was convinced that this family was a menace, and needed to be locked up, but they were also obviously very clever and had, thus far, covered their tracks well. "We should have Kelsey look into Mrs. Clawson," I said, remembering that connection again.

"I can look into her again too," Candice said. "That dream of yours was disturbing, Sundance. The sketch bothers me."

"It was creepy," I said. "I know there's more to it, but I'm having a hard time connecting all these dots."

"We should go back to the hotel and draw it out. Maybe putting it in front of us will reveal something."

"I like that idea," I said.

My phone chirped and I looked at the display. "Kelsey just freed up some time. She wants to meet. Should I tell her to come by the hotel?"

"Yeah. Let's rent out one of the conference rooms if they're available. We need a whiteboard and some thinking room."

"And an area for snacks," I said.

Candice grinned. "It's such a pleasure having a partner so deeply connected to her stomach."

"Speaking of stomachs, have you *seen* mine lately?" I pulled up my shirt and showed Candice my noticeably reduced midsection. In just a few days off the sugar, dairy, and gluten, I now had the abs I'd had in my twenties.

"Lookin' good," she said, before pulling up the bottom of her shirt too. "Soon we'll have you sportin' some of these."

I lowered my lids with disdain for Candice's well-toned sixpack. "Show-off," I muttered.

Candice just laughed.

Thirty minutes later after a quick shower and a gathering of snacks (Candice had insisted on dried fruit and nuts . . . killjoy), we were huddled around a fairly small table in a private conference room at the hotel.

Kelsey and Candice both had their laptops and I was in command of the whiteboard.

"Okay!" I said, pulling off the cap of a purple marker that smelled like grapes. (I love markers that smell like food.) "Let's take it from the top, shall we?" Turning to the whiteboard, I drew a box and labeled it *Bank*; then I drew a much larger square and labeled it *Grave Sites*, including four headstones around the section of the clearing where I'd seen them in my mind's eye. Then I drew an arrow that pointed to the right, and sketched out something that looked like a house, labeling it *The Edwardses*, and followed that with an arrow down to another house and labeled that *The Clawsons*. I filled in a few other houses nearby to make it look like a neighborhood, and then made a very quick copy of the sketch I'd created on paper of my dream. Finally, I put in some mountain ranges to the far right, and what I hoped looked like a computer among them with an arrow that was labeled *Missing Computer.*

When I turned back around, I saw that Candice's face had gone red and she was staring at the final sketch I'd drawn and shaking her head subtly.

My eyes widened, especially when I saw Kelsey squinting at that section of the whiteboard. "What missing computer?" she asked.

Dammit. Sometimes, I'm an idiot. I opened my mouth to try to answer, but no words came out. Candice looked ready to kill me. Still, it was she who managed to keep her head on straight, and she casually said, "We peeked into the Edwardses' windows this morning when they weren't home. One of the windows I looked in was to Edwards's home office. It appeared to me—although I can't be sure because I was outside—that one of his three computers has been removed from the home. Abby and I believe he had evidence on it that might implicate him in the robberies."

Kelsey stared at Candice like she knew a bullshitter when she saw one, but all she said was, "Ah."

I took the opportunity to get us back to the basics. "It seems obvious to me how all of these are now related," I said. "I think that Trace Edwards is a violent psychopath, and last year he murdered Trevor Hodges. I know that sounds like a huge leap, but, Kelsey, if you saw this kid up close, you'd see what I'm talking about. He gives off this . . . vibe. It's *evil.* He's like, Michael from *Halloween* creepy."

"How old is he again?" Kelsey asked.

"He just turned fifteen," Candice said.

Kelsey typed something into her computer, then looked up at me. "Can you give me anything other than saying he's got a creepy vibe that might help connect him to Trevor's murder?"

I shook my head. "Nothing, I'm sorry. When I saw his picture in the La Cañada middle school yearbook, there was this look in his eyes—you know the look that some psychopaths give off? That Charles Manson sort of evil glint and that smirk?"

Kelsey nodded. "I know exactly what you mean."

"Yeah, this kid's photo perfectly captured that, which prompted me to focus on his energy to see what I could get off it, and it was clear to me then that he'd killed before and was anxious to do it again."

"The photo she saw of Trace was taken by Trevor," Candice said, lending a tiny ounce of credence to my theory.

"So, they were classmates?"

"Yes," Candice said.

Then she pointed back to me. "Didn't you say you followed him home a couple of nights ago?"

"I did. He was poking around the excavation site."

"And did he give off a vibe then?"

I shrugged. "He might've, and I might've picked up on it if I hadn't been so focused on keeping out of sight as he led me to his house. Honestly I was more concerned with the clue I'd come looking for, which was one for the bank robberies, so I flat-out missed the opportunity to point my radar at Trace and pick up on the psychopath vibe."

"Okay," she said, seemingly satisfied with my answer. "What else?"

"I think that Trace is the one who'll be responsible for the three dead girls I saw in my vision when I first came up to that clearing where they planned to put that development. I think he's taunting us by putting a few of Trevor's bones in the pit with the tribal remains, wondering if we'll identify Trevor, and he's gotta know we won't be able to prove that it was him."

"We won't?" Kelsey said.

I shook my head. It made me mad as hell, but my gut said Trace would continue to get away with it. "I've looked and looked and looked into the ether on this, Kelsey. He's never convicted of Trevor's murder."

"It makes sense," Candice said. "According to your medical examiner, Trevor's bones had been in the ground at least two years. Any physical evidence we could've had linking Trace to Trevor's death is probably long gone by now, and if the kid truly is a sicko, there's no way he's going to confess to the crime."

Kelsey frowned. "Any case that rests entirely on loose circumstantial evidence is a tough one to convince the prosecutor to bring to trial."

"Yep," I agreed. "There's no smoking gun here. No clue I can pull out of the ether that I can lead you to that'll be the nail in the coffin. He's gotten away with it—at least, as far as I can see, he has."

Kelsey seemed very troubled by my words. "I don't know that I can simply give up on looking for more evidence just because you say we won't find the smoking gun, Abby."

"Oh, I don't think we should give up," I said, quick to clarify. "I can be wrong. Kelsey. It's rare, but it happens."

"Good," she said. "Maybe we'll get lucky and he bragged about it to someone."

I shrugged, but I knew that a kid like Trace had kept his mouth shut. He got more satisfaction out of knowing no one was onto him than he did out of bragging about it. "Anyway, along with keeping an eye on Trace, we'll need to work the bank heists and target Trace's father, Will Edwards."

Kelsey sat back in her chair and considered me skeptically.

"Why not just turn our suspicions over to Perez and Robinson?" she said. "After all, they're already working the case, and it would free us up to pursue Trace for Trevor's murder, which, I should remind you, is the directive Rivera gave us anyway."

I thought about that for a minute. I actually did want to hand it over to Perez and Robinson, but something was niggling at me and I couldn't let it go. "No," I said after a bit. "There's still more that we can uncover that Perez and Robinson won't. We're wrapped up in the case for a bit longer yet."

"Is that what you're pulling out of the ether, as you like to say it?" she asked.

"Yes. We need to work both cases, side by side."

"Okay," she agreed. "My plate's already full. What's a little more?"

Candice grinned. "That's the spirit."

Kelsey then gestured to the whiteboard. "Talk to me about that sketch," she said, indicating the drawing I'd made of the imagery of my dream.

I told her about the dream and meeting Mrs. Clawson and her daughter at the nail salon, then following them to the store where they bumped into Mrs. Edwards and, finally, home to a house in the same neighborhood as the Edwardses.

"What makes you think that Mrs. Clawson is involved with Edwards in the bank heists?" she asked, then added, "And don't say that you have a hunch, Abby, because I need a little more to go on than that."

I pointed to my sketch again of the dream. "See?" I said. "In my dream the vine had hundred-dollar bills for leaves and I'm in a bathtub of warm water, which I think is symbolic for mother. The vine is obviously Ivy, and the bath is her mom."

Kelsey narrowed her eyes at the sketch. "Those are bills?"

"Yeah," I said, trying to make the money a little clearer and managing only to really mess up the sketch on the whiteboard.

Candice reached into her bag and pulled out my sketch. "I had this saved just in case," she said, and slid it over to Kelsey so she could see.

Kelsey took the sketch and her brow furrowed. "Why is the vine severed at the base?"

Candice and I traded a look. "We think it's possible that Ivy may become one of the young girls that gets murdered by Trace and is buried at the excavation site."

Kelsey's eyes widened. "That's a hell of a leap," she said.

"Yes," I agreed. "But if Mrs. Clawson is involved with the robberies, it would explain how the bank robberies and the murders are linked together."

Candice said, "I snooped around in Mrs. Clawson's background. She's had three speeding tickets in six years, but other than the lead foot, she looks clean. At least on paper. Same for Mr. Clawson, except he's got a clean driving record. There's no criminal history for either of them, and they're both pretty active in the community."

"Doesn't mean one or both of them aren't criminals," I insisted, but even I was starting to doubt my own theory.

"I've only taken a preliminary look at Cindy Clawson," Kelsey admitted. "I looked into both her and Will Edwards."

That surprised me. "You did?" I asked.

She grinned. "Yes, Abby. I can be proactive too. And at the time, I figured if you two were so focused on Edwards, it must be for a reason. Nothing that I looked at came back as overly suspicious, but just to be sure I asked Rivera to sign off on a subpoena for Edwards while I was in his office convincing him to sign off on one for Cindy."

"Did he?" Candice asked. "Sign off on both?"

"He did," she said, "and without a lot of questions when I told him that both leads came from Abby."

"Seems I've created another convert," I said with a smug smile. "What happens once you get the subpoena?"

"I file it with Edwards's Internet and cell phone provider, which I did this morning, and now I'm just waiting for them to grant me access to his accounts."

It's a little-publicized fact that the FBI can snoop around in all your electronic files simply by submitting a subpoena for them. Now, they don't do this a lot, and it's got a fair amount of oversight attached to it, so if there wasn't anything in Edwards's electronic files that was incriminating, it could lead to Kelsey being in hot water with the higher-ups. Risky to be sure, but I was certain we'd find something if we kept on digging.

"How long will it take?" I asked.

"Oh, it's usually pretty quick. I'd expect it sometime today or early tomorrow."

All of a sudden I felt a sense of urgency I couldn't quite explain. There was something shifting in the ether; some new action or direction had been taken to alter plans, and it was going to make things harder on us if we didn't move fast. "Can you press them to hurry it along?" I asked.

"I can, but I hate to do that unless time is of the essence."

"Time is of the essence," I said.

Candice looked from me to Kelsey and said, "Get on them. She's usually never wrong about that kind of thing."

Kelsey nodded and began typing—I assumed she was sending someone somewhere an e-mail.

When she was done, Candice said, "We interviewed Phil, the security guard at the La Cañada branch, again."

"Again?" Kelsey said with a note of alarm. She already knew through Rivera that we'd interviewed him the first time.

"Yes," Candice said. "We kept wondering about the coincidence of him being indisposed at the time of the robbery. Turns out he had a severe case of the trots, which we think was brought on by his morning tea."

"The robbery was at four o'clock in the afternoon," Kelsey said.

"Yeah, but Phil was talked into trying a different herbal tea than he normally purchased from his favorite Starbucks. He told us that a new girl was working there that morning, and she coaxed him into trying a blend that tasted like peppermint. He also said it was very strong, and about seven and a half hours later he was locked inside the men's room."

"Smooth Move tea has a minty taste to it," Candice continued. "I think this new girl slipped him a dose of two bags, which were sure to have an effect in about seven to seven and a half hours' time."

"Did you follow up with the Starbucks?" Kelsey asked.

Candice's face went red again. "We did, but I blew it."

"How?"

Candice explained what'd happened and Kelsey frowned. "You're right, Candice. You did blow that one. They'll circle the wagons and I'd have to get a warrant for their employee records and no way would Rivera allow me to pursue the lead. He'd want Robinson and Perez to follow up on it."

"Tell them to reinterview Phil," Candice suggested. I could tell she really felt bad for blowing our only solid lead. "Maybe when he tells them about the girl and the tea, they'll want to follow up on it."

Kelsey tapped her lip with her finger. "Couldn't we simply go to that Starbucks tomorrow morning and look for her?"

"According to Phil, she quit right after the banks were robbed," Candice said. "He hasn't seen her since."

"Hmmm, now that *is* suspicious," Kelsey said. "Okay, I'll pass along the advice to Perez and Robinson, but there's no guarantee they'll do it."

But something about what she'd said gave me an idea, and I vowed to follow up on it later.

I got back to the whiteboard and stared at it for a long time. All these weird pieces that didn't fit—but did somehow. We were missing the common link. I felt so strongly if we could just identify one or two more key pieces of information, we'd be able to put it all together. At least, I hoped we could.

"There's something in his past," I said, tapping the house marked *Edwardses.*

"Whose?" Candice asked. "Will's or Trace's?"

"Will's," I said, a bit distracted. "There's something that connects him to the heists in his past, and it has to do with work."

Kelsey looked up from her keyboard. "I did discover that he used to work for the company that made the video cameras for the banks."

I turned and pointed to her. "Yes! We learned about that too. I almost forgot about it. We have to follow up on that."

"Okay," she said. "I'm not sure how much more there is to follow up on. I confirmed through his tax filings that he worked there for a little over six years before being recruited to work for the drone company."

I tapped the marker to the board. "How long has he been with the drone company again?"

"Two years," she said.

I felt out the ether. It was murky and fuzzy at best, but I thought I had a pretty good thread leading from Edwards to his previous employer. "There's information at his former employer's. Info relevant to this."

Kelsey stared at me blankly, but Candice was all over it. She tapped a little on her keyboard, then picked up her cell and began to dial. After a moment she said, "Yes, hello, I'm calling for a reference for a Mr. Will Edwards, and he's listed on his application that he used to work for your company. Could you connect me, please, to his former supervisor if he's available?" There was a pause; then Candice lifted her gaze to wink at me. "Yes, I'll hold for Mr. Scott. Thank you."

I moved forward and took a seat at the table, my Spidey senses tingling.

"Hello, Mr. Scott? Yes, this is Cassidy Sundance. I work for Metcon Industrials, and I'm calling for a reference on a Mr. William Edwards. He listed you as a reference. Can you confirm that he worked with you from"—she turned her head to Kelsey, who quickly scribbled on a pad of paper next to Candice—"August of oh-seven to October of twenty thirteen?"

I gave Kelsey a thumbs-up and focused again on Candice. "You can confirm that? Excellent. And what was the scope of Mr. Edwards's position?"

My foot tapped as Candice scribbled on the pad. "I see," she said. "Right . . . uh-huh . . . uh-huh . . . excellent . . . uh-huh . . . my . . . all that? You certainly kept him busy!" Candice laughed lightly and I rolled my eyes. She was playing this up a bit. "Well, all of that sounds excellent, Mr. Scott. I can hear in your voice that you were very pleased with Mr. Edwards's employment. You must have been sorry to see him go. Uh-huh . . . uh-huh . . . you don't say? Oh, that's so good to hear. We thought he seemed like a genuinely good person and, as you say, very loyal. Thank you so much for your time, Mr. Scott. Please have a wonderful day."

Candice hung up the phone and raised a fist victoriously. "Jackpot!"

"What?" I asked. "What?"

"We got lucky with Scott. He's a Chatty Cathy when it comes to our buddy Will. According to him, Edwards was such a good guy that, a couple of months ago when the company discovered a problem with a system Edwards had been an integral part in creating, Scott contacted Will to see if he'd do some freelance work to help fix it, and Scott said Will was instrumental in getting it back up and running.'"

"The virus!" I exclaimed. "They looped him back in when they discovered the breach in security!"

"Yes," Candice said. "At least, that's what it seems like."

"Whoa," said Kelsey. "That's good, you guys!"

"It explains how he knew about the security cameras being down," I said, so excited now that we had an actual link that could crack the case wide-open. "And why it took so long to get them back up. He could've easily sabotaged the system a little more to drag it out so that he and his gang could hit as many banks as possible."

"We need to talk to this Mr. Scott," Kelsey said, making herself yet another note.

"But didn't you guys already talk to him?" I asked. "I remember you saying that you'd been stonewalled by these guys when you requested the video from the bank."

"We were stonewalled, but not by this guy. The head of the company was the one who interfaced with Agent Perez—his name was Meadows, I think."

"I still don't get that," I said. "I mean, you'd think he'd do everything he could to assist the FBI with the investigation."

Kelsey shrugged. "You would hope that the head of a company would want to cooperate fully, but in a world where even the smallest scandal can destroy a company's reputation, he was probably smart to try to keep this under wraps."

"So how do we get Scott to talk to us without Meadows, Perez, or Robinson shutting the conversation down before we even have a chance to ask our first question?" Candice asked.

Kelsey smiled. "We'll meet with him for a late lunch and a little chat," she said, like it was simple as that.

Chapter Fifteen

. . .

Kelsey set things in motion by calling Scott directly. She claimed to be a recruiter for a major defense contractor and said she had come across his profile on LinkedIn. She told him she was very interested in speaking to him about an opportunity that would definitely be worth his while, but she had only an hour and asked him if he could meet her for a late lunch. At first, Scott seemed to resist, but she was persistent and slyly persuasive. In the end it took her only five minutes to talk him into meeting with her.

Little did he know, he wasn't even going to spend the time speaking to her. He was going to chitchat with us instead.

"I'll be at the next table," she said as we walked toward the hotel bar, where he'd agreed to meet.

"I get that in order to interrogate him, you'd have to identify yourself," I said, mentioning the reasoning she'd offered as to why we'd do all the talking. "But I don't see why you can't just sit at the same table and listen."

"I'd have to identify myself," she said simply. "If I didn't, and Scott mentioned something he shouldn't that could land him in hot water with us, then it wouldn't be admissible in court. But if I'm sitting at the next table and overhear, then I can testify as to what he actually said. He can't have any expectation for privacy in a crowded bar."

At that moment we arrived at the hotel bar, which was empty of patrons except for two guys at the actual bar. "Or even an empty one," she added.

"Kelsey," Candice said. "You sit at the bar and Abby and I will be at the table right behind you."

Once we were all set, we waited, and thank goodness, we didn't have to wait long. Scott showed up exactly three minutes early. A tall, thin man, with a gray beard and a ring of hair around a shiny pointed dome head, he wore steel glasses, slid a bit down on his nose, and a maroon sweater with black dress slacks. He looked very much like a professor, and Candice waved him over. He seemed a bit confused at my appearance at the table, but he smiled gamely and didn't hesitate to sit down. A wave of aftershave potent enough to choke a horse sat down with him. "Peter Scott," he said, offering me his hand.

"Abigail Cooper," I said to him as my eyes watered.

"Candice Fusco," Candice said when he offered her his hand.

Scott blinked. "I thought I was meeting a woman named Brenda," he said.

"She got tied up at the last minute," I said easily. "We're her replacements."

"Oh," Scott said, that big wide smile of his faltering only slightly. "She had said on the phone that she wanted to talk to me about an opportunity at Boeing?"

Candice placed her hands on the table and laced her fingers together. "Actually, Mr. Scott, that was a lie."

He blinked again. "I'm sorry?"

"It was a lie she told you to lure you here, away from the

office, so that we could speak to you about something else entirely," Candice explained.

"I don't understand."

"We want you to tell us about Will Edwards," I said. "And his recent involvement with the security cameras at various banks around the region not recording footage of five bank heists all committed by the same gang."

The blood drained from Scott's face. "Who are you?" he asked us point-blank.

I was glad he didn't automatically get up and walk out. That he wanted to know who we were was a good sign. "We're consultants," I said.

"Consultants?" he repeated. "For who?"

"I believe you mean for whom," Candice—the grammar police—said. "We consult with the FBI, Mr. Scott. They've recruited us to find out more about Mr. Edwards's possible involvement in the bank heists, and we've uncovered a few suspicious inconsistencies that we'd like your feedback on."

"The FBI is now hiring consultants?" he said, like we had to be joking.

"They are," I said. "You know how it is—resources at the federal level are stretched so thin these days. Farming out what they can to professional investigators like us is becoming the norm."

Scott's eyes shifted back and forth between me and Candice. "I don't think I should talk to you," he said.

Candice made a casual sweeping motion with her hand. "Of course you don't have to talk to us, Mr. Scott," she said. "But I guarantee you that if you don't talk to us, we're going to think it's because you've got something to hide. I mean, you worked closely with Mr. Edwards for a few years; maybe you two were both involved. And it's that kind of thinking that's going to make us head right over to the FBI and tell them that we think you're a person of interest."

"I had nothing to do with that!" he said sharply.

"We didn't really think you did," Candice said. "But Mr. Edwards is a different story."

"Why would you suspect Will?" he said, his tone defensive. "He worked long hours trying to clean up and rewrite the software."

My brow shot up. We'd suspected, but hadn't been certain, that Edwards had been involved in the software development, and now we knew that he was. I said, "It's more that it took such a long time for him to get it working again, I mean, what was the delay?"

Scott stared at the table for a moment and tugged at the collar of his sweater. "It wasn't his fault," he finally said, and I breathed a sigh of relief. He was going to talk to us. "We were alerted to the problem when one of the banks called to tell us that they'd discovered their cameras weren't recording. They'd needed the footage to review a slip and fall at the lobby's ATM. I assigned the issue to the man who replaced Will, but he's not nearly as good at identifying issues within the code, because he didn't write it, so I called Will and asked him to take a look. He found the virus almost immediately. He even pulled it out and sent it to me so that I could see that it was sourced out of Russia, and then he told me the entire code would have to be rewritten because the malware had been that invasive.

"I didn't trust Will's replacement with the project—after all, he'd been the one tasked with regularly inspecting the software for viruses, and it was obvious that he hadn't been doing his job—so I got the sign-off to hire Will as a consultant and we agreed that he would rewrite the code from scratch, working at night after his regular day job. He said it would take him about ten days, and we kept our fingers crossed that he'd do it before anything happened.

"Unfortunately, while he was rewriting the code, the first bank robbery occurred. Our company is in the middle of negotiations with a much larger conglomerate, and Bill . . . Meadows—he's our CEO—he wanted us to keep a lid on the malware attack, and he had us send a tech out to the bank to inspect the cameras and convince the bank that it was just a temporary glitch.

"The next week there was another robbery, and it started to look very bad for us. I put a lot of pressure on Will to finish the code, and he came through for us, but as soon as we implemented it, we were hit again by the very same virus, only this time it erased other bits of code too. While we were in the middle of trying to restore our systems, the third bank heist happened, and the FBI began demanding to see the video footage of the heists, but we didn't have any to give them.

"Meadows was going ballistic of course, and my job was on the line. I spoke to Will and told him that we needed to identify specifically where the viruses were getting into the system, as well as re-create the code again, which was fairly easy for him, as he did it on his laptop."

My radar pinged as he said that and I sat up straight in my chair. Scott had just given us a major clue.

"So then what happened?" Candice said. She'd been taking notes the whole time.

"Will re-created the code three times," he said. "Each time it was corrupted by the malware, which was somehow duplicating itself and entering the system. In the meantime, another bank got robbed. Finally, though, he said that he'd identified the sources of where the code was coming into the system, told me he'd put up a firewall targeted specifically at that entry point to prevent any further corruptions; then he personally delivered me the new code, and that version got the camera recording system functional again. And, I'll add, they were up and running in the nick of time, because that very day a fifth bank was robbed and that footage we were able to give to the FBI."

"And it even leaked onto the news," Candice said.

Scott's cheeks turned crimson. "I had nothing to do with that."

Liar, liar, pants on fire . . . rang in my head. Scott had everything to do with it, but I could hardly blame him. It'd probably been important to his job security that he publicly demonstrate the system was once again functional.

Still, everything else he'd said had rung with the bell of truth to my intuitive senses. He wasn't lying. Not about what'd happened with the malware or Edwards's involvement. And yet, I still had the very strong feeling Edwards was directly involved with the heists, but beyond his being involved with the code to the system, I wasn't sure how.

Then I had a thought and asked, "Did Will have access to the camera feeds while he was working on the code?"

Scott cocked his head. "Yes," he said carefully. "He'd need that in order to test whether the cameras were recording in real time."

I looked pointedly at Candice. "He'd also need it if he was interested in casing out the branches remotely without being seen. It would've provided him with a perfect window to observe the employees and each individual branch without ever having to step foot inside the banks."

Scott's face reddened. "I really think you have Will all wrong," he said. "I know him. I worked side by side with him for seven years. He'd never risk his freedom or his family for money. He's a good man."

I had no doubt that Scott thought so, but nobody knows

everybody's secrets. "Did you know that Will Edwards had a girlfriend named Flower?" I asked, wanting Scott to recognize that maybe he didn't know Will as well as he thought he did.

"I did," he said, casting his eyes at the table as if he was embarrassed that I'd mentioned it. "He met her online, or that's what he told me. He said she was beautiful, didn't mind that he was married, and didn't want anything from him other than what he could give. He's been seeing her for several years now. I think he's in love with her."

Candice and I traded another look. That surprised both of us.

We asked Scott a few more questions about Edwards: Did he know Edwards to ever associate with members of a gang, or thieves, or even an organized crime group? He appeared genuinely shocked by that one, and swore that he had no knowledge of Edwards ever associating with anyone below board.

"What about his home life?" I asked Scott. "Did he ever talk about it?"

"I'm not comfortable discussing the man's personal business," Scott said.

"We don't really care if you're comfortable with it," Candice said bluntly. "But we need to know, Mr. Scott. Lives may depend on it."

Scott scowled. "Lives?" he said. "Really?"

Candice looked him in the eyes. "Really."

He rolled his eyes but said, "Will is a good man. He works hard for his family every day. If I had to say anything about what I know about his home life, it's that he's underappreciated."

"Have you ever met his kids?" I asked next.

Scott's gaze was guarded. "I have."

"Thoughts?"

His scowl deepened. "His daughter is quite accomplished.

Will is very proud of her and talks about her a great deal. His son . . ."

"Yes?" I pressed.

"His son has been a difficult young man to raise. If there is one thing that I think Will regrets, it's not trying to get his son some therapy at an early age."

It wouldn't have helped, I thought.

"And he and the missus?" Candice said. "If you had one word to describe their relationship, what would it be?"

Scott pursed his lips and seemed to think about that for a beat. "Strained."

We ended the interview with Scott very shortly thereafter, thanking him for his time and promising not to reveal anything that he'd said to us to anyone else. Of course, my fingers were crossed behind my back when I made that promise, and I can't really speak for Candice's fingers not being crossed too.

After he'd gone, Kelsey came to the table and set down her laptop. I'd thought I'd heard the tapping of keys behind me. "Everything Scott said checks out," she told us.

"You verified all that, that fast?" I asked.

"Edwards's telecommunications company granted me access about fifteen minutes ago," she said. "I have the e-mails between him and Scott to prove that he was hired as a subcontractor to rewrite the code and logged all the issues week to week that Scott claimed he had. Edwards appeared earnest about trying to find the source of where the code kept replicating itself within the system and wreaking such havoc. Three weeks ago he confirms with Scott that he's identified the source, and assures him that it won't break into the system again. The last communication is him stating that he's rebuilt the code from the ground up and wants to deliver it to Scott."

"Still, he could've taken his time, right? He could've orga-

nized the heists to come during the time he's supposedly rebuild-
ing the code."

But Kelsey's expression was skeptical. "I don't know where he'd
find the hours to do that, Abby. The guy was working full-time at
his current job, then coming home and working on the code until
well after midnight, at least according to the time stamps on the
e-mails back and forth to Scott. During that five weeks he couldn't
have gotten more than five hours' rest a night."

"Okay, so the guy didn't sleep," Candice said. "If he got away
with a couple hundred thousand dollars, maybe that was incen-
tive enough to forgo some snooze time."

Kelsey shook her head. "See, it's more than just that. The
heists all occurred at between three fifteen and four thirty on a
weekday afternoon. I've confirmed with his employer's HR department that he was at work on all of those days at that time."

I sighed. "He's involved," I insisted. "I mean, if he wasn't,
why would he get all cagey when Candice and I confronted him
and then go off and hide his computer somewhere we'd never
find it?"

"I don't know," Kelsey said. At that moment her cell phone
chirped and she looked at the display. "Damn," she said. "The
federal prosecutor's office wants a meeting with me and Rivera
to discuss the Grecco case. I've got to go."

"Okay," I said, trying to hide my disappointment. We needed
Kelsey's full attention on this case, but no way could we ask for
it under the circumstances. Candice and I would have to keep
on working without her.

"We'll keep at it," Candice said as Kelsey gathered up her
things.

"I can come back after the meeting," she told us. "But I'm not
sure how long it'll be."

"We'll be here," Candice assured her.

Kelsey smiled, offered us a wave, then hurried out of the bar. The second she was gone, I said, "Feel like some coffee?"

Candice eyed me curiously. "You have that wicked glint in your eye, so I'm guessing you want more than just coffee."

"You would be correct," I said. "I want the name of the girl who spiked Phil's tea."

Candice's mouth quirked into a sly smile. "The plot thickens."

Twenty minutes later, dressed in a ball cap and sweats, I walked into the Starbucks across from the library. To my delight, it was all but empty. Only one patron was in the place, over in the corner, sipping something hot and reading the paper. Two baristas were behind the counter, one at the register and one scrubbing the espresso machine.

There was no sign of the manager Candice had freaked out the night before, which was a good sign. I approached the young woman doing the scrubbing at the espresso machine, rubbing my neck a little. "Excuse me," I said. She looked up. "Sorry to bother you, but I'm developing a sore throat and about three weeks ago I was in here and one of your coworkers mentioned a tea that was amazing. I get these chronic sore throats—bad tonsils or something. Anyway, she recommended a brew that really helped, but I don't remember which one it was."

The young woman smiled sweetly and said, "Do you remember the way it tasted? Maybe we can figure it out that way."

"Well, it was a little minty. . . ."

"Mint Majesty?"

I made a face and shook my head. "I don't think that was it. There was a little citrus to the aftertaste."

"Jade Citrus?"

I bit my lip and tried to look perplexed. "I don't think that was it either. You know, I think she might've combined two of the teas to give me the best result."

"Oh, really?" the girl said. "We're not supposed to do that."

I smiled and said, "I know. She was new. She told me it was her first day. Is she here by any chance? I'll gladly pay for both teas—I just really want to get the recipe right."

The girl bit the inside of her lip. "She was new?"

"Yes. I only saw her that one day, but she was so sweet to me."

"You said it was about three weeks ago?"

I nodded and felt my heart rate tick up. The girl looked like she knew the barista I was talking about. "I think that was probably Ivy," she said. "She only worked here for like, two days. I trained her, and you're right, she was super nice, but she's not here anymore."

My breath caught and I took a step back from the counter. Every single loose thread from this crazy complicated case came crashing into my head at once and it left me stunned.

"You okay?" the barista asked me.

I stared at her like I was seeing her for the first time. "I'm . . . perfect," I said. "But I have to go." Fishing into my purse, I pulled out a ten and left it on the counter, then dashed outside and ran straight to the car.

Candice was there waiting for me, her earbuds in and her phone resting on the dash. She had a look of utter disbelief on her face.

The second I opened the door and got in, Candice and I both shouted at each other, *"I know who robbed the banks!"*

From there it was a struggle to shout over each other how we knew, because we were both so excited to finally have all the pieces in place. "Ivy Clawson was the one who spiked Phil's tea!

The barista in there just told me that she trained Ivy to work there, but Ivy only worked for two days before quitting! She was the one who gave Phil the Smooth Move tea!" I yelled.

Candice shouted, "Emma and her cheerleading friends were the gang of thieves! They were talking about it on their lunch hour!"

It took my brain a second to catch up to what Candice had just said. "Wait, what?"

Candice yanked the earbuds away from her ears and pulled them out from her phone jack. "Listen!" she said as she fiddled with her phone. "My audio surveillance app sent me a flag on the very first recording from the Edwards house, and at first I thought it was a glitch, but you have to hear this!" With that, Candice pressed the Play button and the speaker function and set the phone on the dash again.

The voices coming out of the mic were tinny, but there was no mistaking the giggly sounds of a group of teenage girls. "Ohmigod, Emma," said one girl. "I can't believe I'm never going to see you again after next week. It's like, breaking my heart!"

"I know, Ives," another voice said. "I'm so totally sad too. And I'll never forget what you guys did for me. Like, ever."

There were small mewing sounds coming from multiple speakers; then yet another voice said, "Are you sure it's enough? I mean, after our cuts it's only like seventy thousand. How long can you live on that?"

"In Thailand? For, like, a really long time, you guys," said Emma.

At this point I felt myself grinning ear to ear. We had them. We totally *had* them! "Confirmation!" I said to Candice.

Candice pumped her head up and down and held up a finger as if to say, *Wait for it.*

Ivy's voice suddenly rang out of the phone to say, "I'm worried that it's not enough, Em. I mean, my dad makes a lot more than that and Mom is always complaining that we don't have any extra money. What if you run out and you have to come back here? What if he hunts you down and finds you?"

"We could go for it one more time, you guys," said a third unidentified voice. "I mean, we've been averaging almost sixty thousand a bank and no one's caught on to us yet. Well, except your dad, but he's not going to say anything, right?"

"No," she said. "He won't. I don't think he knows if it's me or Trace, but he found my ninja costume in the garage and threw it out along with his laptop, you guys. We'd have to go into the next bank and actually look around."

"Would we?" said Ivy. "They're all laid out pretty much the same, right? Except for one lobby being a little bigger than the other, they're all basically the same. And we did think about that bank in Glendale before calling it quits. We already know what the inside of that branch looks like."

"And as for your ninja outfit, we could totally get you another one," a fourth voice said. "They sell those online for, like, cheap."

"We can't buy it online, remember?" Emma said. "The police are probably looking at anybody who buys one of those on the Internet."

"Then we'll go back to that costume store in Torrance and buy you another one," said Ivy.

"We'd have to get new shoulder pads too," said the third voice. "God, those were a pain to sew in, right?"

"At least your mom didn't find your top on her sewing machine," Ivy said. "God, I almost had a cow when she came into my room with it and wanted to know what it was."

"I loved your answer," Emma said. Mimicking Ivy's higher-pitched voice, she added, "It's for Spirit Week, Mom."

"Yeah, which isn't for like, four months!" said another one of the girls.

They all laughed. Then, someone said, "Melanie, you should have Ivy fix that left shoulder pad. I swear it's still crooked."

"So we're actually considering this?" said someone other than Ivy or Emma.

"I think I still have the screenshot of the lobby from the Glendale branch hidden upstairs, you guys," Ivy said, excitement in her voice. "There's no guard there and we can practice the routine this weekend at Mel's place."

"Ohmigod," said one of the unidentified girls. "We totally should do this! And I'd be willing to give my whole portion to Emma this time, just to make sure she had enough to last a long, long time."

Emma became emotional. "Valerie," she said sweetly through choked-back tears. "I love you so much, girl."

"Awww! We've got your—" There was an abrupt halt to a third girl's speech, and then, "Was that the garage door?"

Silence followed; then, in a hushed voice someone said, "Ohmigod! I think he's home!"

What sounded like the opening of a door could be heard faintly on the recording; then a male voice said, "Are the hens huddled around the henhouse?" Nobody answered. "You know how they kill chickens on a chicken farm, right?" he said next. My skin crawled. It was obvious to me that Trace had entered the kitchen and all the girls gathered there were both alarmed and frightened by his presence.

"Come on," he coaxed. "Emma? You're so smart. Want to take a guess?"

"Get. Out. Trace," she said firmly, but there was a quaver in her voice.

"The farmer wrings their neck," he said, then made a sort of choking sound. "It's easy 'cause their necks are so skinny. Kinda like yours, M&M."

Again, no one said a word, but there was the sound of first one chair, then a few more sliding back from the table. Without another word from anybody, there were only footsteps and a door opening, then slamming shut. After that, only the sound of Trace's wicked laughter filled the room.

Candice paused the tape and she and I simply stared at each other. "That's why they looked so tight and efficient in their movements," I said. "The tape of the robbery was like a cheerleading drill, but I couldn't make that connection until just now."

"Yeah," Candice said, nodding. "The shoulder pads threw me off. I never guessed they were girls."

"They must've practiced their movements quite a bit to look more like men," I said. "And I have to say, they kind of nailed it."

"They did. They fooled all of us. Even you."

"Yep," I agreed. Then I looked at Candice. "So what do we do with the tape?"

"We can't use any of the recording in court," Candice said. "And no way am I going to admit to Kelsey that I planted a bug inside the Edwards house, so we'll have to go with what you found out about Ivy working on the morning Phil's tea got spiked."

I grimaced. "That's a little flimsy, though, don't you think? I mean, suspecting that Phil's tea was tampered with isn't enough to get us a warrant to go hunt for Ivy's share of the money or the costume she wore to rob the banks, right?"

"It's not," Candice said. "But it might be enough to bring Ivy and Emma in for questioning. Let's loop Kelsey in on this and see what she wants to do."

Chapter Sixteen

• • •

It took two hours to get ahold of Kelsey. She'd been locked into a long meeting with the federal prosecutor's office, discussing the Grecco case, and as we were feeling pretty confident, when she invited us to her offices, we didn't hesitate to say yes.

Kelsey met us at the elevator and walked us up. "Rivera would like to be included in our discussion if it's okay with you," she said.

"It's not," Candice said immediately.

Kelsey looked taken aback. "Really?"

"Yes," I said. "Kelsey, we've obtained a recording that proves our suspicions about who robbed the banks, but we can't play it for you, and we can't tell you how we obtained it. Still, we need to tell you what's on it."

Kelsey's expression became cautious. "I'm assuming the recording you're speaking of was obtained without anyone's permission?"

"You can assume anything you'd like," Candice said easily. It was all the affirmation Kelsey needed.

"I see," she said. "Okay, then let's start off in one of the smaller conference rooms. We can speak there in private."

Once off the elevator, she led us to a section of the office that was sparsely populated and into a room with a very small table and four chairs. We sat down and Candice and I took turns telling Kelsey what was on the tape.

As I suspected, Kelsey was as shocked as we were by the revelation that Emma Edwards and her BFFs were the orchestrators of the robberies. But then Candice pulled up the video of the fifth robbery at the La Cañada Flintridge bank, and it became obvious to us in little ways that the thieves were girls in padded outfits. They moved with precision and grace, like acrobats used to doing drills over and over with one another.

Once the tape ended, I said, "Emma had access to the computer her father used to rewrite the code. She could've easily used the software to spy on the various banks, casing them out remotely so that neither she nor any of her cohorts ever had to set foot inside the banks prior to the robberies, so there was no risk of ever being recognized by anyone inside the banks."

"She also would've had access to the virus," Candice added. "It was right there in the e-mail her dad sent Mr. Scott."

"Yes, but what would Emma know about computer coding? Isn't this girl only seventeen?"

"She's literally a genius," I said, and motioned to Candice to affirm that.

"She is. She's a member of Mensa, and recently won an award for building a robot with a group of other teens. She was either the engineer or the computer coder, and I'm guessing she was the coder."

"Wow," said Kelsey. "So how do we *prove* this if we can't use any of the information on the tape you acquired? We've got to have probable cause to even search the girls' residences. Give me something that I can use to obtain a warrant."

"There is one thing," I said. "I discovered that Ivy worked

at the Starbucks where Phil got his morning cup of tea. The girls probably saw on the footage of the La Cañada branch that the security guard always brought a cup of Starbucks tea with him to work every day. Ivy could've easily skipped school, gotten a job at the Starbucks for a day or two, and swapped out the tea bag."

Kelsey frowned. "That is some flimsy evidence, Abby. There's *no* way I'm going to obtain a warrant on something as threadbare as that. I'm sure we don't even have a tea bag to connect her to the crime, right?"

"No," I said. "We don't."

"What about bank records for the girls?" Candice asked. "Maybe we'll get lucky and see that at least one of them deposited some of the stolen money."

"You'd need a warrant," Kelsey told her.

"Okay, how about getting a subpoena for the girls' online accounts? Maybe they texted or e-mailed something incriminating to each other," I said.

"Now that's something, but it'll take time, and if these girls are getting ready to hit another bank, then I'm not sure we have time to spare. Once they set the robbery in motion, the chances of things escalating climb exponentially. I need actual evidence that supports the claim that these girls did it. Or a whole lot of small stuff that adds up to something bigger than Ivy working at the Starbucks where Phil got his morning tea and the possible online purchase of a ninja outfit. I'll need at least one more substantial thing."

We all thought about it for several moments, but there was nothing I could think of that might sway a judge that we were on to something. Candice finally said, "We could call the girls in for a chat and see if they crack," she said. "Maybe we can get them to turn on each other?"

"That'd be a stretch," Kelsey said.

"Yeah," I replied, feeling tingly excitement for the idea. "But if they didn't crack, the girls might panic, and attempt to ditch their costumes and maybe even hide their money. I bet we could spook them into making a move like that."

"How're we going to bring the girls in without tipping our hand that it's about the bank heists, though?" Candice asked. "Emma already has her ticket and passport ready to flee, I'll bet. The second we tell her we'd like her to come down to the FBI offices, she and her girlfriends could hightail it out of town."

"Not if we tell her that the chat is about something else," I said.

"Won't that sound like a trap?" Candice countered. "This girl is really smart, Abby. We can't play her for a fool."

"No, but we can feed into her fears. We can tell her that we'd like her to come down to talk about the disappearance of Trevor Hodges. We think she might have some valuable information for us."

Candice pointed at me. "Ooo, I like that!" she said. "Emma's terrified of her brother, right? That's why she's trying to run away. She might even know or suspect Trace had something to do with Trevor's murder. She'd come down to talk to us about that, I'd bet."

"She would," I said.

"How old is Emma again?" Kelsey asked.

"Seventeen," Candice said.

"Well, she's a minor. She can't be questioned without her parents' permission."

"Crap," I said. "I hadn't thought of that. No way will Edwards allow her to talk about Trace to us."

"How old is Ivy?" Candice asked.

My eyebrows rose and another lightbulb went off inside my

head. My mind went back to the prophetic dream I'd had about the bathtub and the vine, and I now understood why the dream had seemed to reference a symbol for Ivy's mother. "It doesn't matter," I said, now knowing exactly how to play this. "Let's start with her. Bring her in, with her mother. And, Kelsey, can I question Ivy with you?"

Kelsey nodded. "I'd have to clear it with Rivera," she said, "but I think it'll be okay."

"Good, and make sure that Emma comes down with her dad. We can't have him dispensing with any more evidence. And for that matter, maybe it's smarter to have the entire family here," Candice said, her eyes unfocused and staring at the far wall. "Let's gather the Edwardses, and keep them in pairs of two. Mrs. Edwards with Trace, and Mr. Edwards with Emma." There was something else in her statement that I found curious. A note, or a hidden message of some kind, but when I looked at her questioningly, she merely smiled sweetly.

"Why?" Kelsey asked.

"Just trust me," Candice said, getting up from the table. "I swear it'll pay off. In the meantime, there's an errand I have to run."

I pulled my head back in surprise. "You're leaving?"

Candice squeezed my shoulder as she passed me on her way out the door. "I am. But I'll be back. You guys carry on with the plan."

With that she left us, and Kelsey looked at me as if to say, "What was that about?"

All I could do was shrug.

It was nearly seven o'clock when we had everyone in place. The entire Edwards family was there, separated as Candice had suggested, and as the final girl, Melanie Michaels, showed up with both her parents and was shown into a room with a camera feed back to Kelsey's iPad, Kelsey and I headed toward the interview room with Ivy Clawson and her mother, Cindy.

On our way to the room, we had to pass Perez and Robinson. Perez looked shocked, but Robinson looked pissed enough to spit nails. I made sure to smile extra sweetly at him.

Rivera stopped us at the door and said, "You two got this?"

"Yes, sir," Kelsey said.

I, however, merely looked at him like that was a stupid question. "Do you?" I asked him in reply. We'd told Rivera that it was very likely we'd need a warrant issued even before we were done with the conversation with Ivy and her mother. He swore that he and one of the assistant prosecutors would be listening in and ready to move the second we had something actionable.

He sort of snickered at me, but stepped aside to allow us to enter the room. Kelsey went ahead of me and I glanced over my shoulder but couldn't see Candice anywhere. Since leaving us earlier, she hadn't come back, and I didn't know where she'd gone off to, but I knew there was something up her sleeve and it worried me a bit.

I didn't really have time to focus on it, however. I had a confession to get.

Ivy sat with her mother in a room with no table, but a couple of chairs. Both of them looked nervous, but Ivy especially so.

Kelsey introduced herself as Special Agent Hart to both of them, extending her hand as she did so; then she motioned to me and introduced me as Ms. Cooper, without explanation about who I was or any assigned title.

We took our seats and I noticed Mrs. Clawson's brow was furrowed in my direction. "You look familiar," she said.

I nodded as if I should look familiar to her, but I didn't explain. Instead I let Kelsey take the lead. "Mrs. Clawson, I know we spoke over the phone about a case we've been working where a young boy from your area went missing about a year and a half ago."

"Yes," Mrs. Clawson said. "Trevor Hodges. I know his parents personally. They're devastated. But I understand you recently found his remains?"

"We did," Kelsey said. "And we believe we know who committed the crime. But we can't, at this time, support our theory with any proof. And the proof is key, because without it, Trevor's killer will remain free, and we think he'll likely kill again."

Mrs. Clawson subconsciously put an arm around her daughter. It was easy to see what a loving mother she was. I planned to use that to my advantage. "How can we help?" she asked.

"Well," said Kelsey. "We've drawn up a profile of who we think the killer is. We believe he's young, maybe no older than fifteen or sixteen. We believe he's a bit of recluse, has very few, if any, real friends, and is unable to form close bonds or relationships. We believe he still lives at home, and could be a threat—a serious threat—to any siblings he might have, especially if he has sisters. He could also be a serious and dangerous threat to his sister's friends. And this is the part of the profile I believe that's the most troubling, because psychopaths like him plot their murders with precision. Their victims never know it's coming. It could be an innocent walk home from school, exactly like what we suspect happened to Trevor."

Mrs. Clawson had gone pale. I thought that she might be wondering about our description of the young killer. Ivy had probably mentioned on more than one occasion how creepy Emma's brother was. "And you say this young man is still in the area?" she said.

"Most definitely," I said, because it was now my turn to speak. "We think he's very close by."

"There must be something you can do," Mrs. Clawson said.

"I'm afraid the only thing we can do at this moment is take away the temptation."

"What does that mean?" she asked me.

"Well, Trevor's murder isn't something we can solve at this moment. But there is a series of other crimes that we're very close to solving. And that's really where *you* can help, Mrs. Clawson."

"I don't understand."

I took from my back pocket a set of blue latex gloves, and reached for a large manila envelope, the contents of which we'd purchased and put together just a half hour before. Reaching into the envelope, I pulled out a shiny sateen shirt, which bulged at the shoulders.

As I held it up, I thought Ivy was going to fall out of her chair. "Do you recognize this, Mrs. Clawson?"

She stared at the shirt, the shoulder pads sticking out of it, and said, "It . . . isn't that . . ." Turning to Ivy, she said. "Isn't that your shirt for Spirit Week, honey?"

Ivy's breath caught and her eyes watered. "Oh, Mom!" she said.

I set the shirt back into the envelope. "No, Mrs. Clawson. It's not Ivy's shirt. It came from Melanie. See, you can tell, because the left shoulder pad is a little crooked. We conducted a search warrant on Melanie's house, and found this hidden away along with about seventy thousand dollars, the serial numbers of which all match those stolen from the very bank you told me was recently robbed."

Mrs. Clawson stared at me like I was speaking a foreign language she could almost understand, but not quite. I'd told her a complete fabrication. We hadn't issued any warrant, but we weren't obligated to tell her the truth about anything.

Pulling her eyes away from me, she turned to her daughter, as if seeing her for the first time. And I knew then that she'd put two and two together and understood that her own daughter could be involved. "Ivy?" she said, her voice shaking. "What have you done?"

Tears streamed down Ivy's cheeks. "We had to!" she told her mother. "Mom! We had to!"

Mrs. Clawson shook her head. "Why?" she said. "Oh, my God, child! *Why?*"

Ivy cried harder. "It's Trace!" she said. "Trace killed that boy! And he wants to kill Emma! But her parents won't believe her, so we figured out a way to get her some money to go to Thailand and be free!"

"How do you know that Trace killed Trevor?" Kelsey asked very softly.

Ivy wiped her eyes, but the tears kept coming. "He drew Emma a picture. It was this stick figure lying on the ground with blood coming out of his head. Next to it he wrote Trevor's name and he stuck the sketch under her pillow while she was asleep. She woke up to find it on the morning when her parents were away visiting her aunt. It was the same weekend that Trevor went missing.

"Emma was going to take the sketch to the police, but Trace got it back and destroyed it. She told her parents about it, but they brushed it off like Trace was only kidding with her. But he makes comments, you know? Like all the time about how to murder someone. He only says it to Emma and to us sometimes. He sneaks into her room and leaves disgusting things on her bed. One time he left a dead rat under the covers with her. She's tried locking her door, but he still gets in."

"Why didn't Emma go to the police?" Kelsey asked next.

Ivy rolled her eyes as if Kelsey had just asked the dumbest

question. "Like they'd believe her," she said. "Her own freaking parents don't even believe her!"

"Did Trace ever confess to the crime?" I pressed. I knew it was hearsay, but maybe we could build on it.

But Ivy shook her head. "Emma tried to record him confessing on her phone once. He never said it out loud. He just kept laughing and talking around it, but we all know he did it."

"Do you know where he might've killed Trevor? Or hidden his body?"

Ivy shook her head again. "No. He sneaks out of his room in the middle of the night all the time, and where he goes, none of us know."

"So, if Emma couldn't get her brother sent away," I said, "then you, her best friends, had to help her get enough money to hide from him forever, right?"

Ivy nodded. "It was for her safety," she said on choked tears. "I swear."

Mrs. Clawson hugged her daughter, but she looked very pained. I felt for her. But I didn't feel for Ivy.

I said, "See, the part of that which is hard for me to swallow, Ivy, is that you guys didn't give up your share of the money. If it was *truly* just for Emma, then none of you would've taken your split."

The sobs coming from Ivy halted abruptly. She knew she was trapped by her own greed.

Mrs. Clawson was also looking at me as if she was suddenly aware of just how bad this all was. She started to open her mouth—I suspected to tell us she was getting her daughter a lawyer—and I made sure to speak again before she had a chance to get that out.

"I think you're in a great position here, Ivy. I think you're in the position to help yourself first, and your friends second. If you confess . . . *everything* and tell us where the money is, and tell us every detail of the robberies themselves, then we can recommend that the federal prosecutor will ask for the minimum sentence. If you decide not to talk to us, not to confess, then we'll gather all the considerable evidence I'm quite sure you and your friends have accumulated, and make our case in court. We'll prove that you robbed the banks not out of any sort of empathy for your friend, but out of pure greed. And I doubt you'll get out of jail in time to celebrate your fiftieth birthday."

Ivy's jaw dropped. So did her mother's.

I stood up and nodded at Kelsey, then turned back to them. "The choice is up to you. But I'm going to head into the next room, where your friend Valerie Sampson is sitting, and I'm going to offer her the same deal. If she confesses before you do, then she'll get the lighter sentence."

I then turned and began to walk to the door. "Wait!" I heard both Ivy and her mother say. "I'll confess," Ivy cried. "I'll confess!"

Chapter Seventeen

. . .

Ivy wrote out a full confession, which took a good hour and a half. Kelsey pressed her for as much detail as possible, and once she was done, warrants were issued for all four of the girls' homes.

It took surprisingly little time to amass a team of agents and local law enforcement big enough to search all the homes. They started with Ivy's residence and moved on to Emma's, Valerie's, and Melanie's.

They found more than enough evidence, and all of the money, which was hidden in each of the girls' rooms.

There was also one additional piece of evidence that got reported back to us around midnight, and what was even more curious was that it came just about the time that Candice— who'd disappeared to God knows where—showed up back at the bureau offices.

"Where have you been?" I demanded. I'd texted her, but had only gotten back a text saying that she was tied up with something and she'd be back soon.

"Taking care of business," she said with a wink.

I didn't know what she meant by that until Kelsey came over to where we were sitting and said that one of the detectives assisting with the investigation had discovered a kilo of heroin jammed into the back of Trace's closet. Kelsey said they discovered the drugs easily, as they reeked of gasoline.

"Trace is a drug dealer?" Candice asked, all innocent-like.

Kelsey shrugged. "If he is, he's a bad one," she said. "We didn't find any drug money, but maybe he was still trying to figure out how to unload the ruined drugs. Even if he couldn't sell them, it doesn't matter. He was in possession of a kilo of smack, and we'll throw the book at him."

"Huh," I said. "How much time is he looking at?"

Kelsey pursed her lips. "The minimum sentence is twenty years for a quantity far less than what we found. He could get life if the judge decides to be a hard-ass."

"Even if Trace is a minor?" I pressed. I wanted that little bastard to spend the rest of his life behind bars, where he couldn't hurt any innocent young person ever again.

"Oh, we'll try him as an adult. I'll make sure of it," Kelsey said with a determined look in her eye. I knew she too was thinking of Trevor.

"Perez is in with Trace and his mother now," Kelsey said next. "He's not admitting to anything, but Perez is grilling him hard about Trevor's disappearance and the drugs. Our tech says that he thinks a few of the execution videos we also found on the kid's hard drive might make a good case for Trace heading down the road to radicalization. We plan to file multiple charges."

Next to me, Candice wore a satisfied smirk. I knew I should've been upset that she'd obviously planted the drugs in Trace's closet to frame him for a crime he hadn't committed. But I wasn't at all upset with her. In fact, I wanted to hug her for thinking of it and getting a psychopath off the streets. I wondered what she'd had to pay for that kilo, though. Candice was quite wealthy, but that didn't mean that she had an endless supply of money to throw around. Maybe I'd give her all of the office pool money.

"Awesome," I said to Kelsey as we wrapped it up.

She wiped a stray hair out of her eyes. It'd been a long day for her as well. "Oh, and, Abby, Rivera would like me to extend a formal invitation to conduct some of your intuitive training classes here. He says if you're willing to stay until Friday, he'll throw in a little extra money for your hourly rate, and make sure that everyone under his command attends."

"Huh," I said, surprised for a second time. "Sure," I said. "Tell him I'd be happy to."

"Great," Kelsey said. "I was hoping you'd say that. Okay, I gotta get back. The girls will need to be booked and processed, and I'm going to oversee it to make sure they're handled with as much care as possible."

We waved good-bye to Kelsey before turning to leave, and as we headed out of the building, I bumped shoulders with Candice and said, "You know what, Candice?"

"What?"

"You can be my Huckleberry any day."

"For sure, Sundance. For sure."

Epilogue

* * *

Candice and I stayed the week and split the betting pool money. I tried to give it all to her, hinting that I knew she'd invested in the tainted heroin from Flower's drug-dealing client, but Candice insisted that she'd gotten a very good deal. "Trust me," she'd said. "He was happy to unload it."

Anyway, it went a long way to relieve the stress of teaching a bunch of field agents a new skill they couldn't always identify as "real." Still, no one was more surprised to discover he was an absolute natural than Agent Rivera. That man could do readings for a living, given his test results.

And yet he wasn't even my most dedicated student. No, that title would belong to Agent Perez, who'd actually turned out to be a really decent guy. I found his attention and thoughtful questions during my lectures to be a refreshing revelation.

I'm sure you're surprised that my most dedicated student wasn't Agent Hart, though, huh? Well, she had reason to be a little distracted. Whitacre had chosen her to be the new special agent in charge for the Phoenix bureau office. She'd have to fill some pretty big shoes after the loss of SAIC Barlow, but I had no doubt she was up to the job.

On my last day in L.A. she even approached me about going to Arizona to teach her new agents a thing or two. I told her we'd see.

One more funny note about the boys from L.A.—I heard that shortly after we left, Agent Robinson resigned. He showed up a few months later in some new Netflix series as a supporting character in an FBI drama. He played the brooding field agent, a part my experience with him suggested he was born to play. (I knew those movie-star good looks would be put to better use someday.)

As for the Edwardses, well, that whole family was indicted. Mrs. Edwards confessed that she'd been the one to find the ninja outfit hidden in their garage, and had suspected that one of their children might've been involved with the robbery cases. Mr. Edwards had assured her that he'd take care of it, which he did only after we paid him a visit, so both of them were charged with obstruction.

Trace was indicted on multiple charges, and last I heard, the prosecutor was pushing hard to have him tried as an adult. Last I checked the ether, Trace was going to be in jail for a long, long time, so I was certain that was a battle we'd win.

Emma and her pals ended up getting fifteen years apiece. They'd be in their early thirties when they got out, and I felt bad for them on the one hand, but not so bad on the other. Mostly I was sad at all that lost potential.

Meanwhile, Candice and I planned a vacation to Bermuda together with our winnings. Feeling charitable, we even allowed our hubbies to come along. I mean, a girl needs someone to help her put sunscreen on those hard-to-reach places, after all. . . . (Wink.)